Bobbie Darbyshire w(
National Academy of
Review Creative Nonfic
as barmaid, mushroom
cabinet minister's priva.. ....,, ...
volunteer adult-literacy teacher, as well as in social
research and government policy. Bobbie hosts a writers'
group and lives in London.

Praise for Bobbie Darbyshire's earlier books

Truth Games (Cinnamon Press, 2009)

After the hippies and before the yuppies, between the advent
of The Pill and the onset of AIDS, between the 'summer of
love' and the 'winter of discontent', the newest game in town
was sex. In London, in the baking, dry summers of 1975 and
76, a group of friends get out of their depth in infidelity.

'Shows the deft touch of a psychologically astute social
satirist.'

'Leaves you with that taste in the mouth: a blend of loss,
innocence and cynicism.'

'I read this novel like a hog eats its share of strawberry tart.'

Love, Revenge & Buttered Scones (Sandstone Press, 2010)

A comedy of errors with dark, serious threads, in which three
troubled lives become mysteriously tangled in the Inverness
public library.

'The brilliantly plotted narrative grabs you by the throat and
doesn't let go... A triumph!'

Published by Cinnamon Press
Meirion House
Tanygrisiau
Blaenau Ffestiniog
Gwynedd LL41 3SU
www.cinnamonpress.com

ISBN 978-1-909077-45-4

British Library Cataloguing in Publication Data. A CIP record for this book can be obtained from the British Library.
Designed and typeset in Garamond by Cinnamon Press. Cover design by Jan Fortune and Adam Craig from original artwork 'Sydney Harbour Lighthouse' by Ben Mcleish © agency: Dreamstime.com

Cinnamon Press is represented by Inpress and by the Welsh Books Council in Wales.
Printed in Poland

To Nesta

OZ

BOBBIE DARBYSHIRE

Best wishes

Bobbie Darbyshire

CinnamonPress

INDEPENDENT INNOVATIVE INTERNATIONAL

This one is for Jason

CYCLONE

November 2008, Monday

By the time I've walked back to Clapham Junction it's dark. A bitter wind cuts through the crowd on the platform, but that's not why I'm shaking. I pull out my mobile and dial Hove. 'Dad,' I say.

'Mark.' His surprise crackles in my ear. 'Nice to hear you. It's been a—'

'Dad, I've something to tell you.'

I imagine him at the window of his flat, looking out at a turbulent sea. The phone's clamped to my cheek. 'She's dead,' I say.

'Who?'

'Mum.'

I hear his intake of breath, but his words are drowned by the station announcement. '... seventeen twenty-one... calling at Vauxhall and London Waterloo.'

He wants to know how, of course. I close my eyes, breathing short, difficult breaths. It's a joke in bad taste. My brain can't bypass the words, so I'm blurting them out. 'She fell under a bus.'

'What?' he says.

'Whitehall. This morning. Not looking.'

'Oh—no—'

'St Thomas's rang me. I went there, I saw her, and now,' I'm choking, 'now her house, Dad—it's as if she's due back any minute—'

'I'm so sorry, Mark.'

I stall. *Sorry.* The word's wrong.

I need him to protest. To tell me this isn't happening.

'Are you?' I say.

'Of course. Terribly sorry.'

For me he means, not for her. He ran out on her twenty-five years ago when I was small. The old anger surges. Useless.

'Mark, are you all right? Where are you?'

'On my way home. Look... Dad... Train's here. Got to go.'

I snap the phone shut, panicking, staring around me, trying to shut out the image of Mum on the mortuary table. Not true. A mistake. As the train draws in and pulls to a halt, a child is taking me over: a lost little boy who if he weren't shivering in this press of strangers would burst into tears. She will surely come soon and find me.

I've just been to her little two-up-two-down house along by the railway line, but she wasn't there. Only last night the place was crammed with people, partying, celebrating her birthday. I'd taken along a *Best of the 80s* CD, and I watched her dance with her mates, more like thirty-six than fifty-six, a glass of wine in one hand, half a poppadum in the other, hair flopping in her eyes, singing along to Cyndi Lauper. *Girls Just Wanna Have Fun*. Two hours ago when I eased open the front door there was no music, no dancing, just a faint smell of curry. Everything was as she'd left it this morning, the CDs piled by the player in the kitchen, her scuffed trainers on the hall floor, a stack of ironing in the living room that she must have hidden out of sight for the party. Upstairs, a crumpled towel on the landing, the cap off the toothpaste, some bills and scribbled notes beside the laptop in the back-bedroom-turned-study. And then in her bedroom a nightdress, a hairbrush, a paperback face down and the sleepy old cat waking and yawning. Beside the bed were two photographs of me, one as a baby being lifted from a bath, the other taken with Gina and Matilda on Brighton beach this summer. Big smiles.

If I had touched nothing, told no one, all might still be well.

Passengers stream from the carriage, and the crowd surges forward, carrying me with it. I'm in among the winter coats, the averted eyes, the flapping *Evening*

Standards, the ears white-wired to iPods, the mixed smells of damp people wishing themselves at home. I'm big, a head taller than most, but inside right now I'm small and scared.

For a long while I sat at the top of Mum's stairs looking down at the mosaic of coloured floor tiles. Through the wall came sounds of kids home from school: a shriek, a laugh, a woman's raised voice. I got to my feet and went down the stairs slowly. Stood a while in the hall, looking at Mum's raincoat hanging on a hook.

At Waterloo I'm stumbling from the train and with the crowds down into the Tube, following the Jubilee signs, and soon I'm on another packed platform, watching another train roll up and open its doors. So many people streaming off, pushing on. Mum is surely still out here somewhere if only I knew where to look.

I'm kidding myself. She's gone.

In her house the silence was rising like floodwater. I couldn't breathe. I dumped the bag of her things the hospital had given me on the kitchen table and fled along the hall to the street, pulling the door shut behind me. I had to fight to get control of my face and my voice before ringing the bell next door.

The neighbour was shocked, kind, sympathetic. Of course she would have the cat. We went back and fetched him.

My feet drag as I turn into our street in Kilburn. Gina told me to pack up and get out this morning, and part of me was ready to leap at the chance. The dilemma feels blurred now, as though it concerns someone else.

The entranceway, shared with the bookie, is littered with fag ends and betting slips, and there's the usual stink of piss and cider. Matilda hears the turn of my key and comes hurtling downstairs, so fast I'm afraid she'll tumble. 'Daddy! Daddy!'

'Hi, Little.' I sweep her up for a hug, warm and alive. Her tangled red hair smells of chlorine.

'Daddy, I can do the doggy paddle.' She demonstrates in my arms, twisting onto her stomach so I stagger, nearly dropping her.

'Without wings? Without me holding you?'

She flails arms and legs. 'I took my toes off the bottom, and Miss Barrett said I was swimming. I only swallowed a little bit, and I kept my eyes open.'

'Good for you, Matty.'

As I set her down, she squeals with excitement, displaying the gap in her front teeth. She's perpetually astonishing: the whole reason I stay. The red hair, the freckles, the green eyes are mine; the curls and a smatter of genteel Americanisms come from Gina.

The stairway above us hums with toxic vibes. I'm reluctant to climb, but Matilda plants her palms on the seat of my jeans and shoves me upwards. Does she know something's wrong? Gina and I have been waiting until she's out of earshot to hiss and whisper at each other, but she must sense the atmosphere.

'Can I have a bicycle for Christmas?'

I'm not falling for this one. 'Have you asked Mommy?'

My head clears the banister rail, and I'm looking into the galley kitchen, where my wife, still in the monogrammed fleece from the bookshop she works in, stands sideways on, jaw rigid, her hair scraped back in a scrunchy, savagely peeling a potato.

The wall clock shows nearly six, and I remember it's Monday, my half-day, no afternoon class. I should have been here by two-thirty, should have made the tea. My phone's been switched off. She probably thought that I'd left her.

I need to tell her straightaway about Mum. I'm opening my mouth to ask for a moment alone, but—

12

'Santa will bring me a bicycle,' shouts Matilda. She seizes my hand and runs around me so I rotate on the landing, turning my head like a dancer to keep looking at Gina, trying to catch her eye.

She glares at the potato. 'She's been at me from the minute I picked her up.'

I disentangle myself and step closer, willing her to look up.

Matilda leaps at me, knocking me off balance. 'It's thirty-one sleeps to Christmas!'

She's using me now as a climbing frame. 'Matty, please don't. I need to talk to—'

'Fifty-two sleeps to my birthday!' She dangles by her knees from my arms.

Gina shakes her head helplessly. 'I haven't sat down all day, and then she wouldn't take off her coat until I'd worked out the sleeps.'

'Stop calling her "she".'

'Stop dodging the issue. Have you been with Alison?'

She looks at me at last, her eyes hard and angry, the peeler in her hand like a weapon.

'Who's Alison?' says Matilda.

'No one,' we both say.

Still upside down, Matilda sings tunelessly.

'No, I haven't,' I say.

A snort. 'You expect me to believe that?'

Matilda's the right way up again, smacking my stubble with her palms. 'Naughty Daddy.'

'Quit it, Matilda,' says Gina. 'Give me a goddamn break.' She meets my eyes over Matilda's head. 'She's ADHD, Mark.'

'She's not, nothing like it. Please stop saying that. She's just a bit charged. There's no space, we can't swing a cat, so we fight, she rampages.'

'Miaow!' Matilda is loud in my face. 'Can we have a cat, Daddy?'

'Be quiet, for Pete's sake.' Gina furiously attacks another potato. When Matilda carries on miaowing, she closes her eyes. 'Give. Me. A. Break.'

I beg Matilda to shush, and she does for a moment. Gina shoots me a look of despair. 'Five minutes ago it was a bicycle.'

'*Can* I have a bicycle, Daddy, please, please? It can live on the stairs.'

'How many times, Matty, no!' Gina yells. 'There's no room. We'll fall over it. There's nowhere to ride it. We don't have the money, *okay?*'

'We might have the money,' I say.

She flings the potato in the sink and swivels to face me square on. 'How dare you? Can't you see what she's doing?'

Matilda slithers down my body and runs into the living room. 'I'm not HD,' she shouts. 'I could swing the cat in here. I would look after it properly and feed it, I promise.'

'I mean it,' I say quietly. 'We might have the money.'

Gina's mouth is pinched as if she's holding pins in it. Quickly, speak. 'Mum was killed this morning, crossing the road.'

She frowns, not sure if I'm joking.

'I've been at the hospital, the undertaker, Mum's house. That's why I'm late.'

A tug comes at my elbow. 'Granny Jonnson?'

God, what have I done? My child's face is blank with dismay. I fall to my knees, seize her hand.

She's staring at me. 'Is Granny all right?'

I'm this little girl's father. A grown up. I have to find the right words. 'I'm so sorry, Matty,' I say, 'but the sad thing, the really sad thing that should never have happened is Mum was on her way to work, nearly there, crossing the road to her office, and she didn't look properly, didn't check—you know how you *always* should

14

check? She stepped off the pavement, and... and a bus was coming... and the bus...'

Even for my child it seems I can't soften the truth.

Gina bends over us, her hand on my shoulder. 'The bus hit her, honey, and Granny died. Her body stopped working, and now she's in heaven.'

Matilda's green eyes are open as wide as they'll go.

'She didn't feel any pain,' I tell her. 'She wasn't hurt or frightened.'

That's what the doctor said as he led me to identify the body. Knocked unconscious, he said.

'Will her body work again?'

My throat clogs. I shake my head.

Gina squeezes my shoulder and says, 'She's very happy in heaven.'

Matilda withdraws her hand from mine, then brings it up in a fist as if she would hit me. She begins to wail. 'I won't see her. I wanted to go to her birthday, and now I won't see her.'

'It's okay. It's okay.' Meaningless, but what else is there to say? And I'm trying to hug her, but she refuses to be hugged. Her wails mutate into howls.

Gina has her fleece off and wrapped round Matilda. 'Don't worry, hon,' she says, rocking her. 'Granny didn't mind that you weren't at her birthday.'

Gradually she quietens as Gina carries on talking and soothing. Gina's Connecticut accent is softly convincing. It had me falling for her, way back at the start. It mesmerises the kids at the bookshop when she hops up on her stool and starts reading a story. But the thought nagging at my mind is how yesterday, in this same, relentless, soft accent, Gina backed Matilda's preference for tea with a school friend over a 'duty trip to her grandma'.

I stand up, observing the curve of Gina's arm around Matilda, the corkscrew wisps that have come loose from the scrunchy, the knobs of her spine showing through the Vassar College sweatshirt.

'There's tons to do,' I say, hearing the chill in my voice. 'There'll be an inquest, but they're releasing the body. The hospital put me on to the undertaker, and he's talked me through everything. I have to go to the registrar. Then there's notifying people, sorting out a solicitor, planning the service. I'll take tomorrow off work.'

She straightens to face me, holding Matilda close. 'I'm so sorry, Mark.'

Our eyes lock. She looks scared. Part of me wants to shout, Like hell you are.

'It's not your fault,' I say.

'Why did you go there?' she whispers later.

'What?'

'Why did you go to Nancy's house?'

It's dark in the bedroom. We lie side by side, naked but not touching. Matilda's asleep in the other room.

'I went to the undertaker first.'

'But then to your mother's.'

'Yes.'

'Why?'

'I don't know. It was only ten minutes' walk. The cat, I suppose. The neighbours have taken him.'

'It seems weird to me. I think you're in shock.'

I wish she would stop talking. She's been asking about what happened—the call at work, the taxi to St Thomas's, what the doctor said, what I saw—and I've been mumbling answers. So I'm lying here, looking at the patterns the orange streetlamp is making on the curtains, hearing a distant siren and remembering Mum on the mortuary table, when I feel Gina's hand on my chest.

'All this stuff...' she says huskily.

I say nothing. She snuggles up under the duvet, the

soft weight of her breasts on my arm.

'I mean Alison.' The name pains her. She pauses. 'All of this fighting we've been doing.'

Her hand goes down to my limp cock, which she hasn't touched in two weeks.

'I mean, this is a wake-up call, isn't it? A chance to see what's important.'

She falls silent, stroking me, and I'm wondering what she thinks is important. Our fragile mortality? Mum's money? My cock?

'Matilda,' she whispers. 'You and me.'

I don't want this, not now, it feels wrong, but she's getting me going. She rubs her cheek on my shoulder, and I'm turning to face her, putting my arms round her. We cling for a moment, and then she's clambering on top of me. Straddling me, tickling my face with her dark curls that smell of shampoo, and I'm feeling the kindness of it as she kisses me and guides me in.

I come quickly, and for a while we lie still. I want to be comforted; I want to feel close to her, but it isn't happening. I'm thinking of the verbal abuse she's been dishing out, which okay I've deserved, but this morning when she told me to leave it felt like an option, a kind of relief, and when she lifts her head and looks at me now I don't know what I feel. My head's in a mess; all I can think of is Mum.

I roll out from under, reaching for a tissue. Her hands follow me, stroking my back, and all at once it's too much. I'm out of bed, escaping the room—'Where are you going?' she says—and I'm across the landing into the kitchen, where I slam open a cupboard, grab a glass, screw the cap off the Smart Price whisky and pour myself a slug.

Jesus, Mum, you were dancing, tipsily showing off to your mates on your birthday, and then, bam, knocked out. You were wearing green nail-polish; did the bus

17

mess that up? What was under the mortuary sheet? Were you squelched by a wheel, your guts all over Whitehall?

Her face was okay, I tell myself. The bus didn't smash up her face.

I've swallowed the whisky, and I'm back on the landing with horror jabbing in my brain. And I can't stand to be with Gina, and I can't risk showing this confusion to Matilda, asleep in the living room, and sure as shit Gina will come looking for me, and I'm damned if I'm going to hide in the bathroom. I feel huge. Caged. This pokey flat can't contain me. I duck back into the bedroom, shutting my ears to her voice, grabbing my clothes, stuffing a few things into the rucksack. I get dressed on the landing.

She comes out of the bedroom, her mouth still moving, her eyes flashing anger. I shake my head. I take keys, wallet, coat, and I leave.

In less than an hour I'm back on Mum's doorstep, turning the key and stumbling inside, anxious to find her whisky bottle.

But then, smooth and swift, there's something in the house that calms me. Beneath the curry a more persistent smell of home. Behind the silence a sense of belonging and safety. She just popped out. She'll be back soon.

I find the single malt in a cupboard, her best tumblers in another. I pour two generous measures, add water to both and carry them into the living room. I shift the ironing from the armchair, as she would do, and sit down. I lift a glass, clink it against the other and drink a silent toast to my mum.

Tuesday

There's a god-awful buzzing, a sick lurch in my skull. A digital clock face shows 5.59, and I clutch at it until the racket stops.

Memory kicks in. I've spent the night in Mum's bed. I didn't want to—smashed though I was, I couldn't bear the idea of crawling between sheets that smelled of her —but the settee downstairs wasn't long enough, and the sofa bed in the back-bedroom-turned-study refused to unfold—the desk got in the way—so I was left with no choice. On the floor is the heap of sheet and duvet cover I managed to strip from the bed before crashing.

I'm seeing her again in the mortuary. Her hair combed back from her forehead, showing the grey roots. Her eyelashes. Her eyes that don't open. I throw myself belly down, smother my breath in the pillow and imagine her eyes opening, her face waking. Peek-a-boo.

For a while I can't move, can't allow time to go forward.

Matilda. I need my little girl. I roll off the bed onto my knees and fumble for the lamp. The light attacks me, I can barely see, but between blinks there she is, in the gilt frame by the clock radio, in her sundress with cherries, on the beach at Brighton, holding an ice lolly. On one side of her Gina leans in close, wearing a swimsuit, her curls loose and wild. On the other sits a man who last summer was me. His freckles are belligerent pink. His red hair sticks up from his scalp as though it's seeking the sun.

'Smile,' says my dad.

I can feel the hard pebbles under my arse, taste the salt wind, hear the thunder of a breaker and its rattling drag back into the Channel. I'm looking at Dad, who crouches in the stones, peering at the image on the back of Gina's camera.

Matilda looks ecstatic. Her face is alight. One hand grips the lolly stick; the other grabs at her daddy's T-shirt. I try to imagine it, the feel of her small fist against my ribs.

The other photo in the frame was taken by Dad too. Me as a baby, being lifted from a bath by Mum's hands.

He left before I was five.

Gina says I'm married, a father, I have to face my responsibilities.

I switch the light off again. It was hurting my eyes.

I've showered and drunk a load of orange juice. On my phone were three missed calls from Gina and a text: *Where are u please call me.* I've replied: *At mums sorting funeral will get back to u.* It's the best I can do for now.

Another text reads: *Hi mate. Pub with the lads this Fri? We're forgetting what you look like.* No need to answer; they'll assume they're my Alison alibi again. There's a text from her too: *Enjoying conference but don't worry no one here half as dishy as you.* There's no need to answer her either.

I'm shaving in the half dark with the landing light on and the bathroom door open, finding the stubble with my fingers. I forgot to bring shaving kit, but there was a disposable razor on the side of the bath and the hand soap is lathering okay. This blade last scraped Mum's armpit or leg, I'm thinking. This mirror last reflected her smile.

I have to get past a registrar and a solicitor. They must see everything from incoherent anguish through to brazen good riddance, but what will they make of me? I screwed up with the undertaker yesterday; he didn't understand me at all, mistaking my distaste for him for glibness about death or my mother. Everything about him seemed false. The plastic flowers in his pokey office. His sombre face and dark suit. His ritual condolences.

His tasteful, glossy catalogues. Younger than forty, pretending to be fifty. Off home later for his tea, not a second thought.

'What will happen to her?' I asked him. 'Where will she be until the funeral?'

'She'll be looked after respectfully. Every care will be taken.'

'But where?'

For a moment I thought he wasn't going to answer, it seemed to pain him so much. He fingered a cufflink. 'We have the use of excellent premises in Kingston.'

My jaw tenses now at the memory. I'm in danger of cutting myself. I lean back from the mirror, ambushed by the image of a wagonload of corpses bombing down the A3.

He wanted to know what kind of service. Offered to put me in touch with a minister.

'She was an atheist,' I told him. 'She used to say, over her dead body did she want any mention of God over her dead body.'

I must have grinned, but he didn't. 'In that case, the humanists? Or you may prefer to conduct your own ceremony?' He held out a booklet. 'This offers an outline and a choice of suitable music and poems. Christina Rossetti is popular.'

Not Cyndi Lauper, then. I began glancing through the brochures. The coffins were hideous, the prices outrageous.

I chuck the razor in the basin and rub my face with a towel. Then as now I couldn't shake off the image of Mum's waxy-white skin, the way she looked dead not asleep, the skull beneath all too evident. 'So,' I said bleakly. 'Cold storage in Kingston.'

He puckered as if I'd made a bad smell. 'That's *not* how we see it. Your mother's remains will be treated with dignity at all times in a temperature-controlled environment.'

Bastard. Making me out to be flippant. Couldn't he see I wanted the solace of straight talking. The reality of death, its ordinariness and inevitability. Isn't it his job to give every mourner the story they need?

'Would you prefer to peruse the options and give us a call?'

Preferring his pompous, preposterous jargon.

'No, thanks. I'll choose now.'

I picked the cheapest coffin, as Mum had more than once told me to do. Then spent a fortune on flowers. 'White,' I said. 'Masses of white flowers.'

'The florist will be informed of your wishes.'

I'll have to go there again. He offered a choice of 'robes' for her to wear in her trashy coffin. I said she wouldn't be seen dead in them; I would bring her own clothes in. I try not to think of his hands on her broken body.

I'm back in the bedroom, rooting through my rucksack in the dark for clean pants, noticing the smell of spilled whisky. It's freezing in here; the radiator must be off. I pull on pants and socks, then T-shirt, sweater, jeans. Battling to get the second leg in, I collide with the heap of sheets and nearly fall over. And suddenly I'm furious angry—with the undertaker, with the tangle of bedding, with Mum. 'How the hell could you do this to me?'

I grab the heap and her nightdress and head for the door. There's a laundry bag hanging there. I swipe it from the hook, scoop her dropped towel from the landing, and I'm down in the kitchen in the faint light from the hall, on my knees, ramming the whole lot into the washing machine. I find powder next to me, chuck some in, slam the door shut, twist the dial and press go, lean my head against the cold metal. There's a pause, then the dull thump and judder of released water, the first turn of the drum.

I groan as I get to my feet, from pain or grief I don't know. I don't know who to be, what to feel. I hold on to the machine, needing its pulse, its matter-of-fact energy and purpose. Minutes pass.

Coffee. I flip on the kettle, watch it boil, fill a mug. Then I sit awhile, nursing it, sipping it slowly, watching Mum's last wash go round.

I'm thinking about my fifth birthday. It must be years since I replayed the memory, but it springs into life. I close my eyes and I'm back there, somewhere in south London, hiding behind the sofa in the flat that Dad has recently abandoned me and Mum for. I'm pulling at a hole in the brown-tweed upholstery. There must have been presents, and a cake, and perhaps I had some fun earlier, but in my memory I'm lying low between skirting board and sofa, my nose prickling with dust, pulling at the hole to make it bigger and watching my tears drop on the carpet. The other kids have gone home. Dad's girlfriend was here pretending to like me, but she's disappeared. There was music but it has stopped, and now they're looking for me: my mum and my dad.

'You've upset him,' she says.

'Don't be daft, Nancy. He's had a great time.'

'I knew this was a mistake. He'll be upset for days.'

'He needs his dad, Nance.'

There's a horrid pause as if they're both shocked. Then, 'Say that again,' she dares him.

Silence. I strain my ears and then jump because Mum's looking at me over the back of the sofa. 'I've found him. He's here.' She smiles in the way I know is not a real smile. 'Come along, Piglet. You and me have to go home.'

'What did you call him?'

She doesn't reply. She grabs hold of my wrist, hooks an arm round me and drags me up and over. I land in her lap and she hugs me. Her eyes glisten with tears. Her shoulder is bare. I want to sink my teeth into it.

'What did you call Mark just then?'

She says nothing. She's up on her feet, yanking me across the room, her fingers clamping my wrist.

'He needs a dad, Nance.'

She swings round, shoving my face into her skirt. 'If you say that once more, God help me I will kill you.'

Don't say it. Please don't say it again.

Dad says nothing. Mum says nothing. My nose is squashed against her belly, which smells of the car and the sunshine outside.

Then we're moving, fast, out of the room, through the hall towards the open door, the bright street. I'm resisting, but she's stronger than I am.

'Come on, Piglet,' she says.

She slams the door as we go, but too late. Dad's voice follows us, mocking. 'Oink, oink.'

Dawn is breaking outside. I cross the kitchen to roll up the blind but then drop it again double quick. Mum's cat was on the sill looking in—I've barricaded his flap—but worse, the neighbour and her two kids were an arm's reach away, leaning over the low fence between my kitchen door and their kitchen door, shaking a packet of cat biscuits. One of the children has started to wail. I must have scared him.

Shit, I don't need this.

The key's by the sink. I fling the door open. A freezing wind smacks my face, and the cat scurries in past my ankles.

'Sorry. We didn't know you were there,' says the woman.

In the grey light she looks older than she did yesterday, mid-thirties perhaps. Her face is sleep-creased. She has the small boy in her arms, and she's clutching her dressing gown to her throat.

'No. Yes. I'm...' Piss off and leave me alone.

The child howls. 'Hush, Christopher, it's okay.'

'Where's Nancy?' the older child demands.

'In Kingston,' I say.

The woman translates. 'She had an accident, Josie. That's why we're looking after Mog.' She hesitates. 'If you still want us to, Mark?'

'Yes... er... Jean, if you don't mind.'

'It's Jane. And don't worry, we love Mog, don't we, kids?'

The cat's sniffing his empty bowls in the kitchen. I march him back and dangle him over the fence. The little girl clamps him to her chest, glaring at me.

'I'm sorry,' I manage, 'if I seem... It's been a shock, and—'

The washing machine crescendos to a deafening spin, spewing suds into the drain by my feet.

'A dreadful shock,' shouts the woman. 'I mean Nance. She was great. It's not fair.'

'I may be staying,' I shout back, 'but the cat...'

'It's okay, Mark. I'm fine with the cat. Come on, Josie.'

She turns and goes into her house.

For a while I drift, making toast, drinking more coffee, wishing I hadn't given up smoking, and thinking how we're all heading for Kingston, until finally I pull myself together enough to look for the will, which I'll need to give the solicitor.

It takes no time to find it. For all her dancing in kitchens, Mum spent thirty years in the government legal service, so she knew how to file. In the back-bedroom-turned-study, in a box labelled 'personal and finance', in a folder tagged 'key documents', there it is, tucked in with her passport and certificates of birth, marriage and divorce.

She's left everything to 'my son, Mark Daniel

Jonnson'.

It's still too early to arrive at the registrar, so I fetch a refill of coffee and hack into her laptop. Password *Matilda*, what else? Her emails include an online utility bill, five happy birthdays, what looks like a spate of round robins from her library book-group, two offers of penis enlargement and a savings-account update. I leave them unopened and scroll through her contacts.

Here they all are: her best mate from Kent, various Muswell Hill neighbours she's kept in touch with, her school and university friends, office colleagues, many names I don't know. Everyone who cares must be listed here. I log into my own account and start composing a message. *I am sorry to tell you that on Monday 24 November my mother, Nancy Jonnson, was knocked down by a bus...*

Thank heavens her parents are dead. It would have been tough breaking this to them, not knowing what emotions to offer or expect. I hardly knew them. She never spoke much about her childhood, shook her head if I asked. 'No love lost,' she would say. 'I don't know why they bothered to have me.' On the infrequent occasions I went with her to Kent, her mother, falsely bright, radiated anxiety that I might make a mess, move a cushion or something, while her tall, craggy father, silent and self-absorbed, barely concealed his impatience for us to be gone. When they were dying, fairly briskly one after the other, Mum never suggested I visit them in hospital; I made do with looking solemn at their funerals.

Oh Jesus, I'll have to invite people here for some kind of wake. I stand up, fuming and mutinous, knocking the ceiling lamp with my head, dislodging dust. I don't want to do this, Mum, even if I knew how. I don't want to make sandwiches for your mates and hear their condolences.

I drop back on the chair and start jabbing the keyboard, deleting the spam and the library stuff. I try to calm myself by opening the birthday greetings, picking over each message for fragments of her. I find only clichés—*Hi Nance... sorry it's late... hope you had a great day*—but one catches my eye.

Happy Birthday with Love to my Beautiful Sexy Nancy. How is my Darling? Me I'm still driving the bus, whinging that it would make more sense to do something else, but you've heard that B4 and I stay in my Groove. Relationship-wise, well on we go. Things seem good at the moment but last month we nearly seperated. It would be Nice if just ONCE she could conceed a point if you know what I mean. You've heard this B4 too but I still hope to get back to see You who I don't say lightly is still steaped with love in my soul. Now I've looked at a certain Photograph of you I have some energy to get behind the wheel. Lots and Lots of Love, Oz XXX P.S. I will send a proper card soon.

Nerdy but tantalising, and I'm breathing more easily, sensing how Mum would have smiled at the spelling mistakes. I can see her tapping out a reply, tongue between teeth, and the thought makes me smile too, although I have to say the liaison surprises me. She had romances now and then, the odd fling, but with professional types, as you'd expect. It seems feelings went deep here, on his side at least, and Mum never got in deep. Each bloke I heard about was soon history.

There was a guy who moved into the Muswell Hill flat with us a couple of years after Dad left. His name wasn't Oz. I can't remember what it was. He was decent enough but it didn't take either with Mum or with me, and he eventually pushed off.

In recent years she's seemed immune to the need for male company, cheerfully self-reliant. 'Friends are more important than lovers,' she once told me. 'I've nothing against men, but they either bore me or I get in a muddle with them. Not their fault—it's the way I'm programmed. I'm best off steering clear.'

This Oz guy is married. Did she get in a muddle with

him? He doesn't sound like someone she would even go on a date with.

The other emails can wait, but he needs answering. I click reply, paste my draft in and play with it. Given his job, I decide not to mention the bus.

Oz, I am sorry to have to tell you my mother Nancy was knocked down yesterday, crossing Whitehall on her way to work. She died instantly, felt no pain. The funeral will be at Putney Vale Crematorium, 2pm Wednesday 3 December, white flowers, and you're very welcome to come. Mark Jonnson

I click 'send'. Off it goes. From her email address not mine, which seems okay for this one. He's hotmail, so who knows where in the world he's stuck in his Groove. Will he be broken-hearted, I wonder, or was he just dishing out randy patter?

Time to go. I log off. Beyond the window there's a pale blue sky chased by wispy clouds and blurred by the tears in my eyes.

Going to fetch my wallet, I stall in the bedroom doorway, shocked to see the mess I've made exposed by the daylight: my things scattered across the floor, the spilt whisky smell on the unheated air.

Grief smashes into me. I can't see Mum in this room any more. I'm losing her too fast.

I cross to the bedside and pull open the drawer, looking for her. Among the jumble of pill bottles and half-used tubes of cream, there's a small vibrator, the colour of candy-floss.

I pick it up, turn it on. It buzzes gently then subsides, its battery flat.

My legs give way. I sit on the bed, grinning and crying.

June 1978

Oh God. Harry. What the hell had she done?

Her mouth was parched from smoking his Gauloises. Her sweat smelled sour. Her head thumped and stabbed. Nancy swayed upright into blinding sun. She'd been flying too high when she got home last night to bother closing the curtains.

There were record sleeves all over the floor. She vaguely remembered yelling along with John Travolta and Olivia Newton-John before Laura in the bedsit next door had banged on the wall.

She began stumbling around, gulping water, washing her face, scrubbing at her armpits, pulling on a blouse and yesterday's crumpled black skirt. She leant into the mirror, avoiding her eyes, trying to make sense of her hair, trying not to remember, trying not to feel shame. Because, bloody hell, Harry. His hands up this skirt, tugging down her tights, squeezing her bum, finding her wetness, while she wriggled her fingers through his pin-striped fly to give him the best hand-job his Y-fronts allowed.

No amount of shame could undo it. She was super-intelligent, for heaven's sake. She'd outshone her peers to get a foot on the ladder of one of the most prestigious legal careers going: drafting the laws of the land. She should have the sense to at least pretend to be decent and dignified. But last night she'd downed five halves of Guinness with her married boss in a pub near Baker Street Underground station, then jerked him off in a shop doorway before letting him hail a cab for her to come home alone in. Her back still hurt where it had been jolted against the door handle.

And now she had to go into work and face him, had to be all day in the same room as him. She wanted to ring in sick, but that would be cowardly. She must set off at once before she lost her nerve; keep moving—the Underground, the Trafalgar Square crowds. She wouldn't falter. She would march up to the demure, eighteenth-century frontage of 36 Whitehall and in through the smart entranceway. She would nod to the security guard and keep going, keep going, into the big, square office where Nerys would be chewing her nails checking the typing, and Edward's face would brighten, and he would get to his feet and say, 'Good morning, Nancy.' And there by the window would be Harry. Oh God.

He would make some clever-dick comment about her torrid love-life keeping her in bed of a morning. He would loll back on his chair and arch an eyebrow as if to say he could lift his big wooden desk with his erection. And she would smile and say, 'Sorry, I'm late,' and slink to her place by the door.

And Edward would come and stand in front of her desk, blocking her view. He would say, 'Actually, you do look a bit under the weather. May I fetch you a coffee?'

2008, Friday

It's two-thirty and I'm unlocking the door to Room 306.

'I'll get the blinds up,' says Keith.

I'm functioning better: still holed up in Battersea at night but back at work in the daytime, doing my damnedest to avoid more condolences. I'm safe from them in class; it doesn't occur to my students to ask after my wellbeing.

It's stuffy in here as well as dark. The altruistic part of me I call Teacher Guy spreads his papers on the front table and pastes a smile on his face. 'Thanks for arriving on time.'

They nod, hungry for praise. Teacher Guy cares passionately about his job, would dearly love to get them reading, wants to give each of them personal attention, but he's stymied by their mixed abilities and the rigid curriculum. Today he'll whiz them, uncomprehending, through the differences between formal and informal letters before heading back to the phonemes that may conceivably yet change their lives.

This year's English 1 students are the usual miscellaneous misfits: unschooled immigrants who lack the literacy for an ESOL class, plus a few home-grown inadequates. The same few as ever are punctual. Keith, built like a professional wrestler, tugs at a window cord, eases a blind past its sticking point. He's a retired labourer who knows everything under the sun except how to link sounds to letters. He could learn this too if he let himself forget his embarrassment, stopped joking and covering up.

Wayne knows his way to the bus stop. His face is pockmarked and his eyes don't quite focus. He's forever slipping out of class for five minutes, returning with alcohol on his breath. Teacher Guy stopped coaching him on spelling the months of the year when he realised Wayne had no use for them, guessing when prompted that there might be thirty-six and unable to say which one contained Christmas. But Wayne makes small breakthroughs. This term he's learned that I-N-G spells 'ing', and he announces this happily whenever he sees it, which gives Teacher Guy a buzz.

The other two eager beavers are grandmothers, Congolese Patricia and Pakistani Nazish, who've devoted their lives to parents, husbands and children and now itch to live for themselves.

My mother is dead. The thought comes at intervals.

Today began with another hangover. Tuesday, Wednesday, most of Thursday, I stayed sober. A mountain of tasks kept me from brooding. But after I'd notified Mum's friends and fielded their telephone calls, more or less planned the service, looked through her finances and delivered her files to the solicitor, decided beer and crisps will have to do for the wake and weathered two days of condolences back at work—I was overdue last night to hit the bottle. I tried to lose myself in my library book first—*Germinal*—poverty and wretchedness in nineteenth-century France—but the words danced on the page. This probably isn't the best time to be reading my way through the complete works of Zola with Hemingway as light relief.

Waking in Mum's house feels less spooky now. The bed has clean sheets, the radiator's on and at seven *The Today Programme* starts murmuring the latest batch of gloom about the collapsing economy. My head was thumping this morning, and I was tempted to ring in sick, but an inner voice nagged me upright, gave me a shower and a shave, insisted I ate egg, toast and orange juice and marched me through the drizzle to the bus stop. There was no call to short-change my students.

Oddly, the inner voice sounded female. Not Gina.

Too jolly and down to earth. Maybe Mum?

I close my eyes, grit my teeth hard, hold grief at bay. I think of Matilda doggy-paddling in my arms.

One bit of luck: Alison is still at the management conference. Since the shit hit the fan with Gina ten days ago, Alison's been angling for me to move in with her, and I can't face that pressure today. It's tricky that she's my boss; I wasn't thinking too cleverly when I succumbed to her charms. I don't usually find blondes attractive, and Alison's interests don't extend much beyond clothes, middlebrow fiction and television reality shows, but she's quick-witted, funny, energetic in bed. Our affair was never going to be serious. I assumed she'd understood that, but it seems that she hadn't. I'm in no hurry to tell her I'm spending my nights solo in a double bed this side of the river.

While the interactive whiteboard boots up, Teacher Guy writes the lesson objectives on the flipchart for the benefit of any passing inspectors. The grandmothers begin laboriously copying them, though he's told them many times there's no need.

You will understand the difference between formal and informal letters.

Fat chance.

You will be able to hear, read and write words with the 'oo' pattern.

Maybe. A little. If they listen and practise and have one-to-one attention from someone between now and the next class. In short, fat chance too.

I can't face explaining formal and informal letters yet, so I write two large, round Os on the board.

'We did this on Monday,' I say. 'Anyone remember the sound?'

'Oh-oh,' says Keith, then roars with laughter.

I add 'f' and 'd' to make 'food'. 'Who can tell me what this says?'

They fidget and smile. Four days, and their memories are wiped clean. Nazish knows, but she doesn't dare speak, and when Teacher Guy prompts her she dissolves into giggles.

Mum is dead. It's as incomprehensible and unspeakable as the double 'o' sound is to these four.

Teacher Guy smiles as he takes them through some examples. He hands out slips of paper: pictures and words, *moon, spoon, school, tool, boot, root.* His decency is soothing if vacuous. If people don't bug me, he tricks me into operating as though Mum's alive and I've a happy family to go home to.

People do bug me, though, tiptoeing around me. 'So sorry to hear about your loss. If there's anything I can do.'

A gust of shouts from the corridor blows in two more students. Comfort, a gorgeous young Ghanaian who has never-ending trouble settling her baby in the crèche, and Lloyd, a teenager, all bling and baggy jeans, here only because the Job Centre requires it.

'Hey, man,' Lloyd shouts, slapping Keith's back. Keith ignores him as he does all 'coloured people'. I don't think he has anything of substance against them. He's never said so; they're simply off his radar. He whiffs a bit, so the others keep their distance anyway.

Comfort murmurs apologies and holds out a hand for the moon-spoon puzzle. I go to shut the door that Lloyd has left swinging open. 'Well done for getting here. Do you remember what sound we did on Monday?'

'Oo,' Comfort says.

'Hey, give me a pen, man,' Lloyd bellows just as his mobile goes off. He's immediately engrossed in a call to a mate.

My own phone has been vibrating. I glance at it while they try to match words to pictures. It's a text from Dad. *Ring if you need help with the funeral or want to talk.*

On Tuesday, after the registrar and solicitor, I went back and faced up to opening Mum's wardrobe. Out wafted a smell of stale perfume. I chose a blue dress with white swirls, plus a linen shirt to cover her arms if they're broken. Shoes didn't seem right for a coffin, but I found satin slippers, the sort of thing dancers wear, and put them in the bag along with knickers, a bra and some tights. Then I set off to walk to the undertaker's.

He wasn't there. A stout, elderly woman was minding the office, which stank of air freshener.

'I'll be laying her out,' she said. 'What a beautiful dress.'

Her eyes were kind and forgiving. The muzak was mournful. I could have wept in her arms. 'You'll go to Kingston?' I said.

She shook her head. 'She'll be here the day before the funeral. You can see her. Did he mention? It costs a bit more as we'd have to embalm her for viewing.'

I said no. One viewing was enough, and I wasn't having anyone else gawping at her.

Was there anything else I wanted to know, she said. Anything at all, I mustn't worry. She knew how little things could prey on people's minds. So I asked about the ashes. What would be in them? Just Mum, or the coffin as well? 'The coffin as well,' she said, 'though they take out the handles and screws and so on.' She read my expression. 'It's not easy to think about, is it?'

Teacher Guy tugs me back to the present. My students are staring off into space.

'Okay. Something new. Tell me, when do people write letters? The kind of message you put in an envelope and send through the post?'

He nudges them into a halting brainstorm, and Patricia pipes up, 'Is why I wanting to larn. So I's writing to my sister back home.'

'Excellent, Patricia,' he says brightly. 'That's a good

example of what people call an informal letter.'

Her eyes glaze, and Wayne slopes off for a nip. I could fancy one myself.

The mobile's vibrating again with a text, this time from Gina: *We need to talk!*

I haven't been back to Kilburn.

Teacher Guy pushes on, explaining examples on the screen, as two more students bustle in: Annetta and Amelia, large, middle-aged Jamaicans smelling of joss sticks. 'Hello ever-body. How it rain, how it rain!' And here's Wayne behind them, grinning, eyes vacant. Everyone stops pretending to care about the layout of a job enquiry to Sainsbury's.

Close on their heels comes the crèche nurse. She looks about fifteen, but I suppose she must be older. She stands in the doorway and raises her eyebrows at Comfort, who sighs, gets wearily to her feet, gathers her things together and sets off to quieten her baby. What are crèche nurses for, I ask myself, not for the first time.

Lloyd's mobile erupts again. He stares at it, then starts thumbing keys. And Teacher Guy wonders how do texts work for a youngster who can barely read or spell. Lloyd isn't stupid: it's attitude that's holding him back. He might learn fast if we started from his texting vocabulary. Words with short vowels that end in 'ck'. The way an 'x' actually sounds like a kiss.

Oz sent Mum kisses. Oz the bus driver, stuck in his Groove.

They've suspended the driver who killed her, pending the inquest. He's offered to meet me, but I've said no. I'm afraid I might thump him, or bawl my eyes out. The solicitor wants me to sue, but I don't think I will. The word is that Mum didn't look.

The door opens again. A blonde head comes round it and a big, cheeky smile. 'Ah, there you are, Mark.'

'Alison. You're back.'

She thinks I'm pleased to see her. There's a flash of her naughty look before she rearranges her expression. Her blue eyes go soulful. 'I'm *so* sorry about your *mum*. Bernard just told me.'

Bernard's her boss. She holds the door wide, wanting me to join her in the corridor.

My throat seizes up. 'Hey, Ali,' I croak, 'we're on a roll here. Catch up with you later?'

'Sure thing.' She blinks sympathy. 'I'll be in my office.'

The door closes. I turn back to the class.

'*My* mum has arthritis,' says Wayne.

I try to escape without seeing her, but she spots me in the corridor, steers me into her office and puts her arms round me.

'You poor, poor love. What a terrible thing to happen.'

She pulls my face down to her level and kisses me. Leads me to the chair in front of her desk; makes me sit on it.

I don't want to be here.

'She wasn't looking,' I say. 'She ran out in front of a bus.'

Alison hunkers down at my side. Her eyes swim with understanding. 'You must be so shocked.'

I nod, swallowing hard. 'I saw her the evening before. She was dancing. Her birthday party—'

'Mark, how dreadful. How old was she?'

'Fifty-six.'

'Oh my God, that's no age. You need someone to listen. Come home now with me.' She gestures at the desk. 'I can leave this.'

She's grabbing her coat from the hook, shrugging it on as she logs off from the PC.

'Hey, Ali,' I say.

She looks up.

'Do you mind if we don't? Not today.'

Her face falls. Her eagerness evaporates.

I edge towards the door. 'Truth is I've so much to do. I'm up to my neck sorting stuff, and arranging the funeral—'

'Of course. I should have realised—'

'No—'

'But I should.' She steps close; takes my hands. 'I was being selfish.'

'You're fine, Ali. It's all fine. I just need... I don't know, to—'

'To get the funeral done. To grieve in your own way. Of course, and I shouldn't have... but listen, Mark, listen.' Her face is grave, but her eyes are irrepressibly mischievous. 'When you're feeling better, when you've done all you need to do, the minute you need a cuddle, here I am.'

I head fast for the street. It's dark and still spitting rain. My collar's turned up; I'm catching no one's eye.

Home to Kilburn by Tube takes less than an hour, but the best way to Mum's is by bus. There's a crowd at the stop, and a 77 is arriving. I squeeze onto it, grabbing one of the last seats downstairs. As the doors close, Lloyd comes running, as fast as he can in those jeans, and the driver opens up again. 'Cheers, man,' says Lloyd. He spots me, and for a moment I'm trying to be Teacher Guy, but he only nods as he slides past a group of school kids and leaps up the stairs out of sight. The bus edges towards the traffic lights, and I begin to relax. We've cleared the lights without killing anyone's mother, and the rain's battering the windows as we pick up speed along Garratt Lane.

I taught Lloyd and the rest of them nothing today. I try to squeeze real teaching in around nonsense like when to use *yours sincerely* and *yours faithfully*, but there's never enough time. The syllabus is about passing tests that will earn them certificates and secure the college's funding and the politicians' targets. My students don't want certificates. They want me to teach them to read, and I cheat them by training them to perform party tricks and pinning rosettes on them.

Alison likes it when I rant about this—her eyes light up, excited—but she doesn't try to change anything. No one challenges the system; we churn pointlessly on.

The illiterate are too easily ignored and discounted. They apply so much ingenuity to hiding their secret. Who realises that the nice chap who paints their woodwork has to copy his address from the dog-eared card he keeps in his wallet? That the woman on the checkout can't spell the names of her children? That the cool teenager on the Tube is only looking at the pictures in *The Sun*? It's the first thing I say to my students: It's okay to come clean here with me and each other, admit you can't do it so you can start learning how.

Some continue to dissemble, sneaking peeks, cribbing off their neighbours, performing heroic feats of short-term memory to bluff me, freezing when I ask them a question. But others are brave and determined. I saw from day one that Comfort is as fearless as they come if the world will only give her a chance. She's young, her spoken English is good and she seems free of learning difficulties and negative attitude. She's desperate to better herself. She didn't go to school. No one taught her to read. She wants me to teach her to read.

The mobile vibrates. Gina calling.

She's cold and clipped. 'You've had four days. Any chance you might tell me what's going on?'

I've no answer. What in hell *am* I doing?

'Mark?'

'You were right, I'm in shock about Mum. Still in shock. How's Matty?'

'She's driving me nuts, that's how, and dealing with it solo is not okay, Mark. She insists Santa is bringing her a bicycle, screams her head off if I say otherwise. I'm on my way to pick her up now, and I've decided I'm gonna burst her bubble. There's no Santa, honey—'

'Hey, go gently—'

'Speaks the absent father. She's old enough. Oh, and I met with her teacher about the ADHD—'

'No, Gina—'

'Don't give me a no. You have an attention deficit yourself, you unbelievable jerk, taking off like that when I foolishly offered you an olive br—'

'What did the teacher say?'

'Same as before, that she's disruptive. She yells at the other kids, even hits them sometimes, talks back, dumps her lunch on the floor, refuses to colour in the letters—'

'What letters?'

'To learn what the shapes are—'

'She knows what the shapes are.'

'Listen to yourself. Taking the side of a six-year-old.'

'Nearly seven. She can read Roald Dahl, for God's sake. She doesn't need to be colouring in letters. There are no sides, Gina.'

'Is that so? Me and Alison, for example?'

'You're changing the subject.'

'Darn right I am. You're with her now, aren't you?'

'No.' I clear my throat. The woman next to me is earwigging. The bus has stopped to let on more people. Half a dozen dishevelled, wet strangers are touching their passes to the reader and adding their bodies to the crush.

'Look, tell Matty I'm coming tomorrow. I'm sorry she's giving you a hard time. Has she been swimming again?'

'Where are you, Mark?'

'On a bus.'

'Don't be smart.'

'Staying at Mum's.'

There's a pause.

'And that slut is there with you.'

'Gina, listen.' I try to speak plainly. 'She's not, and I swear I'm seeing no one but solicitors and undertakers and ghosts.'

She pauses a long time. Her voice softens. 'So what *are* you doing, Mark? Are we separated?'

I take a breath. 'I don't know. I'm sorry—Mum's dead —that's all I can think of.'

Silence. Then she says, 'Are you okay?'

I can't cope with her being nice. 'Look... Gina... I'll see you tomorrow.'

The bus rolls on. I stare out at the rain and the darkness, trying to face Gina's question. If it's over between us, what will that do to Matty? We should be trying for her sake.

I haven't been trying hard enough in I don't know how long, perhaps not since Matilda was born. One January morning back in 2002 we were a couple with big smiles and a proud tummy-bump to match, strolling through the sharp frost in Regent's Park, remembering the good sex we'd just managed to have. From the next day Matilda was with us day and night, screaming and raging, and we were dealing with that and with the stares of our neighbours, and there was no time left for sex, or for smiles except the help-me-I'm-drowning kind. Gina's rare laughs used to collapse into tears. 'Don't *you* start,' I would tell her. 'One crying woman's enough.' We fed Matty, changed her, picked her up, put her down, sang to her, left her to howl, sat her in front of small-hours TV, took her into our bed, pulled faces at her. Nothing worked. She stormed on at the indignity of existence, spurning our cuddles and hurling our offerings aside. Was she in pain, was there something wrong with her, was it our fault in some way? Why the hell wasn't our little girl happy?

The first time she smiled at me, I wept. It was three in the morning. I was exhausted, barely functioning, but her smile swept me away. It was all I could do not to wake Gina and drag her to see it. At breakfast I said, 'She smiled. Have you seen her smile?' and Gina nodded blearily. 'Sure, between bawling her head off.'

We thought, maybe a year. We can manage this maybe a year. But Matilda kept going. From the minute she could crawl she stopped screaming and instead took to rampaging at night, climbing from her cot, sticking her little fingers into everything, putting God knew what in her mouth, throwing stuff, laughing and demanding food and amusement.

Gina's mother on the phone from Connecticut said we were indulging her. We should restrain her, put her straight back in her cot, buy some earplugs.

It didn't work. Caging or tethering felt cruel to me though Gina insisted they weren't, and Matilda proved to be an escape artist anyway.

Mum said, 'Keep her awake all day and all evening. Wear her out, and she'll soon be sleeping through.'

'You must be letting her nap in the daytime,' I would accuse Gina.

'When else am *I* gonna sleep?' she'd snap back. 'Are you saying I gotta stay awake all day, entertaining her, just to give you a night's peace?'

'Jesus Christ, Gina, to give us both a night's peace!'

From the day Matilda was born until the weekend before she was three I don't think we had one uninterrupted night. My only dreams were hallucinations of sleeping. I was half dead, halfway down the slope towards madness, groping from one must-do to another. And when at last she closed her eyes and slept peacefully that miraculous weekend in January 2005, the smug couple who'd strolled through the hoar-frosted park hand in hand were nowhere to be found.

I escape from the bus in a small explosion of released passengers and set off through the rain, down the steep incline that falls away north of Lavender Hill. The bus was crawling in nose-to-tail rush hour, but there's zero traffic in this low-lying wedge of Battersea marooned by the railway line. It's a maze of backstreets, its pollarded trees and wan streetlamps reflected in puddles and in the windows of Victorian two-up-two-downs.

My steps quicken. I'm feeling the relief of Mum's presence. I'm starving hungry, and she's going to feed me. She went shopping last weekend. There are still eggs in the fridge, cheese, the remains of the curry she cooked for the party, some fruit and veg. When the fridge is empty, I'll move on to the freezer, which is crammed full of her soups and stews, labelled and dated. After that there's a cupboard full of tins.

A few other nine-to-fivers are hurrying home, laptop bags slung from shoulders and umbrellas aloft. The grey suit ahead carries a supermarket bouquet of chrysanthemums. The miniskirt on the pavement across from me shrieks into her mobile, planning some tryst for tonight. It's Friday. The population of London is moving from work self to home self, heading into a weekend of seduction or argument or partying or cosy domesticity or relentlessly wakeful baby.

Or silence, in which I need to be.

1978

At lunchtime she was alone in the office. She'd been wrong about Harry; he wasn't here smirking and crowing. He had rung in and told Nerys he had a stomach bug.

Edward and Nerys were out in the sunshine in St James's Park, eating their sandwiches. Nancy's stomach was growling, but she hadn't gone with them. The day was poison. Everything she did was septic. She needed to be alone. She slumped head and arms on the desk and tried to block out the memories of the pub and the Guinness and the doorway and Harry—

The phone jumped her upright, and in her ear came his voice, solemn and husky. 'Hello, you. Any eavesdroppers?'

Her mouth dried. She felt stupidly confused but managed to say, 'They're feeding the ducks.' It was their running joke about Edward and Nerys.

No laugh from Harry. 'How are you?' he said.

'Not too bad. You?' She fished out a cigarette.

'Pretty rough.'

He sounded dreadful. She supposed five pints was worse than five halves. She struck a match. Inhaled. Felt the rasp of the smoke as it went down.

'Look, Nancy,' he said. 'I've made a decision. We have to draw a line under this.'

Eyes closed, she imagined a line, thin, black and quivering. She let the smoke go. 'Good decision. I agree.'

Harry's voice shrank to a murmur. 'I'll remember last night, though.'

She tried to answer, but the breath was sucked out of her.

'Nancy?'

'I'm here.'

'Are you all right?'

'Mm,' she said. 'Was Cathy okay when you got back?'

'Not really.'

'She didn't suspe—'

'It was the drink she was angry about.'

'Of course, yes, she would be.'

'But, Nance.' His voice had her again—a hook through the guts. Tugging on the line he had drawn.

'Yes?'

'I'll still be looking at you across the office. You know?'

'Yes,' she said.

'I'll still be seeing you look back at me.'

'Yes,' she said. The bastard. Not letting her go.

'But it has to stop there. Agreed?'

'Yes,' she said.

He whispered, 'Bye bye, love,' and she put down the phone, trying to hate him.

It's gone one o'clock, and we're impatient for the hearse to arrive. Strained awkwardness reigns between Gina and me. We can't discuss what's happening with us when Matilda's listening, and I don't know what to say in the snatched moments she isn't. We're reduced to small talk.

'Obama's asked Hillary to be Secretary of State,' Gina says brightly. 'Isn't that something?'

'Great.'

'She needs to persuade him on mandatory health care.'

I try to engage. 'I thought he was for it already.'

'Sure he is, but not mandatory. He's chicken about forcing people.'

'God, yes, I forgot we Brits are brainwashed. The NHS is a commie plot.'

Today feels unreal and impossible. I want it to be over. Part of me—Chief Mourner, robotic, dry-eyed—labours to hold things together. He's got the booze in, wine, sherry and beer, and Gina has made sandwiches. She said we had to do this the right way. She's brought the food and my suit in two fat carrier bags. She looks like a stranger in her tailored black coat, her curls tamed in a roll on the back of her head. She hasn't taken her coat off or kissed me. I haven't kissed her.

Matilda, in her grey school things and black leggings, is fixated on Granny, repeatedly opening the front door to look along the street, wailing, 'Where is she? She's lonely all by herself.' We try to console her, to convince her that Granny is safe and at peace.

When I got to Kilburn on Saturday, Matilda ran at me frantically—'Daddy! Daddy!'—as though she'd feared I had gone from her life. She wanted me to contradict Gina, to insist of course Santa exists. When I confessed that he doesn't, she wailed inconsolably, an ear-splitting grief that went on all day. Turned out she'd walloped a kid at school who'd mocked her belief.

'You should stay,' Gina said after telling me this. 'You should be helping me.'

I was in danger of wailing myself. 'Just a bit longer, please,' I said, 'till the funeral. Being in Mum's house helps me to mourn her.'

'With Alison?'

'No, I swear. Solemnly swear. Just me.'

She offered wine when Matilda was finally asleep, and we sat, feet up, side by side on the marital bed, sipping it. I didn't touch her, and she didn't touch me.

'So,' she said, 'when you're done mourning, do you plan on coming back here to Kilburn, or do you see us living in Battersea?'

I couldn't get my head round the question. 'I realise how weird I'm being, but give me a few more days, eh?'

We managed a kiss when I got up to go. 'Okay,' she said. 'No rushing to decisions.'

Now she tells Matilda to keep a look-out and follows me to the bedroom, where I've retreated to put on the suit. 'How's it going?' she says.

I shrug wordlessly.

She steps close to adjust my tie, and I'm looking into her hair. 'We'll talk soon, I promise,' I tell her.

When she goes back downstairs, I linger, avoiding her, checking through my speech notes, assessing Chief Mourner in Mum's long mirror, hoping no one will notice his scruffy shoes.

Below I find the front door open and Matilda outside again, hugging her shoulders to keep out the cold. I'm about to fetch her in when Gina calls from the kitchen.

'What?' I say.

She stands with her back to me, looking out at the garden. 'I guess Matty would like it here. She could have

47

her friends round. It's a neat little house, a good neighbourhood.' Her voice lacks enthusiasm.

I'm starting to mumble something when Matilda runs in. 'They're here. Granny's here.'

The undertaker's at the door, his features moulded in tragedy. 'Are you ready, Mr Jonnson?' he murmurs. 'Mrs Jonnson?'

He supports Gina's elbow, guiding her out. I follow, trying to breathe calmly, holding Matilda's hand, feeling its smallness.

The sun's shining, but there's a crisp edge to the air. The neighbour stands at her gate with Mum's cat in her arms. 'It's beautiful,' she says. 'Really lovely.'

I stare at the hearse. The coffin's hidden in a cloud of white flowers, whose scent clings to the suits of the undertaker and his three flunkies standing to attention at the kerb. There are cards inscribed with black italics—*To Mum with all my love, Mark*—*For my Granny, I'll miss you, Matilda XXX*—*To Nancy with love always, Ted* (that's Dad) —and a few more from colleagues and friends. Matilda tugs at my arm. 'Is she in the box? Is she frightened?'

'It's only her body, Little. She's not alive any more.'

'She's up in heaven, looking down at us, smiling and watching,' says Gina.

We sit facing forward, Matilda between Gina and me, in the back of the limo that will follow the hearse. The interior is plush leather, and there's no noise from the engine as we start to roll. The undertaker walks ahead in the road, his top hat pressed to his waistcoat. At the corner he steps up to the pavement, lets the hearse draw alongside, then bows to the coffin before donning his hat, walking solemnly to the limo and taking his place beside the driver.

The chapel has pews and a cross on the wall and a side entrance they open too soon, trying to hurry us, so some of the crowd wander in ahead of the coffin. I want to shout, Stop for Christ's sake; I want the undertaker to tell them they shouldn't.

Dad is here. He and I shake hands, and Gina offers him condolences as though he's the bereaved widower, not Mum's ex. Has he shrunk since last summer? He barely comes to my shoulder. I got my height from Mum's side of the family. Seven years Mum's senior, he must be sixty-three. With a pang I realise I have no blood relatives now except Dad and Matilda. He and Mum were only children, me too, and Matilda looks set to be one. I was keen to give her a brother or sister, but Gina wouldn't hear of it, said one was more than enough.

Matilda hurtles up to each mourner, asking, 'Do you know my granny?' Telling them, 'She didn't feel anything when the bus hit her. She's not in the box, she's in heaven.'

'Shush,' Gina says. 'We shouldn't have brought her,' she whispers.

Gradually the subdued responses dampen Matilda. She stares for a while at a woman who's dabbing her eyes with a hanky; then she breaks into hiccupping sobs. She has me choking up, but Chief Mourner mustn't blub. He needs to safeguard his voice for his words of remembrance. He swallows and rides out the discomfort in his sinuses. A Schubert quintet beckons from the chapel as the undertakers lift the flower-laden coffin. There are heaps more flowers, he notices, white as requested except for one wreath that's a jarring crimson red.

As we go in, he scans the ranked mass of faces. The pews are crammed full; at the back some are standing. Plenty of these people he knows or half recognises, but many are strangers. Maybe one of them is Oz.

He takes his place in the front pew with Matilda and Gina. The undertakers withdraw, the doors close and he's shut in with the coffin and the expectant crush of strangers and the crematorium DJ tucked away in the corner. The air's chilly, but it smells more like a cupboard than a crypt. They've told him how long he has and which buttons to press. All he has to do is squeeze Matilda's hand, then get up and speak.

His feet carry him to the podium. The murmurs fade to silence as he unfolds the notes from his pocket and begins. The trick, he finds, is to steer his mind away from the body three feet from his elbow, to disengage from the words and read them like a shopping list. A brief account of Mum's life. Compliments to her lovability, her outgoing nature. It's doing the job, giving these people something to listen to. He's nearly there, just a couple of lines left, the hardest. He takes a breath.

'What I'm missing most is her laughter—'

The truth of it hits me. Chief Mourner goes AWOL and leaves me to finish this alone. I force my voice on, a raw whisper. 'She always seemed to be laughing.'

One last sentence to speak. 'She was a happy person who made other people feel hap—'

The final word breaks in the middle. But it's okay; it's done. There's a murmur from the congregation, a wail from Matilda. I reach out, brush the coffin with the tips of my fingers and stumble back to the pew.

It's the turn of others to speak: some senior lawyer from Mum's office and an old friend of Mum's, Sally, from Bristol. I barely hear what they say. I've an arm around Matilda. I'm giving her my tissue in place of her soggy one. I'm struggling to reassemble Chief Mourner because when Sally stops he has to get up again.

He makes it to his feet, walks to the coffin and turns. Concentrates on speaking the line from the undertaker's script. 'Let us be quiet for a minute with our own thoughts of Nancy.'

God almighty, that was hard. Whatever I do, I mustn't

think of her. Think, how long is a minute? This long? Or this long? Swallow down.

'And now, in sorrow but without fear, with love, we commit Nancy's body.'

My finger moves to the button. I press it and wait for the crematorium to do its thing.

I decided against music for this bit. I thought accompaniment would be trite, but oh dear, what a mistake. The whir and click of the two gloomy drapes trundling out from the wall is ridiculous. Along the sides of the coffin they go before turning to meet in front of it, more reminiscent of the double zip on a suitcase than a final curtain.

The silence is unstable. I almost expect giggles or boos. I stare at the floor, unable to look up. For a few seconds we stand waiting, until I remember there's another button to press. It summons the undertakers, who open the door and start herding us out, rescued by a nice bit of Bach.

Outside we mill around shivering, unsure what happens next. At least it isn't raining. A mate of mine, Geoff Eliot, has arrived, cursing the traffic and turning to wave hi at Gina. He and I go back to primary school. He fell for Mum when he was seven, he reminds me, polishing the lenses of his fashionable spectacles on his black tie.

A queue is forming, wanting to speak to Chief Mourner, who has no choice but to listen, although most of what they say goes by in a blur. Secretaries from Mum's office gush platitudes about how much they'll miss her. Bristol Sally confesses she always envied Mum's capacity for joy, even when it seemed dangerous or selfish. 'It was just like her to step off a pavement without looking,' she says and smiles as though careless road-crossing's a virtue. Sally's daughter, Grace, startlingly middle-aged since I last saw her, offers quietly, 'When I was little, I wanted to grow up to be Nancy.'

Last in line, Harry, the classy, grey-haired lawyer in crumpled pinstripes whose eulogy followed mine, confides, 'Your mother was a delightful flirt. She's been my fantasy for thirty years.'

There's a moment of relief when I'm left to myself, but then the undertaker sidles up. 'We must apologise, Mr Jonnson. The crematorium has inscribed your mother's name incorrectly on the commemorative plaque in the Garden of Remembrance. Please rest assured it will be rectified on the urn. This way, if your guests are ready.'

The 'Garden of Remembrance' is a joke, just a wind-raked stretch of paving with a low railing. Here's Matilda, staring at her granny's flowers, which are shrunk to insignificance beneath a small pseudo-brass notice that misspells our name in the usual way, 'Johnson'.

Matilda expresses my outrage. 'Heaven won't know who she is.'

Dad arrives with Gina, who says, 'It'll be fine, honey. No one's a stranger in heaven. They get it wrong at your school too, remember, but they never forget who you are.'

Dad bends to examine the flowers. He straightens up, gesturing irritably at the name.

'I know,' I say.

His eyebrows shoot up. 'You know?'

I don't bother to answer. Big deal, they've spelt his name wrong.

He glowers at me. 'Okay. Fine. You can do without me at the wake. I need to be in Hove by five-thirty.'

Bloody hell! He's a driving instructor these days, paid only for the hours he works, but surely he can take one day off for Mum's funeral? I'm about to say so, but he's gone, heading for the car park, pausing to speak to Bristol Sally, gesturing in this direction.

The rogue scarlet wreath draws my eye. It's bugging

me. This isn't the Cenotaph. The flowers aren't even real. Giant silk poppies. Layers of shiny petals, centres thick with black stamens. I stoop and peer at the card.

Nancy. Forever in my heart. Oz.

Back at the house I've no energy or desire to play host. The place is shoulder-to-shoulder with people I don't know who are beginning to laugh and talk about work and children and routes to Romford. I've said hello to them all—none of them is Oz—and I've escaped to sit on the stairs with a whisky.

The doorbell rings, and Matilda runs to answer. It's the neighbour with her two kids. The little girl carries a posy. She and Matilda stare at each other.

'Come on in, Jane,' I call from the stairs. 'Help yourself to a drink.'

I ought to jump to my feet, greet her properly, hear more words of condolence, but I pretend to be caught in conversation. A secretary from Mum's office sits a step down from me, gazing up through lashes thick with mascara. She's gabbling on about what a great person Nancy was, not aloof like the rest of those poncy lawyers, didn't mind mucking in, what a shock, how carefully she herself has been crossing Whitehall since the accident; and I'm nodding soberly, and what I'm hearing, loud and clear, from her cherry-painted lips is, 'I fancy you.'

I sip at the whisky. The air's dry and close, and there's a smell of hot dust. The heating's up way too high. This is Mum's funeral; I mustn't think about sex. My glance slides past the girl's smile to the shadow of her cleavage, the shine on her outstretched black calf.

I steer my mind to the noise in the living room. General chatter. Matilda asserting authority over the child from next door. Gina holding court. 'She sure was young for her years. Had so much energy. What would you call

53

it? *Joie de vivre?* We can't believe she's passed on. It's been tough for Mark.'

I concentrate on how carefully Gina's choosing her words to avoid telling an untruth. 'Truth is the most important thing,' she screamed at me when she found Alison's note in my jeans. 'Don't you see this makes everything worthless? Less than worthless, it's crap. I mean, who *are* you, Mark? I don't know who you are?'

'Nor me, neither,' I said truthfully, although what kind of answer was that?

It's hard to be just one person.

Anyway, the truth is Gina didn't like Mum. She disapproved of her '*joie de vivre*', accused her of absurd eagerness, naiveté about politics and world issues. She would ask, didn't Nancy embarrass me, didn't I agree she should act more her age?

Funny to think of it really. Put those two women together and each acted the age of the other. I snort at the idea, and Mum's little assistant at my feet smiles up at me.

'What's the joke?' she says.

'Nothing. Just a stray thought.'

She drops her gaze to my mouth. 'They're the best kind.'

I laugh, and she grins.

A man steps between us on his way up to the bathroom. When he's gone by, the girl has her head bowed and is fingering the razor-cut hair at the nape of her neck.

I tear my attention away to watch Gina, who's in the living-room doorway now chatting to my mate Geoff. She looks regally beautiful with her straight back and raised chin and her hair swept up like that. Geoff's flirting his eyes at her over his specs, and she's smiling at some joke he just cracked.

'We must meet up for a pint soon,' Geoff said to me

as he stepped through the door. Last time we did he was as reticent about his domestic situation as I was about mine. He works nine-to-five in retail management and has a harassed wife, two pre-school kids and a people carrier.

Maybe Gina should shag him. It would even the score and help clarify what I want. He and she always jabber away together because they're both frustrated politicians. He's a big noise in his local Labour party, standing twice unsuccessfully for a council seat. She dreams of working for US health-care reform. I imagine him closing those few inches now to kiss her. I wonder what she would do, how jealous would I be. The doorbell rings again.

Matilda and the little girl from next door come running to see who it is. Gina opens the door, and it's Alison.

Bloody hell.

Gina smiles. 'Come on in.' They've never met; to Gina this is one more late arrival. 'Let me take your coat.'

Alison looks nervous. She starts unwinding her woollen scarf, then spots me on the stairs. 'Mark, I didn't realise... I should have... I just thought, maybe after the funeral...'

'Who are you?' says Gina.

'Can I get you a drink?' says Geoff.

'I'm...' says Alison, looking at me.

I get to my feet, and I'm suddenly gigantic—Big Man—towering up the narrow stairs, all six foot three of me, above the mayhem that's about to kick off.

Play it straight. 'This is Alison Finlow, my boss. Alison, this is Gina...' I indicate with an open palm, 'Matilda... my friend Geoff...' I glance down, 'and— forgive me, I've forgotten your name.'

'Tracy,' says the girl on the stairs. 'Nice to meet you.'

Alison smiles nervily. 'I just wanted to pay my

respects.'

I'm looking at Gina. She looks straight back at me and reaches for Matilda's hand. 'Okay, fine,' she says quietly. 'It's your call, Mark. Which of us leaves?'

Shit. My mind whirls to no purpose. I turn to Alison. Surely she will back out.

She doesn't. Her blue eyes grow big.

I touch her shoulder. 'I'm sorry, but it's best you go.'

'Oh boy,' says Tracy.

Gina steps close to Alison. 'You heard him.'

I don't like her doing that.

Alison turns pink, holds her ground, shakes her head.

I don't like her doing that.

Gina's mouth is opening. Matilda is watching and listening.

Big Man takes over. 'Pause this,' he says, then jumps down the stairs and pushes past Geoff into the living room. 'Excuse me, everyone.'

They stop talking and look.

'I'm sorry, folks, and grateful to you for coming, but it's been a long day, a long week, and I have to wind up the party now. I hope you don't mind.'

Strangely they don't. They barely seem to blink or consider it odd. They mill about in the hall, finding their coats, offering each other lifts.

'Keep in touch, Mark,' says Bristol Sally.

'All the best, Mark,' says Grace.

'Good luck, mate,' says Tracy.

'We must have that pint soon,' says Geoff.

The front door opens and closes. The temperature in the hall drops to frigid. Big Man notices the glass in his hand and swallows the rest of the whisky.

Alison is sitting on the stairs. Gina, jostled by departing guests, holds to her spot. 'What's the answer, Mark?'

All is clear now in Big Man's head. 'I just gave it. Everyone's leaving. That means you and Alison both.'

Alison nods. She stands and begins rewinding the scarf.

Gina ignores her. 'You can't do this,' she says.

'I need to be by myself.'

Gina wobbles explosively. Then her shoulders go down, and she takes her coat from its hook. 'Whatever.'

Alison is hovering. Big Man shakes his head, and she moves to the door, steps outside.

Gina's bundling Matilda into her parka. Matilda resists, launches into piercing shrieks, 'No! No! No!' and Big Man crumbles to nothing. Jesus, what the hell am I doing?

Matilda's screeching, 'I want to stay,' and stamping as though trying to smash the mosaic tiles. She aims kicks at Gina's shins as Gina manhandles her into the street. 'You can't stay,' Gina hisses. 'You have school tomorrow.'

She pulls the door to behind them. I wrench it open again. 'I'll see you soon, Matty. I'll ring you tonight. Gina. Gina, listen... Thank you for today.'

She straightens up, her eyes burning. 'You asshole,' she says. Then she's dragging Matilda off down the road.

Alison has been lurking by the gate. She says, 'Are you sure you wouldn't like me to stay?'

Matilda's screams grow fainter. I see with sudden clarity that Alison wanted this or something like this to happen.

'For Christ's sake,' I say, shutting the door.

I try Gina's mobile, but it's switched off. As soon as it's possible they might be there I'm dialling Kilburn like crazy, every few minutes, hanging up when the voicemail cuts in. I've been stupid. I haven't understood what's important.

Matilda.

I've been worried about losing her, but that isn't the point. The point is not to let her lose me.

Hang up. Redial. I have to show her I care. I have to prove it, not just now but every day, all the time, so she never doubts it.

Hang up. Redial. Click, yes, at last. 'Gina—'

'Mark, leave us alone, we've nothing to say to y—'

'Gina, I'm sorry. I don't know what got into me. I didn't mean that to happen.'

'Is it Daddy?' Matilda's voice in the background.

'Matty!' I shout.

'Go put your coat away,' says Gina. 'Do it right now.' Back to me, low and clenched. 'This is unfair. We've only just gotten in. She's in meltdown, fighting me all the way home. I can't talk—'

'Gina, listen. I was wrong—'

'Darn right you were wrong. You humiliated me—'

'I wasn't thinking straight.'

Matilda is screaming. There's a scuffle, some thumps, muffled yelling, a banged door, then Gina's back on the line. 'This is it, Mark. We're through. I want a divorce.'

'Please, Gina. Think. You said yourself we mustn't rush into decisions.'

'Are you kidding me? You just made one.'

'I didn't. I ducked it. I absolutely shouldn't have ducked it, you're right.'

I'm pacing the landing with the phone clamped to my ear. 'Alison hasn't been here, not once,' I say. I push through to the bedroom and stare at the bed as if this somehow proves it. 'And she's not coming here ever. That's it, Gina, I promise. I've had it with Alison.'

Silence on the line except for Matilda's outraged cries. The truth of what I've said hits me, and the corollary's simple: Gina and me for the sake of Matilda, the only choice we can make. I'm finding words for this when, 'Who gives a shit?' Gina says.

I catch sight of myself in the mirror: a big guy in a funeral suit, carrot top, flushed face. I take a breath.

'It's hopeless,' she says. 'We both know it is, Mark.

Her words drag at my stomach. Maybe she's right. Hell, what is wrong with me?

'We just need time,' I say dismally, 'to get our heads sorted.'

She erupts. 'More time like *this?*

Matilda is shrieking, 'I hate you, I hate you,' from behind the shut door. Gina must be leaning on it.

'Where's Matty?' I say.

'On the landing.'

'Let me speak to her.'

And suddenly Gina's shouting, out of control. 'You bastard, you asshole. You think you're so perfect? The model father, yeah? She's exhausted from exhausting me all across London, people staring at her on the subway, tutting at me, and you think you have the magic touch because you can calm her? You bastard, you bastard, you bastard.'

'Okay, okay,' I'm repeating. 'Please, Gina... please, let me help you. I can have her here this Saturday. I can—'

'For real?'

'Never more so.'

She laughs bitterly. 'Fine then. You take her. Have her the whole weekend. See how you like being a single parent.'

When I put down the phone, I take in the quietness. The empty bedroom, the open door, the landing beyond. I imagine Matilda here, happy, swarming up me, clobbering me, kicking me in the ribs, bellowing in my ear about what her stuffed animals are saying.

The phone rings. 'Mark, it's me.'

Big Man resurrects himself: strong, cold and businesslike. 'I was going to call you.'

Alison sniffs and speaks wistfully. 'She's so beautiful.'

'Matty?'

'No, Gina. What an idiot. I shouldn't have come.'

'No, you shouldn't. How did you get the address?'

'From your file. Next of kin. I'm so sorry. I thought, your mum's house, there'd be nobody in. I thought the wake would be in Kilburn. But when I saw the lights, well of course, and then, golly Mark, are you and Gina actually separated? When did that happen?'

Her eagerness is repulsive.

'Let's be sure I understand this,' I say. 'You were having a look at Mum's house?'

'Well, I know it sounds silly, but—'

'Not at all.'

'Oh Mark, I—'

'Shut up and listen. You came to size up the property—'

'No—'

'—saw the party was here and decided to ring the bell.'

'It's not how you think. I shouldn't have done that, but please stop being so cold, Mark. I've said I'm sorry. I didn't mean any harm. I thought, slip in quietly, it might cheer you up, even if we can't—'

'Listen,' I say. 'It wasn't okay.'

There's a short silence. 'What are you saying?'

'I'm saying it's over.'

'No.'

'Yes.'

'You don't mean it.'

'You spoiled my mother's funeral, embarrassed my wife, upset my daughter—'

'You did those things yourself. Take a few days to think, Mark.'

'I don't need to.'

Her voice gathers tears. 'I came because I care about

60

you.'

'I don't think so.'

She pauses to blow her nose. 'So, this is it?' She sounds cooler.

'No hard feelings. Let's just forget it, okay?'

'You used me,' she says.

'Oh come on. Don't trot out the clichés.'

'We have to work together,' she says.

It's a pisser, but she's right. I make an effort to put some warmth in my voice. 'We can do that, I hope. We're both grownups, eh?'

Silence.

'So,' I say. 'No bones broken? Are we straight, boss?'

'I'll see you tomorrow,' she says, and rings off.

Saturday

She's asleep in this house.

My daughter.

The frost hardens outside, but she and I are snug. The study is a bedroom again. Thursday I shifted the file boxes to the living room and the desk to the front bedroom, and then last night I vacuumed and cleaned and made up the sofa bed with the girliest sheets I could find.

I've done no more thinking about what I want, because the only thing I've been wanting is to be with Matilda. Never before have I been this eager to have a serious man-to-child talk about Santa, to listen to her chatter, to read her a bedtime story. From a cupboard I've unearthed books from Mum's childhood. *Alice, Winnie-the-Pooh, The Wind in the Willows, The Wizard of Oz.*

Dorothy lived in the midst of the great Kansas prairies.

Matilda fell asleep before the cyclone arrived. Glancing up from *the sharp whistling in the air from the south*, I saw she had dropped off. For a while I stayed, with the open book on my knee, watching her breathe, smiling at her small, perfect hands, her red curls on the pink pillowcase.

The day has gone better than I dared to hope. I expected her to scold and batter me when I arrived at Kilburn to pick her up. I feared she would refuse to come with me, scream all the way, give me a taste of what Gina went through on Wednesday. Instead she was ready with her little packed bag, excited to be crossing London by Tube for the second time in a week. She seems more resigned to Mum's death now and has brought coloured drawings of heaven to show me. 'There are zillions of flowers, Daddy, and birds singing, and butterflies.'

I had lame speeches prepared about Gina and me, how we may get divorced but we won't be horrible to each other, and she probably has friends with divorced parents, and so on. But she hasn't said a word about any of that, too busy being gleeful at having her own bedroom—Mum used to tuck her up on the living-room sofa—and she's been nattering nonstop to her two teddies, who haven't been here before and need things explaining to them. 'Battersea's not by the sea, but it's quite near the river. And "batter" is because at the seaside you have fish and chips.' The trickiest question she's asked me so far is, 'Where's Mog?'

Since I closed *The Wizard of Oz* and crept from her room, I've done the washing up—we had burgers and ice-cream—tidied the kitchen, dug one of Mum's stews from the freezer to feed her tomorrow, and now I'm climbing the stairs again with a mug of coffee, humming *Somewhere Over the Rainbow*. All I need is to be with my child. This, plus my students, some beers with the lads, a willing woman in my bed now and then.

Mum's office-friend Tracy pops into my mind, perched on the stairs, flirting, drawing a laugh from me. I picture her here now, following me into the front bedroom, slipping out of her clothes, standing naked with a corner of the duvet in her hand.

She morphs into Gina. 'What's the answer, Mark?' Refusing to smile.

I don't have an answer, a smile, an erection. I can't think about Gina.

I set the mug on the desk and switch on the laptop in search of distraction. I'll have a go at seeing what I can find out about the mystery lover. Rummaging through Mum's cupboards last night, I half expected to unearth some mementos of him, but I didn't. I thought he might email condolences, but he hasn't. The inbox is empty tonight except for one from Alison, telling me that I'm 'under stress at the moment' and she's 'there for me'. I delete it and cool my annoyance by Googling 'poppies'. *Papaver... blood red... symbol of sleep and death, also of resurrection.*

One of Mum's folders is called 'diary'. I dip in around the time she moved here and scroll through, skimming for the name Oz.

Within seconds a lump forms in my throat. This stuff is tough to read. It spooks me to see her private voice light up the screen.

I let my mind wander last night, drinking wine, dancing alone, fantasising the past and the future. Today I've told myself, 'Quit, girl. Let go of that stuff. It's like cigarettes. You think it's okay to have just one reminisce, but it isn't. Before you know it you're hooked and making yourself unhappy.

I close the file and sit motionless, shocked again that she's gone.

It has been far too easy to make this house mine: there was almost no clutter; she was forever filling charity bags. She detested nostalgia; equated it with self-pity, which she hated even more. When she moved here seven years ago, selling the sprawling Muswell Hill flat where I grew up, she shocked me by abandoning three-quarters of her possessions to a house-clearance firm.

I tried to dissuade her. 'Some of these things belonged to your parents.'

'They're yours if you want them,' she said.

I rescued a few sacred objects, as many as Gina would allow me. Fair play to her: she was eight months pregnant, and the flat was piled high with baby stuff. It was Mum who was being unreasonable.

If I break with Gina, I'll need to rescue those heirlooms again. It would be a decision to collect them and cart them here. The tarnished brass kettle, my grandfather's WWII pilot's logbook, a box of black-and-white snaps of people who look vaguely like me, inscribed on the back with fragments such as 'Diggory at Broadstairs in 1952'.

After Mum's move here from Muswell Hill, I realised she'd chucked out my music cassettes. She was unrepentant in the face of my fury, spouting William Morris. 'Have nothing in your house that you do not know to be useful or believe to be beautiful.'

'Screw William Morris,' I yelled. 'They were useful and beautiful to *me!*'

'If so, I'm sorry, but you haven't played them in years. The past is a chain, Mark,' she said. 'Cut yourself free.'

When I calmed down I could see she was right. The cassettes meant nothing.

She's telling me the same now: Don't get bogged down in my diary. Okay, but I'm still curious about Oz. I run a search of the hard disk, and a long list of files materialises. I open 'diary 2002' and find:

I haven't been away since my three weeks in Oz last February. Now the move here is over, I'm planning Barcelona.

Then:

Stir fry vegetables for 5 mins, add 8 fl oz stock

Then:

Conversation was an effort. I soon saw it was futile. He took it well, as if he had another dozen women lined up!

I scroll up to discover this 'he' was called Patrick and she met him through an internet dating site. Oz probably came later than 2002, but I open an earlier file at random, 1997, and search on his name just in case.

I need hardly record my jubilation at Labour's landslide. It's there in the journalists' boozy outpourings. The Observer's headline was 'Goodbye Xenophobia!' Mark and I stayed up until dawn, drank fizzy wine, bounced with delight like children and have been shooting grins at each other since. My friends say, 'Isn't it wonderful?' Even my father, in hospital, is distracted from his grim slipping away and pretends a smile. I don't know where I am with

Mr Blair, but I pity the Jeremiahs who are already intoning how it will go sour. How sad to be averse to hope. I've bought a pair of red earrings for 99p.

I'm on my feet, trying to outpace the grief. Transported back to that May night in Muswell Hill. Seeing her whooping and bouncing on the battered corduroy sofa in front of the fourteen-inch Sony, alarming Mog, who was young and sleek then.

Blair is a bastard, and Mum is dead.

I go to fetch a whisky. Just half an inch with some water; mustn't sabotage tomorrow with Matilda. I climb back up the stairs.

I was whooping along with Mum that night. Too young to vote, a month away from my eighteenth birthday. To my sixth-form-college mates I pretended political cynicism, but with Mum I dropped the pretence.

I remember her recent excitement over Obama. 'He's different,' she enthused down the phone. 'He bloody well has to be. Obama's no Blair.' For once she and Gina saw eye to eye. She'd rung to invite us to her birthday party the day before she died. Her dancing with her pals, the whole celebration: it was as much for Obama, the planet and humanity's uncertain future as it was about racking up another year.

I shouldn't be reading her diaries. They're bristling with wormholes that will suck me back in time and make me sad.

An email pings in. It's from Becky, a college girlfriend of mine from before I met Gina. She's teaching in Stevenage. *How's things, Mark?* she says. *Robert just dumped me, boo hoo, but actually not very boo hoo because I was just about to dump him. Sod him for getting there first, but what the hell, there'll be another along behind. What is it with me, eh? Can't imagine being married like you, with a kid. For how long is it now? Unbelievable! Spill the beans. Slippers and telly, or adventurous sex, which is it? No, please don't tell—either way you'll depress me. Here we both are, 29, and you're posh and I'm still Becks. You're a pillar of the community and I'm a... what? No, don't answer that either! Love, Bx*

I reply: *Buck up, Becks, you're ace, and wise not to be hitched yet. I'm regretting at leisure. Love my kid though, has to be said. Get out there and party! Love and hugs, M*

I log off. Blow my nose. Look in on Matilda. Brush my teeth. Go to bed.

She slept without dreams. When she woke, she lay still for a long while, noticing the greasy dribbles on the doors of the kitchenette cupboards, listening to the Saturday traffic in the street below, thinking of Harry and Edward.

Edward had been kind yesterday. He must have sensed the raw state she was in—who could miss it?—but he hadn't mentioned it or asked her about it. He'd offered a sort of solid, unspoken, unobtrusive support and then helped her out in the afternoon when she got panicky over the Vaccine Damage Payments Bill. Harry had it pretty much drafted, but big boss Felix stormed in after lunch, demanding to know where Harry was, wanting a loophole he'd found plugged double-quick for a meeting with the Department first thing on Monday. The problem was in the conditions-of-entitlement clause. She'd had an idea how to solve it, but her mind was all over the place, so she'd asked Edward what he thought. Edward couldn't draft for toffee, was forever saying he was in the wrong profession, but he was good at asking the right questions; it wasn't the first time he'd shown her the way through. She'd ended up with an elegant redraft, and Felix had said, 'Well done. Clever girl.'

Nevertheless, when Nerys skived off early she'd jumped up and gone with her to avoid being alone with Edward. Any day now he was going to wind up his courage and ask her out. Not furtively to ply her with Guinness in a pub where no one knew him, but on his arm for a meal or to the theatre. She imagined Harry being there when he did it, head down on the other side of the office, pretending to work, listening as Edward found the words, alert for her answer. Because what would she say? I'm sorry, Edward, I'd rather not? Of course, Edward, I'd be happy to? And then would Harry be jealous?

Not now, anyway. Not yet. Yesterday she'd refused to meet Edward's eyes, filled the silence with chatter and dashed off to the Underground before he could offer to walk with her.

She moaned, swung her legs off the bed and sat for a moment, feeling slight nausea, rallying herself. She couldn't face the idea of going to Bristol, but it was Sally's fortieth, so she must.

Fresh from the shower, she pulled on jeans and a T-shirt, set her hair in large rollers and began packing her bag. She put on a Kate Bush LP, but then took it off again because *Man with the Child in his Eyes* had her wanting to cry. She lit a cigarette, hated it and stubbed it out, tore up the few that were left and dumped the shreds in the bin. She went out to the landing and tapped at the bedsit next door. No answer. Laura often went home for the weekends.

Back in her own room she impulsively crossed to the window, picked up the phone and dialled home herself. Talking to her mother never helped, not at all, but maybe this time, not that she could possibly tell her—

'Hello?' Her father's voice. Tetchy. His deafness had him fearing the phone.

She spoke clearly. 'Hello, Dad. It's Nancy. How—'

'I'll call your mother—ELIZABETH!'

She whipped the receiver from her ear but still heard the clunk as he dropped his on the polished mahogany. She imagined her mother's latest flower arrangement for the telephone table: three display blooms stuck in recycled Oasis, sprigged out with foliage. '*DAD!*' she yelled.

He must have been hovering. He was back on the line, muttering, 'No need to shout. She's coming.'

'Yes, Dad, but couldn't you and *I* find someth—'

'Here she is. Where *were* you, Elizabeth? It's Nancy for you.'

'Nancy? Hello, dear. How are you? I was on my way out.'

Nancy glared through the window at the avenue four floors below. 'I'm fine, Mum. Well, not fine, a bit miserable actually...'

She paused, but her mother said nothing.

She felt her throat tighten. '... anyway, just saying hello.'

Still nothing.

'... so don't let me keep you, Mum. I have to go too. It's Sally's birthday party in Bristol tonight.'

'That's nice, dear. Give them our love.'

Nancy put the phone down without saying goodbye. Not that her mother would notice.

'It's not nice, Mum. Nothing's nice, Mum. *I'm* not nice, Mum.'

2008, Sunday

I'm smiling to myself and humming *We're Off to See the Wizard* as I stir the stew over a low light. It smells good; I think there's wine in it.

Matilda has been here a whole twenty-four hours. She has let the cat back in and next door's children along with him. Josie—seven, snub nose, fair hair—and Christopher—four, snubber, blonder—have been thundering through the house with her, yelling and banging doors, and out into the garden where a pale sun has struggled clear of the chimneypots. The kitchen table's littered with crayons and paper, and one of her teddies lies face down on the backdoor mat. I pick it up and sit it on the chair next to hers.

She bursts through the door in a blast of cold that carries a whiff of decaying vegetation. 'Daddy, come and see what we've done.'

Out I go. They've gathered leaves in a heap.

Christopher jumps on the heap. 'I'm a tiger!'

'Stop it,' says his sister. 'We're tidying up.'

Matilda flashes her gap-toothed grin. 'You can help if you like, Daddy.'

I have the feeling she's testing me. How long before I start tuning her out as I used to do in Kilburn, frowning and saying I'm busy?

So I fetch a bin bag and join in, grabbing handfuls of leaves, half-rotted, crisp with frost, and stuffing them into the bag. The children's noses are pink, and their chatter makes speech bubbles of mist. The neighbour's here too, the other side of the low fence, hacking at her shrubs with secateurs. She's wearing several layers of sweater, and her mousy hair hangs in her eyes. She smiles at me but says nothing, just carries on clipping. There's been no sign of a bloke; she must be a single mum.

The cold's great, and the sunshine and the shouts of the children. Christopher starts hurling leaves at Matilda and Josie. After telling him off they retaliate, pelting him and each other and shrieking with laughter. Some killjoy slams a window shut two doors down. I bury my arm in the bag and hurl leaves in the air, handful after handful, trying to make the small garden like the inside of one of those paperweights.

'No, Daddy!' Matilda chases the leaves, furiously scooping them up and chucking them at me. She stuffs a handful down the neck of Christopher's sweater, and he starts to cry. 'Hey, Matty, stop,' I say, but she runs at him with another.

As I'm helping the little boy flap the leaves from his clothes, Matilda thumps my head with her fist.

'Ow. Hey, calm down,' I say. 'Stop now. Come inside. We have to eat tea soon.'

'No,' she says, puckering up.

'Come on. School tomorrow. Home by eight, Mommy said.'

'No. No. No.' She flings herself on her back in the leaves.

'Our teatime too, kids,' the neighbour calls helpfully. 'Thanks for having them,' she says as I lift her two over the fence. 'Shout when you need the favour returned.'

I reach for Matilda's hand to help her to her feet, but she refuses. Her eyes aren't seeing anything, her face reddens, her lips tremble.

Oh God, here we go. 'Matty, don't do this. We're having such a nice time.'

Her mouth opens and the first scream emerges, shrill as a whistle, piercing my brain. Stop. Please. I don't have energy for this.

I glance over the fence. The neighbour's picking leaves from her kids' hair and clothes, pretending not to be listening.

I lift Matilda bodily—'Come see what's for tea'—but she shrieks and flails, trying to bite me. I bundle her into the kitchen and set her down, closing the door with my shoulder. 'Please,' I beg her, 'don't spoil everything.'

She wrestles the door open again, screeching, 'I want to put leaves in the bag.'

I hold her clear while I lock the door and put the key on top of a cupboard. She starts clambering up the units. She has a foot in the sink.

'Stop it!'

A cupboard handle breaks off in her hand. 'Shit.' I grab her to my chest, shut off the gas under the stew and whip the pan out of range of her thrashing feet.

'Look,' I say. 'Granny has—Matty, stop, please—look, Granny has cooked tea for us—it's her lovely stew—shut *up*, for Christ's sake—I need to mash the potatoes.'

'I hate potatoes. I hate stew. I hate *you*.'

Her scream ricochets off the walls. I can barely think for the noise. I want to yell, I hate you too. I want to hurl her to the floor. I want to slam my way out of the kitchen.

Her heel connects with my shin. 'Ow! Shit!' I hold her at arm's length. 'You like potatoes, and lamb, and tomatoes.' I flip the lid off the pan, and it lands on the floor with a clatter. 'Look how yummy it is.'

She draws a shaky breath, then pulls her disgusted face.

'Don't be silly,' I say. 'You—'

'It's got onions, and onions are slimy.' She squirms from my grip and throws herself to the floor, sobbing.

Shit. Onions. What an idiot I am.

'Okay, you win.' I stand, glaring down at her. 'You *win*,' I bellow. 'So flaming shut *up*.'

She squeals as if I've kicked her. I have to get a hold on this anger, to calm myself down. I close my eyes.

73

Breathe.

I try to lift her, but she resists, hammering her fists on the tiles.

I crouch, my mouth close to her ear, whispering in the pauses in the racket she's making, when she draws breath. 'It's okay, Little... hush... it's no problem... We'll go shopping... What shall we buy?... What would you like to eat?'

At last she is quietening. I see the teddy on the chair, grab it and kneel beside her, among the dropped potato peelings, the broken-off handle, the pan lid, the blown-in leaves.

She sits up, hiccupping and moaning, rocking herself to and fro. When I offer the teddy, she snatches him to her chest, glaring at me, keening as if the end of the world has come.

I stick on a smile. '"Poor old Matty," says Teddy,' I say. '"What does poor old Matty want for tea?"'

Her chin trembles. 'Can I have anything?'

'Anything quick. How's about steak?'

She threatens to dissolve again. 'I want fish fingers.'

I hold tight to my smile. 'Okay, let's go get 'em, eh?'

The tantrum is over, and we're off to the supermarket. It's hard to be warm to her, my shinbone is throbbing where she kicked it, but if I can count to ten, force a smile, get the acid out of my voice, maybe the day isn't ruined.

We're going the backstreet route, following the railway embankment. There's no traffic, no one about, just the trains rolling above us into Clapham Junction. She seems happy enough now, skipping ahead of me, swinging her arms. Is she triumphant? She has on a red coat, a white pom-pom hat, stripy tights.

I got her over-excited out there in the garden. No lunch. Low blood sugar. My fault, not her fault.

74

It could have been worse. Gina deals with this stuff all the time, and then, she's right, I swan in from work or from drinks with the lads or a tryst with Alison and start playing Good Cop.

The school want the GP to check her over for physical causes before they refer her to a psychologist about the ADHD. I've told Gina no way. Am I wrong?

I don't want Matty labelled. Okay, she's a handful, but it's more likely Gina and I who need assessing. I've barely been home lately, and now what am I doing? Hiding in Mum's house, playing at being a weekend father.

Matilda turns and walks backwards. 'Josie says Christopher won't eat fish fingers. They make him cry.'

'He probably thinks fish have hands.' I waggle mine. 'Would you eat fish toes? Or fish knees?'

'Oh, Daddy,' she says, full of scorn.

A bit further along, she stalls so I nearly collide with her. 'Carry me!' She holds up her arms, daring me to refuse. I heave her up and hug her close, burying my nose in the cold pom-pom. It's not too late to mend my ways. I'm going to get better at this. Work out how to do it right. I want her to look back and feel lucky and loved.

'Can I live here?' she says.

'Well...' I say, putting her down.

'Mommy too.'

There's a moment of bleakness, of night swallowing day. I shake it off. 'We'll see, Little,' I say. 'Step by step.'

She falls silent and lags behind, head down, dragging her feet, scuffing her toes.

'Come on. Help me find the fish fingers.'

She ignores me. I take her hand to cross Latchmere Road. We're nearly at Asda, and I make a big effort to recapture the mood. 'Let me think, what do we need... fish fingers, frozen peas... Hey, Matty, let's only buy things beginning with "f", eh?'

She looks up. Sees me trying my hardest. 'Okay,' she concedes.

The game is seductive. It has us giggling and skirmishing in the bright warmth of the supermarket aisles, almost happy again.

'Whisky doesn't have even one, single, single "f"!'

Jesus, look at me, alkie Dad. But she'll be gone in a couple of hours and I'll be needing this bottle. 'It isn't whisky. It's firewater.'

'Don't be silly, Daddy.'

'I'm not being. It's fiery, hot firewater, and it's fundamental to my felicity.'

She laughs, but she's adamant. 'That's cheating, and cheating is naughty.'

'Very naughty, but you can cheat too. Choose anything you want, and I'll eff it for you.'

So we carry back fruit, and fresh milk, and fizzy pop, and five different tins, and fudge, and floss, and two new flannels, one for her, one for me, a cut-price bunch of flowers for Mommy, a litre bottle of firewater, and a fabulous, flamingo-pink T-shirt. She's back to her happy self. No way does she have ADHD. We've got through the screaming; she's had a great time in Asda. Gina needs to relax around her. I need to spend lots of time with her.

It's wintry dark, and the air's freeze-drying my nose. Matilda holds the flowers aloft like the Olympic torch. They're red, which has me remembering Oz. As we come through the front door, I sample the air. The distinctive aroma of Mum's house persists, but it's overlaid now with other things. I can smell the back garden and something that's indefinably Matilda. 'I love you, Matty,' I say.

She doesn't hear me. She has dumped the flowers and is running upstairs to look for the cat.

She doesn't need to hear that I love her if I make

76

sure to show it. My child is going to have my time and attention from today and for as long as she needs me, until one day she says, 'Piss off, Dad, I'm a grown up.'

We haven't much time. I charge into the kitchen, tip the groceries out on the table, skim-read cooking instructions.

She should hear me say it, though.

She comes down. The cat flops in her arms like a rag doll. 'I love you, Matty,' I say.

'I can eff Mog,' she says.

I burst out laughing before rescuing myself. 'A fossilised feline?'

She groans and rolls her eyes. 'No, Daddy. He's furry!'

The effing cat is a downer. Accusingly old, it keeps doing circuits of the house like I did on day one. Now it skulks in the kitchen where I'm rushing to grill the fish fingers and simmer the peas and heat the oven chips that made it into our trolley as 'French fries'. It stands where its bowls used to be and lets out a brief howl.

'Oh, poor Mog.' Matilda drops to the floor and looks into its face. 'He's sad. He wants Granny.'

'It's not Granny,' I say. 'It's the house. The changes have unsettled him.'

Something's burning. I leap back to the grill.

She puts on her talking-to-teddy voice. 'Don't be sad, little pussycat. If you don't like it here, you can come with me to America.'

I swing round. 'America?'

'That's what Mommy says. She says that blonde lady's your girlfriend. She says we might go and live with Grandma and Grandpa Franklin.'

At eight-thirty, Gina won't talk to me, just says, 'You're late,' and shuts the door in my face. Through the door I can hear Matilda trying to explain about the flowers and the effing game, but Gina's not listening. 'Don't start,' she says as their voices recede up the stairs.

My brain boils all the way back across London, and I'm reaching for the whisky when the potted plant on the windowsill catches my eye, limp and reproachful.

'Fuck off,' I growl.

I peel another black plastic bag from the roll and charge round the house bunging greenery into it. Straight in the dustbin out front. Job done.

The cat's back next door, but I've discovered the bloody thing has pissed on the landing. I'm swearing and scrubbing at the carpet when I decide I want rid of the photographs too. I've had a bellyful of encountering the happy-family images of me, wife and child. I do another circuit collecting a stack of them, which I dump on the living-room floor.

There's only one I need to keep seeing. It's Matilda's most recent school portrait. Her curls are pulled into tight plaits and she's scowling, but her eyes are untameable. There's a dark outer ring to her irises that makes the green seem astonishing. I unhook the photo from above the mantelpiece, carry it upstairs and prop it on the bedside table.

Monday

Grandma and Grandpa Franklin have moved into my brain, smiling inanely and draping New England lace over everything. I want to yell obscenities. I want to kidnap Matilda and run. First thing this morning I rang the probate solicitor, and he's booked me an appointment this afternoon with his colleague who does family law.

It's hard to pay attention to anything else. Teacher Guy's on autopilot, steering the class through a curriculum assessment. They have to listen to a taped phone conversation and take a message. Half of them are as tuned out as I am, and the other half can't get the hang of it. Lloyd rocks back on his chair thumbing his mobile. Big Keith stares through the window at the low-hanging clouds. Annetta and Amelia gossip as though in the canteen. Wayne searches the question sheet for 'ing'. Patricia copies the questions, letter by letter: *Who is ringing? Who is the message for?*

For crying out loud. Teacher Guy has carefully explained this, but they won't or can't do it. They could all take a message after a fashion if it meant something to them, but this tape is irrelevant noise. Only Comfort has grasped what's required. She's written the baker's phone number down and is stuck because she doesn't know which of the help words at the bottom of the sheet might be 'baker' or 'Barbara', 'icing' or 'cake'.

I play the tape a third time. Their eyes become glassy.

'*Lloyd!*' He stops rocking and shoots me a grin. 'Lloyd, who is it who's calling?'

'The fucking baker, man,' he says, triggering smirks and grunts from Wayne and a tut from Nazish.

'Okay!' I snap the tape off. They look startled,

uncomfortable. 'We'll stop that and take a look at the double 'e' sound.'

I collect the question sheets, which are mostly unmarked except for their shakily inscribed names.

It's not their fault; it's mine. Teacher Guy should be guiding them, praising them, getting the most from them short of writing the answers himself, but he's held out of reach by my impatience to see the solicitor and by horrified fury at Gina, who wants to transport my little girl three-and-a-half thousand miles and a deep, cold ocean away.

Last night, after murdering the plants and blitzing the photographs, I finally rang her. 'So, what's this about America?'

'It's an option,' she said. 'You have options. So do I.'

'We haven't sorted out what we feel yet—'

'What's to sort out? Alison's important—'

'No—'

'Else you're just messing around. Either way you're messing *me* around, Mark. We should quit.'

'All right, enough, look, move in here. Come to Battersea.'

'It's too late. I want to go home.'

'You don't mean that—'

Her laugh cut me off at the knees. I needed her to qualify, mitigate, but all she did was repeat herself. 'Totally I mean it.'

'And Matilda? What about her options? When would she get to see me?'

'Shit happens. Kids know that. They adapt. You could visit. You could have her visit. You could talk to her on Skype. Whatever.'

'Whatever' sent me over the edge. 'You want our child to be homesick?' I yelled. 'You want to watch her turn into a Wasp?'

'*I'm* a Wasp,' she said icily. 'There are worse things to

be. And at least—'

'At least *what*, Gina?'

Her parents aren't genuine Wasps, more aspiring to be. Grandma Franklin's charity committees. Grandpa Franklin's smug hints about the Masons. Their unthinking Republicanism and distaste for Obama. Their cotton-candy condescension to anything outside their experience. On their one appalled visit to Kilburn four years ago, they refused to sit down, to accept food or drink, to touch anything. Bolting back to the Hilton, they resumed their European tour, taking in the usual proofs of the Old World's quaint irrelevance, and ever since they've been angling to rescue their daughter and grandchild from this incomprehensible hell, to carry them safely 'back home'.

Half of me is there now: the limey son-in-law in small-town Connecticut two summers ago, the whole place with its sunlit clapboard 'cottages' and picket fences manicured and unreal, like Surrey crossed with Disneyland. I'm attempting to sit well on a straight-backed chair at a deep-polished mahogany table. I'm yearning for London's honest chaos and dirt. My eyes prickle at the air-conditioning; my ears hum with its white noise. I nod as Grandpa brags about his golf handicap. Gina's gormless jock of a brother flashes his laser-white grin, and Gina scowls like a teenager. Matilda, perched on a cushion, wields her knife like a hammer and pulls faces at her pork chop.

'Shall I cut it up for you, Little?'

'Good grief, she's a smart girl. She can do it herself,' Grandma says. 'Sit up straight, hon. Has no one taught you how to use your silverware? Watch how I do it.'

'She's only five, Mom,' says Gina.

'Which is way over time to be a young lady,' says Grandma. 'You need to be firm.'

I wink solidarity at Gina, but she glares at her plate.

For all her polish and politics, she's reduced to resentful silence with her parents.

'Little Lord Jesus is watching you, Matilda,' says Grandma, 'and he surely knows how to behave at the table.'

I'm opening my mouth to dispute this, but, 'Is your Tony Blair a golfer?' Grandpa wants to know.

'What?' I say, startled.

Grandma leans close to Matilda. 'What your Daddy means to say, honey, is, "Pardon me, sir?"'

'I doubt it,' I say. 'Blair's no sportsman. Useless at football. He can play the guitar though.'

I catch Gina's eye at last, wink at her, and she tries to smile.

'You mean soccer,' says the jock.

'It's football in England.'

'But you're in the US of A now.'

'I'll venture he's an excellent golfer,' says Grandpa. 'Margaret Thatcher, her husband played golf.'

Oh God, here we go. 'So he did,' I say.

'Sure test of character,' says Grandpa.

Gina wants Matty to live with these people?

'At least I'll be free, don't you see, Mark?' she insisted last night. 'To get a decent job—maybe work for the Democratic Party—I can't believe I'm not doing that—to start my novel—to go on dates goddammit while Mom looks after Matilda—to live some kind of a life.'

Oh Jesus. She's going to dump Matty on her mother. My child is going to be brought up by Grandma Franklin. I can't bear it.

Teacher Guy is sleepwalking the class through a picture-clue crossword with answers that contain double 'e', when the crèche nurse sticks her head round the door. Comfort moans softly and gets to her feet. She picks up her things and locks eyes with me. 'I'm very sorry,' she says.

She's near tears. I'm near tears. 'Excuse me a moment,' I say to the others, and I follow her into the corridor. 'Comfort.'

She turns. Her face is broad and beautiful. Her head is adorned with a shining black mass of hair extensions, elaborately braided and beaded.

'Comfort, do you need to rush off when class finishes?'

Her mouth quivers. She thinks that I'm going to scold her, exclude her or something.

'I could teach you for half an hour one-to-one.'

For a moment she doesn't catch on; then her smile sweeps doubt away. 'Ah-huhn!'

'Come at lunchtime,' I say. 'Bring the baby. Okay?'

Back in the classroom Teacher Guy spends the rest of the lesson working hard to make up for my snappishness. He gets them writing about 'what makes me happy', spelling the words they need on the board. When Annetta asks how to write 'Obama', Lloyd shouts, 'Yay, Barack!'

'Yay,' I echo. I write his name up in large letters. 'He worked hard at school,' I say.

Lloyd shrugs, but he smiles too.

When they leave, I keep tight hold of Teacher Guy, who gets some Scrabble letters from the cupboard and waits for Comfort.

Her baby's crying when she arrives.

'I'm sorry. He is hungry,' she says. 'I don't want to come late. I'm afraid you leave. Excuse me.'

She sits facing away from me on a chair by the window, and soon the baby is quiet. Her yellow sweater is rucked up, showing her bare back and what look like a couple of nasty bruises. I'm wondering about these when she twists her head to smile at me.

'There's no rush,' I say. 'You feed him. That's fine.'

Feeding a baby takes time. I keep the conversation going. 'How old are you, Comfort?'

'Twenty-five.'

'And you never went to school in Ghana?'

She half turns, revealing the dark bulge of her breast. 'My father is Ashanti. He has many wives, many children. My mother, she work and send money, but my grandmother say is not enough. I cook and care for my brothers and sisters.' Her emotion rises. 'They go to school, have good jobs—'

I cut in. 'You know the alphabet, though?' She looks blank. 'Your ABC?'

She nods. 'Ah-huhn. My grandfather teach me.' She bends her head and recites to the baby. 'A... B... C... D...'

Eventually she rearranges her sweater and carries the sleeping baby towards me. 'Matthew,' she says.

'Is he your first?'

Her eyes widen with pride. 'I have three. Luke, Mary and Matthew.'

The baby's wrapped in a long blue and gold cloth. She shakes and refolds it, leans forward, winds it around him and herself and in a few movements has him snugly cocooned on her back. She turns a chair sideways-on to the table and sits. Waves her hands, beams, and confidently announces, 'Now I learn!'

Teacher Guy asks her to write her name and address: Hanbury Close, Tooting, London. Her false fingernails hamper her. She transposes some letters and leaves others out. 'I work hard,' she pleads.

'Don't worry. Tell me, can you read these?' He arranges Scrabble tiles into the words 'cat' and 'dog'.

She bites her lip, shakes her head, and it's my turn to be ashamed. What the hell use is the double 'e' sound to her?

'That's fine,' says Teacher Guy, 'because I'm going to show you how reading works.' He points. 'This is "cat".'

84

This is "dog".' She leans forward, eager to memorise the spellings, but he stops her. 'Two words,' he says, 'fine, but also six sounds.' He separates the tiles, demonstrates the phonemes and asks her to echo him. 'Feel how your mouth makes each one.'

She examines the workings of her teeth, tongue and throat. We shuffle and reshuffle the six letters, sounding them until she associates each phoneme without thinking.

'Time for a new word.'

I pick out C, O and T, and she makes the three sounds.

'Now, can you run them together? What word do they make?'

She's stuck. She tells me the phonemes again. Frowns, straining to understand.

'What does Matthew sleep in at night?' I glance at the little head among the beaded braids on her back. Do Ghanaian babies have cots, I'm wondering, or do they sleep in something simpler and more natural, like this blue and gold cloth?

'A cot,' she says.

'Well done. Cuh-oh-tuh, cot, can you hear it?'

'Ah-huhn!'

I sound out more words. 'Dot,' I say. 'Tag.'

She strains to understand. She nods when I make the leap from phonemes to word but cannot make it herself. 'Got,' I say. 'Got,' she says. 'God,' I say. 'God,' she says.

I gather the tiles up. 'That's enough for today.'

She's dismayed. She thinks I'm giving up on her.

'It's okay. You'll get there. You just need to practise.'

She nods vehemently. 'I work hard for you. After *every* class.'

Hang on, I didn't say that.

'Please. I need so much.' There are tears in her eyes. She wipes them away with a finger. 'Please.' Her hand touches mine. The false nails are intricately painted. The baby stirs on her back and burps softly. I remember her bruises.

'Okay. Half an hour, Monday and Friday.'

She has hold of my arm. 'Jesus, he bless you. I work very hard.'

Friday

Somehow I've made it through another week to be here again in Mum's pitch-dark hall, my back to the door I have just closed behind me. Out spill the groans that choked me as I raced down the hill. The other commuters were peeling off into homes glowing with Christmas lights, but I wanted only this.

I fight to get control of myself. The family-law solicitor says I have rights. Gina needs my consent or a court order to 'remove' Matty to the States. If I contest, the court will consider her welfare, Connecticut versus here: care, schooling, funding. They may want to know her preference, but more likely not; she's a bit young to be asked. Before rubberstamping a move to America, they'll want undertakings from Gina that the 'father-daughter relationship will be fostered'.

My chances of keeping her with me? The solicitor shook her head. 'You can never be certain. It's worth a try, but if I'm honest, not high.'

I would lose. But I can't lose. I mustn't. I'm caught in an anarchy of warring voices: no centre, no sense. I switch on the kitchen light. The container I dug out of the freezer this morning stands in a pool of melt water. Mum's Bolognaise sauce.

Her cat is hunched on the sill outside, eyeing me balefully. Hard luck, puss. You and I can't help each other. I pour whisky, gulp and refill.

I push on through the minutes, hanging over the stove now, raking a fork through boiling spaghetti, reaching again for the glass. Still drinking, not thinking.

I was so panicked yesterday I made the mistake of offloading to Alison.

'How are you?' she said. 'You look dreadful. Do you need to share?'

We went to the pub together. I was hoping for help, a clue to a solution, but all Alison gave me was outrage —'So selfish!'—which is not right or fair because Gina's no more selfish than she is. Plus the outrage was an act. Her blue eyes were greedy. She wants my child in Connecticut and me back in her bed. She even tried squeezing my knee.

Oh Jesus, it's hopeless. I drop the fork in the pan, and for a moment I'm lost in the seethe of spaghetti. But then a life raft takes shape in the steam. It's Saturday tomorrow, and Matilda will be here again. I'm pouring spaghetti through a sieve, blinking in the fog. The lost fork tumbles out. Matty's not in Connecticut yet.

After eating, I'm limp as a shed skin. I need to distract myself, hope for a decent night's sleep. I drink some water to douse the effects of the whisky, then drag myself upstairs and turn on the laptop. Teacher Guy will plan Monday's class and his next session with Comfort.

I saw her this afternoon; the thought has me smiling. The baby was snug on her back, and she was talking excitedly, banging on about Jesus and angels and how she was praying for me and something about one of her kids. I wasn't paying attention. I was fetching the Scrabble tiles from the cupboard while I noticed how musical her voice was, how many octaves it was touching. I was waiting for her to quieten and focus when she wound up, full of pride and expectancy, '... and I'm knowing what this word is!'

I took in her radiant face, the flawless, smooth skin, the triumph in her voice.

'Say again.'

She didn't mind. She liked telling it. She told it several times over. She'd taken a child to the doctor and found the door locked. Printed notices meant nothing, she barely registered them, but this one drew her attention:

she half-recognised the word on the door. It said 'CLOSE', like her address Hanbury Close, and then D. And she'd remembered the sound of a D.

'Ah-huhn! Closed!'

She was laughing, high on the miracle, and I was laughing too. 'That's it! You're reading!'

Teacher Guy getting his buzz. Maybe, just maybe, sometimes he earns me my place on the planet.

Lesson planning done, I decide to keep the demons at bay by blitzing the drawers under Mum's bed. So here I am on the floor, sliding a drawer off its runners onto the carpet. It's stuffed full of maps, guidebooks and pamphlets from holidays. This shouldn't take long. A quick look through, then most of it straight into the recycling bag.

There are some treasures. Her school reports on yellowed paper in faded fountain-pen ink. A few photographs of her as a child: a sweet face but shy-looking, uncertain, possibly unhappy. Her 1962 diary with brief entries in a painstaking, juvenile hand: *Daddy says I am getting more riliable.* Her graduation certificate. An ancient, anonymous valentine. A small, typewritten letter confirming her appointment as Assistant Parliamentary Counsel, asking her to report to 36 Whitehall on 9 January 1978, a year and a half before I was born.

A white envelope contains a thick stack of greeting cards. I slide one out. The message, in blotted blue ballpoint, is chaotic, some letters small, others large, sloping and lurching all over the place.

12 Jan '03 Darling Nancy, sorry this is late for xmas. Things are going OK. Thinking of you wishing and hoping I will one day see You again. I promise to phone you soon. Lots of Love and Hugs and Kisses Oz

I leaf through the pile. All from him. February, November, December. February, November, December.

Valentine's Day, her birthday and Christmas. The earliest seems to be November '94.

Dearest Nancy, I wonder how you are. I still think of you far too much. I am still optimistic for next Year. I will phone soon now I have to catch the post Happy happy happy birthday! Have a Ball! Lots of Love Oz

The latest is last February.

To my Valentine I LOVE YOU. yes, time may pass by—how much I would like to hold you in my arms—just one more Time—it gives me a Warm Fuzzy feeling thinking anyway. here I have let things move far to slowly—I've decided the Bus is not actually a Business but a hobby at the moment. I am optimistic and expect things to get a lot better. heaps of Love and Kisses Oz

What the hell does she see in this wimp? Why has she hoarded this trivia for what, fourteen years?

I'll ask him. I'll email him. I'm up off the floor, carting the recycling downstairs and fetching a whisky while the laptop reboots. It takes a while to decide what to say, steering between offhand and officious.

Oz, Thanks for the flowers, which stood out. Mum clearly meant a lot to you. I see you and she go back fourteen years plus. I'd be interested to hear your memories of her. Don't worry about offending me. It's good to know she met someone she cared about. Kind regards, Mark Jonnson

I fidget with it a bit. It's wrong, but I can't make it right. I swallow the whisky, decide it's okay and press send.

By two o'clock she was on the coach, heading for Bristol, watching London's western suburbs whiz by in the bright sun, then fields, trees and motorway verges. She slumped in her seat, exhausted and angry. At Harry, at herself, at her parents for blanking her phone call like that.

Always she had the sense she was interrupting their lives. Nothing she did awakened their curiosity. One university summer she and a boyfriend, romantic and daring, had thumbed lifts from Milan down to Bari. They'd taken the ferry to Corfu, where they'd slept on beach sand under the stars for an idyllic nine days before returning to Italy through a terrifying Mediterranean storm. With their cash running out, they'd sold blood in Naples, then accepted some dodgy lifts northwards, had an almighty row in Florence, hitchhiked shivering over the Alps and starved on the long train journey back up the Rhine. Her parents had only glanced through the photographs. She'd stopped trying to relate her adventures after the first tale fell flat. Her gift of little Greek coffee-cups carried home in her green-canvas knapsack was gathering dust at the back of their cupboard. They'd disapproved of her travelling alone with a man, living with him at college. They'd feared her grandmother would get to hear of it. They'd been relieved when she and the boyfriend had broken up. But mostly they hadn't been interested.

She'd tried forcing the issue a couple of years ago, insisting bravely that she needed more love from them, and her father had shocked her with an explosion of clichés. She had 'gone off the rails'. He could only hope some 'decent man' would 'take pity' and 'make an honest woman of her' before she spent 'a lonely life on the shelf'. He'd shouted until she had run upstairs crying, and neither he nor her mother had come after her or spoken of the subject again.

A 'decent man' would be great in principle, minus the pity of course, but hell, she was programmed all wrong. Harry and Edward were archetypes of the too-often repeated cast-list of her love life. Harry, the dirty rat. Edward, the decent man her parents would gather to their cold bosoms like a prodigal son if she gave them the chance.

Okay. Fine. Easy. The answer was simple. Re-programme herself. Think about the long haul, the kind of man she wanted to wake up next to for the rest of her life. Nothing like her father for a start. And stop falling for other women's husbands. Stop romanticising danger and sex. Recognise a decent, single man, and say yes.

Except, ouch, here was Harry, still prowling her mind. His five-o'clock shadow, his ironic eyes, his huge intellect, his impatient, cocky dick. She had no wish to live with him, watch television with him, wash his socks, have his babies. She couldn't stomach waking up next to him on some not-too-distant morning, knowing he was having sex with a new conquest. What was wrong with her that she couldn't fancy Edward, smiling hopefully, shuffling from one unpolished shoe to the other? Come on, imagine kissing Edward: it couldn't be so bad. A nice person. Kind, intelligent. Funny in a mordant sort of a way.

The view through the bus window was changing. They were coming into Bristol, semi-detached villas and local shops giving way to high-rise new-build. Sally had moved here from Kent three years ago. She always wrote, 'You must visit us,' but this was Nancy's first time.

The B&B wasn't far from Sally's house. She walked through the afternoon sun, following the map Stuart had sent her. Come on, she told herself, stick on a smile. She checked in and dumped her stuff before exploring the neighbourhood. She wolfed pie and chips at a café, bought a bottle of wine to take along, managed to resist buying cigarettes too, then nipped back to pile on the mascara, put on her party top—diaphanous cotton, violet and gold—and grab Sally's present. She was feeling better, she told herself. She wasn't going to smoke today, not even a puff, and she was going to put Harry right out of her mind.

2008, Monday

It's one o'clock, and I'm leaving the undertakers, where I've handed over a cheque in return for a plain cardboard box. This morning was the last English 1 class before Christmas, and the students brought in samosas and sweets and warm Pepsi. Teacher Guy entertained them with a word quiz and a festive game of Hangman, took them through some phrases to write in Christmas cards, then let them go. Even Comfort dashed off; she had no time for Scrabble today. And Monday's my free afternoon, so I've come to get Mum.

The cheque, released by the solicitor, was for more than three grand. The undertaker has sonorously offered the option of paying extra to have Mum's name included on his 'tasteful seasonal remembrance display', and I've shaken my head. Take your money. Hand over the ashes. I'm gone.

He holds the door open and half bows, his eyes cold, and I'm away, power-walking the pavement. Okay, Mum, I have you. You're safe.

I glance around. Did I say that aloud? It's all right: no one notices everyday madness; they assume that you're talking hands-free. The box is an intractable cube that won't fit in the rucksack. I transfer it from one underarm to the other and quicken my pace. *Ashes to ashes*. I shift it again, hugging it to my chest, resting my chin on it.

I distract myself with thoughts of Matilda. We did fine together this weekend. She threatened a wobbly when she found the kids next door were away, but then jumped for joy—'Yes! Yes! Yes!'—when I suggested a swim at the leisure centre. We ducked and dived in the waves from the machine, and I cheered her first width across the teaching pool. Back at the house, she taught me to play Uno and crowed when she beat me. With the help of Mum's recipe books I managed to serve up roast chicken and mash, which she said was, 'Quite good, Daddy.'

Neither of us mentioned America. Please God, it won't happen. I read her to sleep with more of *The Wizard of Oz. The cyclone had set the house down, very gently— for a cyclone—in the midst of a country of marvelous beauty*. She left some of her stuff here for next weekend, including the pink swimsuit I bought her and one of her minor teddies to guard her room.

It's no use: my mind keeps coming back to this box clutched to my ribs. I'm hurrying through the immense brick-and-iron tunnel beneath the bridges that deliver trains into Clapham Junction. The noise from overhead and from the race of traffic alongside me is deafening. I'm almost running; it's oppressively dark. There's mist in the air, and the people coming at me are dull-eyed and unsmiling, shrugged into their coats. I'm alive, I remind myself, not dead yet, not yet. I suck in deep, chilly breaths to prove it. Above me, above the iron and the rails and the heavy grey sky, I imagine frozen white cloud-tops dazzling with sun.

It's a relief to be out where the pavement widens and frostbitten buddleia overhangs the embankment. The world opens up ahead, busy with shoppers and spangled with Christmas lights reflected in puddles. I pause, panting; rest the box on a ledge beside a poster hoarding. I need to look inside; can't wait. I peel back the parcel tape and hitch out the urn. It's made of maroony-brown metal. I drop it back in the box, twist off the lid and peer in.

The ashes are mottled in shades of light grey, coarser than I expected although some are fine-grained. The underside of the lid is powder-dusted, or was before that gust hit, tossing random flakes into the trampled filth of south London.

I press the lid back on, then snatch up the box and veer left, fast up the hill past Lidl and Boots towards home. I swerve past two women who are blocking the pavement, their baby-buggies festooned with bulging carrier bags. I'm out of milk, I remember, and I'm going to need whisky. I'm about to cross Asda's car park. It seems daft to go home and come out again.

I shift the box from one arm to the other. The store's buzzing. Shoppers stream in and out through the automatic doors. There are only three trolleys left. I look at them for a moment before putting the box and the rucksack in one and joining the stream.

I pause inside, glad of the warmth, unsure if I should be doing this.

'Merry Christmas,' says a greeter with a Santa Claus hat.

I push on into the vegetable section, past mounds of Brussels sprouts. Red and gold decorations swing in thick clusters. Some new Yuletide pop song glitters the air. The aisle ahead is jammed with people scrabbling for potatoes and parsnips, their trolleys piled high with mince pies and wrapping paper, turkeys and sausages. I'm blinking at the colours, breathing the smells. Look, Mum, I'm thinking, orange, green, yellow. Earth aroma of mushrooms. Tang of tomatoes. I drop a bag of tangerines into the trolley, then steer through the mêlée, growing defiant, adding two pints of milk, a granary baguette, a litre of whisky. I'm humming along to *All I Want for Christmas is You*. You see, Mum, the world hasn't come to an end. It's been a tricky three weeks, but here you are in amongst it again. No more treating you with respect in a temperature-controlled environment. I'm treating you with offhand disrespect in a pre-Christmas scrum in a nice, warm supermarket. Now, doesn't that feel good?

A black guy with a child on his shoulders reverses into me. A woman tuts as I step back and collide with her. She screws up her mouth, glaring at my half-empty trolley.

'Merry Christmas to you, too,' I say.

Her eyes slide away. She pretends not to hear. See this box, I want to shout. Say hello to my mum.

Giant red and green balloons float above the checkouts, every one of which is open, so the queues are short. I spot one with no queue at all, load my purchases onto the conveyor and fish for my wallet. Looking up, I meet the checkout girl's eyes.

It's the neighbour, the woman next door, in a Santa Claus hat. 'Hi there, Mark,' she says.

Beep. The tangerines tumble along the ramp. Someone behind bumps me with their trolley. 'Hi... er, Jane... I didn't realise you worked here.'

Beep. She hands over the whisky. 'Flexible hours,' she says.

Beep. Beep. I'm putting the milk into the rucksack beside the baguette. I rest my hand on Mum's box before looking up. Jane is smiling. Alive. 'What time do you finish?' I say.

'Two,' she answers. Her mouth moves. Her eyelids close and reopen.

I put my credit card in the reader and tap in the PIN. 'Do you fancy a drink after work?'

She laughs. 'Why not?' Her teeth are nice.

'I'll bring a bottle to yours. Two thirty?'

'Make it three,' she says.

When she hands me the receipt, I notice the wedding ring.

Her house is the same layout as Mum's, except mirror-image, but it feels totally different. Mum's is uncluttered but cosy: carpets, discreet lighting, comfortable chairs, warm colours. This place is Spartan: exposed floors with the odd threadbare rug, long-life bulbs dangling, cheap furniture, no soft surfaces. The only colour is the Lego pieces scattered everywhere.

I'm here on an impulse. Heat seeking. Running away from the ashes.

This woman is older than I am, and she's wearing a ring. I need this complication like a hole in the head.

The kids aren't home yet. We sit at her kitchen table. She pours the wine I brought into smeared tumblers and tears open a jumbo bag of crisps. The cat's hunkered under a cold radiator. Jane seems acclimatised in a T-shirt and jeans. She lifts her glass. Sips. 'Delicious,' she says.

'Courtesy of Mum,' I say.

She smiles. 'Cheers, Nance,' she says to the ceiling. 'Here's to the good times.'

Her figure's slim and muscular, and her face is appealing, not pretty exactly but vibrant.

'So, what's the story? How come you're checking out groceries?'

'To feed the kids. I'm actually an actress, or trying to be.'

'Really?'

'Don't sound so surprised. I'm fully trained and competent.'

Large eyes, mobile features. Fearless. Easy to see how she would hold an audience.

'On stage?'

'When I can, but voice-work mostly. Radio. I did *Book of the Week* once. I've been in *The Archers.*'

'Middle-aged radio.'

She grins. 'Why not?'

I take in her crow's feet. 'Because you're not middle-aged?'

She tilts her head, frowning, considering this. 'Are you flirting or being ironic?'

'Not sure,' I say, smiling. 'You're wearing a ring.'

'To keep the wolves away.' She's smiling too.

'Wolves like me?'

'Probably.'

We sip wine and look at each other. 'So, what's become of their dad, if you don't mind my asking?'

'Dads plural,' she says. 'This is really good wine.'

She has stopped looking at me. I wait for her answer. She leans back from the table, speaking fast. 'It's a bit selfish, but I just went ahead and had them. Josie by accident, and Christopher sort of by accident and sort of to keep Josie company.'

Suddenly I don't fancy this woman at all. 'Do they know?'

'What? That they have different dads?'

'Did the dads know what they were doing?'

She looks at me a moment, then slowly stands up. 'If that's your opinion of me, perhaps you should leave.'

I stand too, draining my glass.

'For your information, they're both fine with it. I didn't trick them. I wanted my kids to have dads, and they do.'

'I haven't seen them around.'

'Well, pardon me!' She shoves her chair in against the table. 'Next time one of them comes, I'll make sure to alert you. The kids go to see them. They have three lots of doting grandparents. Anything else you need to know?'

I shake my head. I want to know what those two blokes think. How the story looks to them.

'Stop judging me,' she says.

'I'm not.'

'Like hell you're not. Josie and Christopher are fine. Their dads are fine. Three sets of grandparents are fine. And I'm fine. What's happening in *your* life?'

'*Touché*. I'm sorry.' I stare at my glass, then blurt, 'It's in bits actually.'

I put the glass on the table. I'm ready to leave. I don't want to leave.

'In bits because of Nancy?' Her voice is still tight and cold.

'Not only that.'

'Your little girl? Your... wife, is it?'

'My wife, yes, but not just them either.'

'So. Tell me. What gives you the right to disapprove?'

'I haven't... I wasn't... I'm sorry.'

I empty the dregs of the bottle into my glass. Then I'm gabbling, unable to stop. 'I've been... I've been feeling... I don't know, like I'm falling to pieces, losing control... of who I am, what I do—'

She's moving away, picking the cat up. She watches me steadily.

'It scares me. It's as if there's a bunch of odd bods who don't even like each other fighting to be me.'

She goes on stroking the cat.

I should shut up, but I can't. 'I did something freaky today.' It feels theatrical saying this, as if I'm really crazy or pretending to be. 'At least I think it was freaky.' The words keep coming. 'In Asda, the box in my trolley... it was Mum... her ashes. I'd just picked them up from the undertaker. Asda was on my way home.'

I stop. What an idiot.

She waits. Then, 'You wheeled Nancy's ashes around Asda?'

'Yes.'

'Is that all?'

'I suppose.'

She puts the cat down. 'That's okay. A bit odd maybe, but why not?'

'The weird thing is it felt as though I'd rescued her and was giving her a good time. Look, I really am sorry for what I said to you.'

Our eyes meet. She nods. 'Okay,' she says. 'Apology accepted.'

She pulls her chair back out from the table and sits on it. After a moment I do the same, clutching my wine, feeling grateful. We look at each other. She smiles.

There's a small scar on her cheek that tugs at her smile like the ghost of a dimple. I'm really liking that smile. It seems to be the place her face comes to rest. I look at her. She looks back at me. Her large eyes are light brown like her hair.

'What time do you need to fetch the kids?'

'I don't. My mum has them. I'm working the six a.m. shift until Christmas.'

A second ticks by, and he snaps into place: lonely guy on the pull. He holds out his hand, and she looks at it, smiling, shaking her head. Then she takes it.

'I shouldn't do this,' I tell her, half-hoping she'll let go again. 'My wife mustn't know.'

'Understood. You can trust me. Not a word. Solemn promise.'

He stands up. She stands up. He steps forward, bends his head and he's kissing her, tasting the wine on her tongue, tightening his arms around her.

He shouldn't be doing this. There are condoms in his pocket. He doesn't plan on being dad number three.

'Nice body.'

'You can ease off on the irony now,' she says.

'But it's true.'

'Yeah, yeah.'

I rescue my foot from under the weight of the cat, which is curled in a tight, heat-seeking ball on the duvet. My knee bumps Jane's thigh, and she shifts her position.

'Shall I put on the light?' she says.

She waves an arm, finds the cord. Another long-life bulb limps into action, casting shadows into corners. A plug-in fan-heater rattles under the window, but the end of my nose is cold.

The sex was awkwardly polite, and I was out of practice. The only action I've seen lately has been solo, a few feet away through the party wall. Climbing the stairs last thing at night, I've got into the habit of imagining Tracy, perched three steps up. She's become a fixture, there when I need her, rising, her hand on the banister rail, beginning a slow striptease as she leads the way to the bedroom.

Whereas Jane just chucked her clothes on the floor and jumped into bed, yelping, 'Whoof, it's cold.'

It took a while to recover my hard-on. Once I did, everything worked after a fashion, but there was no heart in it and not much sexiness. Now her head's on my shoulder, and I'm looking at the watch on the inside of my wrist, thinking I'll give the pillow talk twenty minutes, then say I have work to do.

I drop my hand to squeeze her arm. 'Well I never. Biceps. You're really quite fit.'

'Yeah, yeah,' she repeats, and we're quiet for a moment.

'Are you back together?' she asks.

'Come again?'

'You said you were falling to pieces.'

'Oh... that... I was probably exaggerating.'

'Fair enough.'

Another pause.

'Nancy said you teach adults to read?'

'I try to.'

She interrupts my fidgeting hand and links her fingers through mine. 'And you passed up promotion to stay in the classroom?'

Uneasy morph into Teacher Guy. 'I hate paper-pushing. Don't want to be anyone's boss.' I free my hand on the pretext of stroking her hair from her eyes. The gesture feels awkward, and my other arm, beneath her, is developing pins and needles.

'Nance was proud of you.'

I laugh. 'Now who's being ironic?'

'But it's true.'

'Yeah, yeah,' I say. Another pause. 'How many times have we been round that loop?'

'It must be the scripts I've been reading.' She's half sitting, so I can no longer reach her hair. 'I auditioned for Pinter last week.'

I ease my arm out from under, glancing at my watch again. 'You met Harold Pinter?'

'I mean for a Pinter play. I won't get it. My money's on the director's girlfriend. She was hanging around, patronising us, spouting about RADA.'

'Young and pretty?'

'Bastard. Don't rub it in.'

We're silent for a minute. Now I've stopped pawing her, she slides down beside me, contemplating the ceiling and smiling her smile. I like the way she's not fishing for what happens next. For some reason I'm wondering if she knows about Oz.

'How come Mum told you I'm a teacher?'

'Why wouldn't she?'

'Chats over the fence?'

'Her kitchen. My kitchen.'

'You were pals?'

'Sort of. She was a friendly lady.'

'Did she confide ever?'

She turns to face me. 'About what?'

'Well... this may sound odd, but... about any men in her life?'

Jane gives me a quizzical look. 'Are you jealous?'

'Of course not.'

Shit, she thinks I'm a mother's boy. I rush to explain. 'There's a mystery ex-lover called Oz who sent flowers to the funeral.'

'Nope. Sorry. She never mentioned him.'

Damn Mother's Boy. I grab hold. The smooth curve of her hip.

She shows me her profile again, the scarred side of her smile. 'Your mum reckoned she was "all passion spent". She had plenty of mates, you know.'

'Never short of a friend,' I agree.

'And she loved having your little girl to stay.'

'So... no men then?'

'I think she preferred her own company.' Jane's voice is soft and unhurried. The smile comes and goes. 'She told me she did some internet dating when she first moved here, but gave up on it. She said the unattractive ones were sad bastards and the attractive ones all had baggage. She reckoned she had enough baggage of her own; she wasn't her best self with a man. She said it was a relief to be over fifty because her libido had stopped ruling her head.'

Enough about Mum. I press closer and whisper, 'Well, Jane, I'm a sad bastard with baggage. Bad news all round.'

She rotates in my arms, presenting me her body and her full smile, scar and no scar. 'There's no escaping bad news these days,' she says. 'Just turn on the TV. All this economic disaster, and global warming.'

We're laughing. It's getting warmer under the duvet.

'And worse luck, we still have our libidos,' I say.

After her chilly house, mine feels warm and welcoming. I've switched on the heating, and the radiators are clicking and banging. We opened another bottle and ordered in pizza, which we gobbled in bed. Then she said she needed her sleep, an early night before another six a.m. shift. So I pulled on my clothes, said, 'We must do this again,' and slipped out through her front door, stepping over the low wall between her front path and mine.

I'm knackered and tipsy. Mum's box is on the kitchen table where I dumped it in my rush to find a bottle of wine. I'm drawn to look at the ashes again; it feels safer now.

Off comes the lid. Grey-white powder and grit: all that's left of the woman who gave birth to me. Although actually nothing is left.

Except me. I'm still here, solid and six-foot-three. How peculiar.

My mobile's on the table. There's a text from Gina—*Call me goddammit!!!*—another—*Come on, you sad fucker. Forget the bit on the side. Find your way to the pub*—and two voice messages, the first one, 'Hi, Mark. Geoff Eliot here. D'you fancy that pint before Christmas? Give us a bell,' and the second, 'Hello, Mark. It's Alison... (laughs) Are you hiding? Well... um... here's the thing... Christmas... it would be... you know, bygones, good will to all... we're grownups... I'd be happy to spend it with you... Matilda too, of course, if... (laughs) *Damn*, I hate voicemail. Anyway... cool... you probably... (laughs) *Shit*, I hate voicemail. Ring me, eh? Bye.'

My eyelids are drooping, but I suppose I'd better call Gina. I scoop up the landline phone in the hall and sit on the stairs, next to Tracy, who slides her make-believe arm round my waist.

The dialling tone's intermittent. I hit 1571.

You have... two messages.

'Mark. It's your dad.' Long pause. 'Gina said I'd find you here. Look... well... she says you've split up and... you know I'm not judging, it's just... if you need someone to listen. I'm sorry I lost my temper at the funeral. Don't be a stranger... Okay... Speak soon.'

The second message explodes in my ear. 'Damn you, Mark, how come it's my responsibility to tell Ted what's going on? I've had all I can take of this crap. Working my butt off to make life normal for Matty, hanging tinsel, trying to give her a regular Christmas. It's driving me nuts. I've talked to my dad, and he says come right on home, he'll pay for our flights. So that's what we're doing, and I need you to sign the consent.'

God. Too fast. This can't happen.

I dial Kilburn, and Matilda picks up. Her voice is small. She sniffs after saying hello.

'Are you all right, Little?'

'Daddee!'

'Hello, sweet thing. What's up?'

Gina comes on the line. 'Where have you been, Mark?'

'Nowhere—'

'Did you get my message?'

'I did, but—'

'I can't wait any longer, we have to go to Connecticut—'

'You hate Connecticut—'

'We've been over that. Now here's the deal. I need to tell Dad and Mom when we're coming. Like, for Christmas, or New Year, or when I've—'

'Gina, hold on a min—'

'I'm done holding on, Mark. There's a limit.' Her voice wobbles. 'You don't know how hard it is, doing everything by myself, day after day in this shitty apartment.'

There's an agonised wail from Matilda.

'Calm down,' I plead. 'You shouldn't do this in front of—'

'Don't give me lectures, you asshole. Everywhere here is in front of her.'

'Gina. Look. I'm working till Wednesday, but then I'm free if you want me to have her. If you want a break.'

'And then what?' she says hopelessly. 'It goes on and

on, Mark. I really want to go *home*.'

The word hangs between us.

'Please don't do this,' I say. 'Come and live here with me. Please think about it. One more chance.' I strain my ears for sounds of Matilda.

She pauses. 'It's no use. We're washed up. We're through.'

I'm refusing to believe her. 'We're not. We can do this, Gina, I know that we can. I've been a bastard, but I won't be again. I promise, hand on heart. Solemnly. On Matty's life.'

No answer.

'Gina, let's please try to do this for Matty, okay? She needs her daddy.'

No answer.

'For us too. You and me.'

We're silent, I don't know for how long.

Finally she sighs. 'I guess.'

I imagine Tracy's cynical pout as I climb the stairs with a whisky. 'Good luck, mate,' she says, but I hold to my optimism. It's not luck I need now, but loyalty, common sense and, yes, love. Gina's my wife. I still want to love her; I still want her to love me. We can turn this around.

They're coming on Saturday. Gina will give notice to the landlord and rent a van for our stuff. I'm to get there mid morning to help her load up. Meanwhile I've to get Matilda a new school for January and book her a GP appointment for the physical once-over her old school wanted done.

I haven't argued. Wait till they get here. One step at a time.

Gina will be happier here than in Kilburn. So will Matty, I'm sure of it. We'll find ways to manage her together without getting her labelled as ADHD. She is going to be seven, and now that we've weathered this storm she'll be calmer, and maybe Gina can go after a more fulfilling job. She's been fretting to do that for years, bored out of her educated mind slaving in that bookshop and managing Matty.

In the bedroom I switch on the laptop to glance at my emails and, like a good omen, here's an answer from Oz. I'm curious to know more about him and Mum. But it reads like a slap.

Mark, Thanks for yours if you don't mind I would rather just leave it that is probably best thing. Kind regards Oz

Christmas Day

I'm on the living-room floor playing Monopoly with Matilda, with half an eye on the closing scenes of *The Curse of the Were-rabbit* and half an ear on Gina in the bedroom overhead.

'Why is Mommy mad at us?'

'No reason,' I say. 'Or maybe she isn't mad at us. Maybe she just feels like having a thump.'

'Thumping's good,' Matilda says. 'I like thumping.'

'Don't I know it,' I say, and she grins at me.

Gina is stuffing the contents of Mum's wardrobe into bin bags for me to take to a charity shop next time they're open. It's fine, I'm telling myself. I would have done the same weeks ago if I'd needed the space, but I didn't, so I left it, and now Gina needs the space, so it's fine.

She bristled when I tried saying, 'Sit down, relax, you deserve it. Monopoly's better with three.' She didn't answer, just scowled, charged upstairs and started banging about. I'm interpreting this to mean that I'm a lazy git who doesn't deserve a break from work and why haven't I helped her more with a whole list of things she hasn't time or energy to point out to me.

Like polishing my heirloom brass kettle, which now gleams in the light of a real fire. 'I've started—find your own job,' she said when I tried to take the Brasso cloth from her.

She has barely paused for breath, let alone conversation and certainly not sex, since she got here six days ago. She has powered her way from one task to another, cleaning and decorating, shopping and cooking, wrapping presents for Matilda, in between working extended pre-Christmas hours at the bookshop halfway across London, right up until late closing last night.

When Gina's not here, the house seems to exhale. Matilda and I share activities and find our own speed. When she is here, there are suddenly things we're not doing that we ought to be doing, and we're doubly at fault for needing to be told what they are. Playing Monopoly on Christmas afternoon is not one of them, it seems.

'Will I like my new school, Daddy?'

'I'm sure you will, Little. And they'll like you too.'

I'm suppressing annoyance; counting the day's many blessings. The living room's warm and festive, hung with gold tinsel and cards on red ribbons. Matilda has on a pink Disney-princess outfit Gina got in a Woolworth's closing-down sale, and her hair's restrained in true princess-fashion by a circle of braid. Spending Christmas Day in the doghouse is unimaginably better than being holed up here on my own, desperate about losing Matty, eating baked beans or Mum's defrosted stew and fielding predatory calls from Alison. Alison's face fell a mile when I told her Gina and I were back on.

From dawn until five minutes ago, I thought Gina had finally thawed. We woke up smiling, opened our presents, expressed thrill and gratitude, had a bacon-and-egg breakfast, then strolled off through the frost to Battersea Park to road-test Matilda's pink-and-grey bicycle. We saw coots and geese, mallards and moorhens, a heron and countless squirrels. We spotted the parakeets screeching from treetop to treetop, hobnobbing with magpies on the bare branches above the Peace Pagoda. Gina and I stood side by side, our gloved hands on the wall not quite touching, looking out across the Thames tide churning in the wind, while Matilda pedalled up and down, yelling, 'Look, Daddy. Look, Mommy,' laughing as pigeons took flight around her.

Back home, we ate roast duck with our fingers, wowed Matty with a Christmas pudding licked by blue flame, piled on the brandy butter and sank a bottle of wine. We shared the washing up without a single harsh word. But now this—another shedload of passive aggression.

Matilda throws dice, moves her piece. 'I'm going to be really, really good in my new school.'

'Turning over a new leaf, eh?' I say. 'That's an excellent plan.'

Me too, I think: that's what I'm doing. And if I hang on, keep my cool, that's what Gina will do too before long.

It's no use; another bang from above has me fuming. What the hell kind of family Christmas is it where Mommy ducks out of playing Monopoly with her kid and starts clearing a wardrobe? Gina hardly ever plays with Matty or listens to her properly is what I'm noticing. I feel like running upstairs and telling her so.

'Daddy, it's your go.' Matilda stares at the TV, picking her nose, as Wallace, transformed into a massive bunny, terrorises a giant-vegetable contest.

I throw the dice, and she screams in triumph, 'You didn't see. You're too late.' She's pointing with both hands at the board. Her piece was on one of my stations.

'Ah shucks,' I say. 'I needed that rent. If I land on Mayfair now I'll be sunk.'

I've been coaching her in the principles of capitalism while discreetly failing to invest enough myself. She's piling up the cash and storming towards victory. 'I'm going to be a million, billion, zillionaire.' This is capitalism before subprime mortgages and credit crunches, and it works pretty efficiently.

Matilda flinches at a crash from above. 'Hey, Matty,' I say. 'Having a good time?'

She nods solemnly. 'It's my best Christmas ever.'

Damn Gina. Every time she's looked in the wardrobe she's got tetchy. The sight of Mum's clothes is enough to annoy her. Okay, so I should have cleared them before she got here. I wish I had.

I smile hard at Matilda. It doesn't matter, I tell myself. The clothes aren't Mum any more than her ashes are. She's not watching or grieving for her trashed possessions.

I've thrown a six and a four. 'Land on mine! Land on mine!' urges Matilda.

Mum's urn is safe in its box at the back of a high cupboard in the kitchen. Gina would need to stand on a chair to see it or reach it. I stashed it there before she arrived. The vibrator went into the dustbin. I didn't want her to find it.

My piece dodges between the hotels and lands safely. The credits are rolling on Wallace and Gromit. While Matilda has her go, I get up, shake the numbness from my feet, draw the curtains and glance at the TV guide. The news is coming up next, although nothing much happens on Christmas Day. No crashing stock markets, few shots fired in anger, just various pontiffs pontificating.

Hiding the ashes was idiotic. Gina wouldn't mock them or harm them or throw them out, not even accidentally, because the box also contains a brown plastic label and a printed crematorium certificate.

I used to be mad keen on Gina, back before Matilda blasted us apart. I struggle to re-imagine how she first seemed to me. Try to relive Millennium night. It was her hair that caught my attention, her dark curls shining in the party lights. Then a flash of her immaculate teeth, the muscular body of a gym-goer and the after-trace of a phrase she'd shouted across the room to a friend conveyed to me that she was American.

I was immediately, unquestioningly hooked, starting to detach myself from the girl I was half-heartedly flirting with and sizing up this American's companion.

Some nondescript oik. She was way out of his league. He couldn't take his eyes off her, but she wasn't touching or barely noticing him. Between tracks I excused myself and headed for the door, doubling back from a new angle to land grinning in front of her as a slower number began, steering her into the sweaty centre of the room.

Mission accomplished. She had her hands on my arms. Long, strong fingers. Her cheeks glowed; her smile challenged me. She was looking up at me, waiting to hear my next line.

'I hope you're not a Hollywood film star,' I said, 'because I'm no Hugh Grant.' Okay, yes, it was cheesy, but I was only twenty years old.

Turned out she was twenty-two, doing a postgraduate degree in European politics at LSE, but she didn't mind slumming it with a trainee teacher. We had our first shag in the old century and our second in the new.

I was more or less a whole person back then, I remember, brash and confident, with no doubt who I was. Maybe that bloke is still inside me somewhere, the big ginger charmer that Gina fell for on Millennium night. I need to resurrect him. He would know how to cut through her hostility.

Gina, forgive me. I've been crap, I see that completely, but we can't be here just for Matty. If we are, it's useless, for her and for us, so stop punishing me, eh?

'Daddy. It's your turn again.'

I'm back on my knees on the twist pile, rolling the dice, when my attention's drawn by the brief fanfare for the BBC headlines: three upbeat bleeps, a fragmented, spinning planet and the camera swooping down on the newscaster.

'One of Britain's greatest playwrights, Harold Pinter, has died. He was seventy-eight and had been having treatment for liver cancer...'

I'm reminded of Jane next door. She doesn't seem to be around; I suppose they're with her parents. Will she be upset by the news, I'm wondering, although of course she didn't meet Pinter. And I'm thinking, if I could have chosen, I would have been here with Matilda, not Gina, and I'd have suggested to Jane we spend the day together, our three kids and the two of us, and maybe we'd have gone to Battersea Park and seen the parakeets and the Peace Pagoda, and I might have taken her gloved hand and slipped it out of its glove and deep into my trouser pocket for a Christmas surprise—

'Mark?'

I look up. Gina's standing in the doorway. 'Can you spare me a moment?'

She doesn't seem to be angry. Her eyes are wide, a bit secretive maybe. Her glance at Matilda means she wants me to come on my own.

I nod. I've thrown a double, and my second throw takes me to Bond Street.

Matilda rolls on her back, kicking her feet in the air, bellowing, 'It's mine. My hotel.' She snatches the card from her pile and thrusts it at me.

'One thousand four hundred pounds,' I read with mock horror. 'What a disaster! I'm cleaned out. Well done you, though. You've won. Clever girl!'

She does a victory dance. 'I beat you. I beat you.'

'Calm down,' Gina says.

I clamber to my feet. 'Do you want to put it away, Little? I'll be back in a mo, and we can start on the jigsaw.'

And I'm out in the hall, and Gina's pulling the door to behind me, whispering, 'I've found something.'

'What?'

'I'm not sure. Come and see.'

As she leads me upstairs, I know it has to do with Mum, and there's something about Gina's silence and gravity that has my heart beating faster, as if I'm going to view the body again.

She died instantly. She had no time to know what was happening. She wouldn't have felt any pain.

I'm following Gina along the landing.

The room smells of perfume and dust. The bed is strewn with Mum's dresses and jackets, trousers and jeans. It's almost as if she's here. There's a clutter of shoes on the carpet, a small stack of handbags. Gina picks up one of the bags, a large one, soft leather with buckles and flaps, and hands it to me. It's heavy.

'Look inside of it. I put everything back.'

I lift the flap and see a miscellaneous wodge of paper, two or three inches thick. I'm easing it out. On top there's a greeting card with a photograph of a bowlful of roses, and I'm opening it, seeing the disorganised handwriting, thinking, okay, this is it, here he is.

Nancy, Well, Sorry I can't wait those few days to phone you, so hence a quick note. I came floating back to Lizzie's, steering my head away from passers bye who may have wondered at the beaming Smile I had from ear to ear. Dave perhaps I probably shouldn't say had the indignity to ask did I score and about the wings when I said you were an Angel. I will call you I still have an inner Glow love Oz

'That's not it,' Gina says.

'What do you mean?'

'That's not it. It's the photographs.'

I leaf through the pile, past more notes from Oz, and suddenly there he is, beaming close-up at the lens. And wham, the breath is knocked out of me. Because he's just a boy, a teenager, grinning a goofy smile. His face is sprinkled with freckles. His hair, flopping into his eyes is bright, coppery red. There's a dark outer ring to his irises that makes their green seem astonishing.

'Gina. This is... this has to be...'

'I know,' she says. 'But who is it? A cousin?'

115

And I can't answer her because I'm looking at more photographs of this boy, some alone, some in a sunny pub garden with an arm around Mum, who is... what age? I don't know. Not a teenager, but young, her thick, dark hair cut in a fringe, wearing flared jeans and a print shirt with a big collar. They're lifting their pints to whoever's taking the photo. They're squinting into the sun, smiling. And his face is my face.

JOURNEY

1978

At eight-thirty she was skulking by Sally and Stuart's front hedge with a few others, nobody sure how the surprise was supposed to work. She was overawed by the double-fronted house set back behind laurel bushes. It was bigger than her parents' place, bigger than the B&B even. They must be earning pots of money.

Grace came running out to fetch them. Loud and skinny, grown into an eight-year-old. 'Mummy's not here yet—she's gone to the pictures.' She spun on the doorstep, showing off her dress and her painted nails. 'There's some dishy boys. I'm allowed to stay up till midnight.' Stuart appeared with the baby on his hip. 'Nancy! You made it.'

Her present joined the pile in the hall. The house smelled of grilled sausages and was crowded with people whispering and tiptoeing in the dark. A few lurked with cameras. Only one light was on, in the front room, and the music was classical piano, almost too quiet to hear.

She fetched a glass of wine from the kitchen before wedging herself among the sitters on the stairs. The smoke in the air had her craving a cigarette, but she didn't know anyone well enough to cadge one. She and Sally had no mutual friends. They'd met in Sevenoaks, in the solicitor's office where Nancy had worked for a few weeks between school and university. Sally, a junior partner, had seemed so clever and capable, making Nancy feel special, explaining the cases to her, increasing her certainty that she wanted to be a lawyer herself.

Just after nine-thirty the lookouts stage-whispered, 'She's here!' and the house held its breath. There must have been a hundred people crammed into the hall, up the stairs, craning their necks from the kitchen and living room and over the banisters. The key turned in the lock, and Sally's worried face came around the door as the flashbulbs went off. 'Hello, darling. Come in,' Stuart said.

Sally disappeared, tried to run, but he went after her and tugged her back. She was gawping at everyone, saying, 'Unbelievable, amazing,' as they belted out *Happy Birthday*.

Nancy queued to say hello, battling feelings of envy. Sally had what she hankered after: a loving husband, a live-wire eight-year-old daughter, a baby. Was Stuart an Edward or a Harry, she wondered. Could she imagine herself fancying him? A bit of a stretch, but anyway, hang on, he was someone else's husband, so what would fancying him prove?

The lights were on. The crowd's excitement was fading. After refilling her glass she hovered in the living-room doorway eyeing the polished wood floor. Dancing would cheer her up, but classical music persisted and the crowd was resolving into a party of chattering couples, mostly older than she was.

Better join in somewhere. There was a group on the sofa, dominated by a ginger-haired woman about her own age. She gathered courage, went over, caught the woman's eye and said, 'Hi.'

The woman told her companions to, 'Shove up,' so that Nancy could sit. She introduced herself as Lizzie, a legal secretary in Stuart's office. The older guy, dark haired and dark suited, was her boyfriend, Dave. The teenager with a shock of red hair spilling over the collar of his clashing red lumberjack shirt was her brother, Oz, and the one with glasses and acne was his school pal, Mike.

'Have a ciggy.' Lizzie offered a packet round.

Huge effort. 'No, thank you. Such a pity, this music. I feel like dancing.'

Lizzie jumped up, 'Good idea,' but they hunted through the LPs with no joy.

120

'What are you after?' a woman asked.

'Something with a beat,' Lizzie said. 'Golden oldies. The Stones.'

'Wait,' said the woman. 'I'll fetch mine from next door.'

Someone dimmed the lights, the room filled with dancers and the beat and danger of *Satisfaction* took possession of Nancy. The Rolling Stones were not 'nice'; her mother was clear about that. Here she was, well out of Harry's reach, dancing with Lizzie, but Jagger's sneering voice carried her back to the doorway in Baker Street. Heedless of what passing strangers might think, riding a high wave of arousal, her knees had given way when she climaxed. The memory had them almost giving way now. Harry shoving her hard against the door to keep the two of them from collapsing. God, she needed a cigarette. 'Hey, Lizzie—'

Grace bounded up. 'Dance with me!'

'Where are the dishy boys?'

Grace wrinkled her nose. 'Upstairs, playing Cluedo.' She began jumping and twirling.

Dancing was driving out thought. There was only room in Nancy's head for the drumbeat. When Lizzie bowed out, she pushed herself on, taking Grace's hand, spinning her round to *Brown Sugar*. She could see her reflection in the uncurtained, dark window, her party top sparkling and swirling as if it hardly needed her inside it. Lizzie's boyfriend, the dark one in the suit, was slumped in an armchair, blowing smoke, watching her. He reminded her of Harry. She was damned if she would take any notice. She concentrated on Grace.

It got to be late, and the crowd was starting to thin. Nancy, out of breath, had dropped to the sofa. Soon she would have to find Sally, say goodbye and be on her own

121

again.

Grace was across the room, whispering to Lizzie's brother, the flame-headed teenager in the red-tartan shirt, who had taken over the armchair. They kept glancing her way, then Grace came sashaying towards her. 'Go and ask him to dance.'

'Don't be daft.'

Grace ran back to confer. Something was afoot: a little girl deep in conversation with a lumberjack. Soon she was with Nancy again, pleading, 'He wants to ask you, but he's shy. You have to ask him.'

The boy grinned across the room.

'I've forgotten his name.'

'Oz. His name's Oz.'

'Okay.' She smiled back. 'Tell him, if he asks me, I'll say yes.'

Grace whooped and dashed to deliver the message. The boy shrank into the chair, but she levered him out of it and brought him across, dragging and shoving him. Nancy held out her hand from the depths of the sofa.

Someone else had been choosing the music. This track was too slow to move to. He agreed wordlessly, led her to the record player. They put on Status Quo.

At first they danced without touching, but soon he had her hand and they were jiving to *Caroline*. Hey, the boy was a good dancer. He knew how to lead, how to spin her. Not much taller than she was, he was still growing, probably. When their bodies collided he fitted against her, hand to hand, hip to hip. He gave her new energy; she wanted to dance on and on.

People were leaving; before long they had the floor to themselves. It didn't stop them. No one was watching, but that made no difference. They were dancing for the pleasure of it. They went on until finally they began to stumble, had to agree they'd run out of puff and flopped on the sofa together.

Even now, even not dancing, he was kind of easy to be with. He had a slow, gentle style of speaking, with a slight stammer that didn't seem to bother him, so it didn't bother her. She liked his smile, and he was looking at her in that way, cheeky sod. He was much, much too young. She answered his unspoken question with another. 'How old are you, Oz?'

'How old do you think?'

He looked out into the room while she examined his profile, his puppy-soft skin. She didn't want to insult him. 'Eighteen?' she tried.

His eyes slid sideways to meet hers, full of naughtiness. He said, 'How old are *you?*'

She nearly said twenty-six. She didn't know why because that was five months away. 'Twenty-five.'

His smile was amazing, huge and happy, an exuberant loop between deep, long dimples, and full of white teeth. His eyes were laughing above it.

She kept her face straight. 'You still haven't told me how old you are.'

'Seventeen.'

She couldn't have looked too convinced.

'Seventeen, I swear. Last m-month.' He grinned. 'Would you like to see my provisional driving licence?'

Far too young. But still he was giving her that look. He'd been at boarding school, he was saying, but he'd done with that. He'd never been any good at the academic stuff. He and friend Mike had decided to fly to Australia in September on a six-month visa.

The boy with the acne. 'Where is he?' said Nancy.

'Gone home on his bike,' Oz replied. They were going to backpack all over Australia, he told her, see everything, maybe go to New Zealand as well. He thought, if he liked it, he might stay there for good. He was handy, he said. He could get work on a farm or a building site.

He smiled. 'But n-now I've met you, so I can't stay in Australia. I'll have to come back.'

'Rubbish,' she said.

'Don't you want m-me to come back?'

'We only just met.'

He flashed the big, loopy smile. 'But don't you want me to?'

How ridiculous. She had no answer. She leaned closer and planted a kiss somewhere on the smile.

She sat back, grinning, feeling seventeen herself.

'I'm glad you did that,' he said.

And then he looked at her, smiling, and she looked at him, smiling too, but he was only a boy, and this wasn't going to happen.

'You don't smoke,' he said.

'No,' she said.

The room was deserted now, the music had stopped, but conversation was still loud in the hall. Oz was telling her how he'd been staying with Lizzie since he'd quit boarding school. He was earning his keep by redecorating her kitchen. After a while Grace tiptoed in and whispered in Nancy's ear, 'He likes you,' and ran out again.

He was looking at her, waiting for her to say something. She was wondering how to tell him that this was going nowhere when his face came close, and he kissed her, a brush of his lips, and Grace who had been behind the door watching the reflection of the sofa in the window was screaming and laughing and running about like a mad thing.

He whispered in Nancy's ear, 'If I leave you alone, go and get you a drink, will it confuse her, d'you think?'

Sure enough, Grace followed Oz from the room, pleading with him to stay. While they were gone, Nancy slipped upstairs. She looked at her flushed face in the bathroom mirror. Don't do it. He's only a boy. She'd done enough bad stuff for one week. But oddly this didn't feel bad. He was okay, not a Harry or an Edward. Just a bit too bloody young.

When she came down, the two of them were conferring anxiously in the hall. Grace rushed up to her, pleading, 'Where have you *been*? Don't you like him?' His eyes were asking the same question.

Nancy bent and whispered, 'It's what you do, Grace. Somewhere near the beginning, you pretend you don't care.'

Grace frowned, not understanding, but then shouted, 'Yes!' and ran off. They went back to the sofa in the deserted front room. 'What did you tell her?' Oz wanted to know.

'A girly secret.'

She looked at his big smile, his laughing eyes fixed on her face. She sipped the wine he had brought her. Did she live nearby, he was asking. 'London,' she said. 'Maida Vale. I came on the coach. My B&B's just a few streets away.'

A head came back round the door.

'Grace, you can't keep digging a plant up to see if the roots are growing.'

No use. In a flash, Grace was standing in front of the sofa. 'You've kissed,' she insisted. 'I want to be a bridesmaid at your wedding.'

Nancy laughed. 'We're not going to get married.'

'You are! You are!' She ran off again.

It didn't embarrass Nancy. She felt safe and relaxed. Eventually Oz said what she knew he would say. 'I wonder, can I walk you to the B&B?' And she said what she knew she would say. 'There's nothing I'd like better.' And they both knew he would stay the night, but he didn't know yet that there was a double bed and that she was on the pill. And Lizzie came in and said, 'Dave and I are leaving, Oz. I'll put the keys in the flowerpot.'

When he asked was she ready to go, it struck her she was. She went upstairs for her sweater and bag, followed by Grace. She said, 'Thank you, Cupid,' gave her a hug, then ran down again to where Oz was waiting, smiling up at her in his red tartan shirt.

'Oh, Nancy, we've had no time to catch up,' Sally said.

And Sally hugged her, and Stuart kissed her cheek, and they stood at the front door waving her off past the laurel bushes into the warm night. This felt simple and easy, pretty wonderful actually. He was only seventeen, but why should that matter? He would be fine to wake up with tomorrow. She imagined Grace peeping through some upstairs window as they went arm in arm down the road.

2008, Saturday

I can't stand to be in that house today, not even with Matilda, so I'm on a half-empty train heading for Brighton. Dad doesn't know that I'm coming. I could have phoned him, but I need to see his face as he answers my questions. He's not 'Dad' any more, I keep thinking, just Ted.

I'm sweating from lack of sleep, loosening and tightening the strap of the rucksack. The train's been dawdling, faffing about, but now it's zipping along. To ease my impatience, I fish out the things I've been staring at for two days and two wakeful nights. Photographs of a grinning teenager in an open-necked tartan shirt, and four official certificates—birth, marriage, divorce, death—four tent pegs fixing some facts. A girl, Nanette Julia, born 23 November 1952 in Kent and Canterbury Hospital to Michael James Rogers, bank employee, and Elizabeth Margaret Rogers, formerly Barnes. Married, a spinster lawyer aged 26, on 5 May 1979 to Edward Jonnson, a bachelor lawyer aged 33. Divorce, final and absolute, on 7 July 1986. Death, final and absolute, on 24 November 2008.

She married barely a month before I was born. I knew that. I can't remember since when I've known it. She used to joke grimly about her marriage coinciding with Thatcher's election, so it stuck in my head.

Edward Jonnson. Dad. Ted. He must have known that he wasn't my father. I try to remember how he was to me when I was small. He hated Mum calling me Piglet. 'Oink, oink.' Does that mean he hated me? I strain to reach further back than that miserable fifth birthday party. Please, anything, the tiniest image or clue. I'm sensing green, feeling shadow, and yes, dimly, I'm squatting on grass, there's a frog, and something rears hugely beside me, smelling of tobacco and blocking the light. As enormous to me as I am to the frog. Is it Ted? Is he speaking? Telling me not to harm the frog, helping me name it? Freddie the frog?

I shake myself awake and stare at the certificates. My tired eyes prickle and burn. They divorced after two years' separation the year I was seven, the age Matilda will be next month.

We're held on a signal at Gatwick, where a man sprawls on a bench on the platform, reading the *Mail*. There's a ring on his left hand. Ted's girlfriend didn't last. Mum's bloke after Ted left didn't last. Neither of them ever had a relationship that lasted.

We are off again, hurtling past a gravel works and through scrubby woodland, and I'm gazing at the luminous photographs of Mum with this boy. Nancy, I suppose I should call her: she was nobody's mother back then. Her eyes shine with laughter. Her unlined face glows. I've no other images of her this good. The snaps in her albums are of me, Matilda, her friends, and the cities she explored on her own: Hong Kong, New York, Sydney, Rome, Madrid. Almost none of herself. 'I like to be invisible,' she once told me, 'to see without being seen.' I remember her dancing with her mates on her birthday. Visible. Laughing. Girls just wanna have fun.

The train shakes me out of my dream. We're into a tunnel, nearly there. There's a bit more countryside, but we're heading for hills, the ones that guard Brighton. Sussex Downs. Sussex Ups. A second tunnel, a gap, a third long tunnel, under the Ups and we are out into Preston Park and the small, sunlit architecture of Regency terraces.

I steady my nerves with a pint at the station and buy a six-pack of Guinness. Then a short bus ride and here I am outside Ted's place, steeling myself to confront him, half-hoping he's out. I've not visited in winter before, and I'm unprepared for how dreary it is, this eight-storey block of flats on Hove front, square and grey behind a patch of weedy grass, rotting posts linked with chain, barrels of wind-battered shrubs. There's a meagre glass balcony for each Channel-facing view, but the windows are tight shut today, guarding their few, shabby Christmas trees against the freezing wind and the cries of the gulls.

The entrance bristles with prohibitions. *No hawkers or circulars. Parking of bicycles in the foyer forbidden.* The door to the stairwell's open, and I go up unannounced, still unsure what to say to him. If he's in.

His flat's on the seventh floor. Somewhere near the top I pause, dizzy from lack of sleep. I have the rucksack off my shoulder and unbuckled, and I'm groping inside for that first, shocking close-up of Oz.

So here we are, Oz and I, a comedy double-act, lined up cheek-to-cheek in front of Ted Jonnson's door, and we're knocking.

His footsteps approach, his shape looms through frosted glass. I can feel the cold sweat on my back.

The door's swinging inwards, releasing a roar of canned TV laughter and a fug of cigarette smoke. He looks at me and the photo and frowns.

'So you've decided to talk to me, have you?' he says.

We're in the cramped kitchen, where he's finding me a pint glass. 'I've had years to get used to it,' he says when I ask doesn't he need a drink too. His calm feels unnatural, like something rehearsed. He's dragging hard on a cigarette.

'Why didn't you tell me?' I say.

'She swore me to silence.' He's frosty as well as calm. 'It was between you and her.'

'It was my right to know.'

'Maybe so,' he says, 'but not my right to tell you. Sit

down, eh?'

I duck my head back under the doorframe into the living room, where the television still blares. I'm looking at this cruddy little place with new eyes. The room's chilly; Ted's wearing a fleece; perhaps he can't afford heating. I would suggest we go to the pub, but I'm too knackered.

'On second thoughts...' He's beside me with the rest of the six pack and a glass for himself. I lower myself to the sofa, feeling the wooden slats through the foam. While he turns off the telly and fetches a chair, I slide Oz's picture from my shirt pocket, needing its shiny explosion of green, gold and red.

Ted puts down his Guinness and takes the photograph from me. He shoves his spectacles to his forehead and examines it close up, frowning. I'm seeing his thin features as if for the first time, wondering how come I ever took it for granted that we were related.

'Huh!' For a moment I fear he will rip Oz's picture to pieces. He thrusts it away, dropping ash on the parquet floor.

'So... you know him?' I say.

'Know him?'

'His name. The fact he's my father?'

'All that,' he snaps.

His anger is disconcerting; I wasn't expecting it. I'm the one who should be angry.

'Dear departed Daniels,' he sneers.

'Daniels?'

He nods.

'Oz Daniels?'

He doesn't answer. I let the name sink in. It should have been my name: Mark Daniels not Mark Daniel Jonnson. 'Did you meet him?' I say.

He pulls a sour face. 'To give him a piece of my mind? Sadly not. I only got to see the happy snaps. She showed them to me once, proving some point.'

'Please stop playing games,' I say. 'What point?'

'What a waste of space I was. That sort of thing.'

He glares for a moment, then drops his gaze. His tone softens. 'Look, Mark, it's done and dusted. I don't spend my time thinking about it. I'm not sure what you want me to say.'

I let a second go by before asking, 'Do you know where he lives now?'

He snorts. 'For God's sake.' Then sees my bewilderment and sits forward, paying attention. 'I thought *you* did. The poppies?'

'What about them?'

'His poppies. You were in touch with him, yes?'

'Only by email. I had no idea who he was.'

'You didn't? Oh Mark, I'm sorry.' Ted shunts closer, scraping the parquet with his chair, and grabs my wrist. 'I assumed—I thought Nancy must have told you—'

'No.'

'I was livid, seeing his message. I thought you hadn't bothered to talk to me—you'd moved on to that bastard and airbrushed me out.'

I wish he'd let go of my hand. 'Of course not.'

'So that god-awful wreath was a mystery to you?'

'Completely.' I reach for my drink, escaping his grip. 'I emailed him, asking questions, but he told me to "leave it". He drives a bus is all I know. And now this.' I finger the photo. 'I only found it on Christmas Day. Only realised then who he is. It's a lot to take in.'

'I'm sorry,' Ted says again. 'I shouldn't have jumped to conclusions.'

'I was pissed off with you too,' I say, 'thinking you skipped the wake because you didn't give a damn about Mum.'

'Far from it. Crossed wires.'

He leans forward. Looks at me. 'This has shaken

you, hasn't it?'

'And how.'

He lights a new cigarette, and I suddenly want one myself. 'May I?'

He pauses, holding the packet open between us. 'Last thing you need.'

I battle the urge, and he puts them in the pocket of his fleece. 'A bus, eh? He didn't drive a bus in seventy-eight.'

'What did he do?'

'Just drifted as far as I know. Downwardly mobile middle-class kid. Like me, ha ha. A school-leaver. Seventeen.'

'Jesus,' I say, 'is that all? How old was Mum?'

'Twenty-five. Heaven knows what she thought she was playing at. I never could get any sense out of her on the subject. There was something Oedipal going on—not only with him—with her too—that's my theory.'

'So how on earth did they get together?'

He shakes his head. 'What can I tell you? They met through her friend, the woman with white hair who spoke at the funeral.'

'Sally?'

'That's the one. She'd know more.' He takes a deep hit of nicotine before adding unhappily, 'To be honest I barely knew her myself. Your mother, I mean. I barely knew Nancy before she got pregnant. We worked in the same room, but it ended at five p.m. I knew she didn't fancy me, not in the slightest.'

It's a sad admission. He rocks back on his chair with his eyes closed. When he opens them he's looking at the past not at me.

'She was nothing out of the ordinary to look at, was she? But... well... as you said at the funeral, she was always laughing. It was the same back then. Even later, when she didn't know what to do for the best, even when she was crying over her fly-by-night lover, she could laugh through the tears. She made me feel happy, as if happiness was possible, and I couldn't help wishing... thinking... maybe if I'm patient, show her I care, maybe one day...'

He runs out of words. Stares into his Guinness. 'Foolish.'

It feels cruel to mention Oz again, but I need to. 'So where did he go? Why did he leave?'

Ted lifts his eyes to mine, making me awkwardly conscious that I'm an Oz lookalike. 'Search me. He vamoosed is all I know. Took off without a word.'

'Not true,' I say. 'Cards, messages, valentines. I found them in the house. Heaps of words, right up to the day she died.'

I see how this hurts him and try to downplay it. 'Schmaltzy stuff. Naff, empty, repetitious. Never anything worth reading. Next to no information. So why? I don't get it.'

Ted shakes his head. 'Nostalgia for puppy love? I couldn't take him seriously once I saw the pictures.'

'But *she* must have done.' I try to get my head round it. 'So... Sally introduced them?'

'Yes, summer of '78, at some kind of party. Fair play to Nancy, the age difference put her off—or that's what she said. But he kept up the pressure, pursued her from Bristol to London. Moved into her bedsit.'

He's fidgeting as if his chair is too hot for him. His voice grows sarcastic again. 'Fixed her shelves, bought her flowers with her own money, went bed-and-breakfasting in Devon with her.'

He escapes the chair and takes a pace to the window. 'He had her wanting to believe in happy-ever-after. She stopped telling him it was nonsense. Stopped telling herself that it was. She fell, hook, line and sinker, and then the little bugger buggered off.'

'Because she was pregnant?'

'I don't know. I didn't care, Mark, to be honest. All I needed to be sure of was, was he coming back? She swore blind he was gone, so I said to her, "Marry me." She told me no way, but I kept on at her, wouldn't take no for an answer. Her parents were on at her too. They thought I was the father... your father, and she didn't enlighten them. I told them, "I'll look after Nancy." She said, "I can look after myself," but I could see she was weakening.

'Anyway, her parents were no use to her—disapproving, didn't want to know. "Made your bed, you can lie in it," said her father. Not nice people. She made me swear I would never tell them the truth. No deal otherwise.' He stares out at the grey sea. 'I thought I'd won the pools, more fool me. Only myself to blame. There was someone else I could have married. A nice, ordinary girl. Nerys, her name was. Jesus, Nerys, I'm sorry.'

He's not talking to me or to Nerys. He's railing at fate. 'My life could have been fine—nothing special, but fine, you know—and I had to go after Nancy.'

He stops, awkward suddenly, comes back from the window and sits down. Drags on his cigarette. Stubs it out.

'One thing I can tell you—it's a mistake to marry someone who doesn't fancy you. A kind of living hell, if I'm honest. We stuck it out for five years, and you know the rest. She fancied *him*. Oz Daniels. It got so I couldn't bear to go on seeing that, feeling that...'

I'm hungry for more. 'What else did she tell you about him?'

A shrug. 'She got pregnant. He took off. She loved him. What else do you need to know?'

'Everything. He's my father.'

And all at once Ted is shouting, 'To hell with that,

Mark, *I'm* your dad. He's no more your father than...'

He stops. His logic has nowhere to go. There are tears in his eyes.

I look away, down at my hands. 'Okay,' I say.

'I'm your dad, Mark,' he repeats.

'I'm sorry, Dad.'

We don't say a lot more after that. 'Did we have a garden?' I remember to ask him.

'A garden?'

'Before you and Mum split. I remember a frog. Did we ever have grass, or a pond?'

He shakes his head.

A while later the Guinness is gone, and I get up unsteadily and say, 'I'd best be off.'

When I come out of the bathroom, he's on his feet. He looks ready to hug me, but I forestall him by holding my hand out.

He takes it and squeezes. 'Give my love to the family.' His voice is slurred and hoarse.

He follows me to the door, a hand on the small of my back.

Once the train's through the tunnels, I get Bristol Sally's number from enquiries. Her voice sounds younger than she is and kind-hearted, and she has Mum's Kentish accent, which fills me with an ache.

She confirms that Oz was my father. Mum swore her to silence, refused to talk about it, said it was best left alone, there was nothing to be done.

She says she never properly met Oz, just saw him with Mum at the party. Her husband worked with Oz's sister; the sister brought him along.

She says Mum danced all evening with Oz, jumping and jiving. He looked way too young for her. She's amazed when I say seventeen; she'd assumed nearer twenty.

She says Ted was hurt to see Oz's flowers at the funeral. She'll ask her husband if he knows where the sister is and get back to me. She tells me, 'Take care.' We ring off. Damn, my battery's low.

Her sympathy for Ted has thrown me off balance. I should have let him hug me just now.

I get out the photographs of Oz and Mum, smiling happily, his arm around her, she leaning against him, lifting their pints in the sunny pub garden.

There's a sister, said Sally. My aunt. I have an aunt.

The phone rings. I snatch it up, but it isn't Sally, it's Gina, and then the bloody thing dies on me. I drop it into the rucksack and fish out *Germinal*. Open it up.

It's no use: not even Zola can distract me from my own story. My eyes slide from the words. I stare out at the rushing winter darkness, trying to imagine Mum falling in love with a seventeen-year-old boy.

The world bombarded Nancy with its meticulous, beautiful clarity. From a luminous sky, heat and light pulsed down on the lunchtime crowds in St James's Park. Ducks bustled and jostled on the banks of the lake, gobbling crusts. On the bridge, sparrows perched on outstretched fingers to snatch crumbs from palms. Everyone around her was smiling. Edward and Nerys were smiling and feeding the ducks. Nerys was smiling at Edward. Edward was smiling at Nerys. He was glancing over at her too and smiling, which last week would have felt awkward but today wasn't awkward at all. Edward was no fool. He could tell she'd moved on. The trap she'd been in was of her own making, and now she walked free. Harry was back in the office, tersely grumpy about the pointlessness of feeding ducks in the park. He was sulking because he was no fool either. Who gave a damn any more about Harry?

It wasn't that she was in love with Oz or would ever see him again. It was nothing like that. It was just one evening, one night that had shown her how simple it was to be happy if you looked at life straight. The difference was the change in herself.

A warm dollop of romance had been just what she needed after the humiliation of Harry, but romance was all it was. Through those few hours in the Bristol darkness, the clarity that coalesced and intensified was the sure knowledge that this was ephemeral. Oz had been sent to lift her from the gutter, dust her down and pop her up on a pedestal, but she didn't belong on a pedestal, Oz's or anyone else's.

His quiet voice in the dark had felt somehow wiser than she was in spite of his age and his stammer and the nonsense he was actually talking. But she resisted the illusion. He was seventeen. They had almost nothing in common. If they saw more of each other the romance would evaporate, the gap between them would widen. She wasn't going to be waking up next to Oz for the rest of her life.

Under the covers, he'd assured her earnestly they belonged to each other. She was the one for him, he knew his own mind, and he was the one for her too, he'd insisted. She had only to realise it. 'Maybe,' she'd whispered. 'Maybe.'

It was part of the romance. She hadn't minded at all. She'd smiled back at him through the dark. But all the while she was learning the lesson. She was hearing from Oz the wishful thinking men must have heard from her, felt from her, and she saw all at once how immature and unnecessary it was.

She'd been waiting for love to solve her problems. What problems? Love had become the problem, and now she saw through it. A decent man was a nice dream to have, but so what if she didn't meet one? Her father was wrong. She wouldn't be lonely on the shelf. Male chauvinist rubbish. She was fine as she was.

Back there in the dark, she'd told Oz, 'You don't know me. I'm not what you think.' She'd whispered, 'I can hardly even remember what you look like.'

He'd presented his face close up for inspection: his big smile, his mischievous eyes. His bliss was undentable, and eventually she'd conceded he wasn't completely mad, this was worth something. 'But leave it a few days,' she'd said. 'Let Lizzie give you a good talking to.'

Nothing would come of it. He was a hundred miles away west. He was just a boy, hormonal, impressionable. He scarcely knew her. The few days would pass, and then more, bringing new influences, new trails for him to follow. She would fade into memory. The 'older woman' who took his virginity.

The fact made her shiver each time that she thought of it. Sent a tremor into her belly. She'd deflowered a seventeen-year-old. He hadn't seemed nervous or inept, but still she'd believed him when he said it was his first time. After Harry he'd felt slight in her arms. The soft rustle of the curtains stirred by the breeze, the strange room, the sound of his breath in her ear, had carried her back to her student days when sex had still seemed wondrous and strange. 'You're a good dancer,' she'd whispered.

At some point in the night, she'd said, 'If Grace hadn't made you, would you have asked me to dance?' And he'd said, 'I wouldn't have got up the n-nerve.'

That's all it takes, she thought now. Everything you want can be yours if you have the nerve to want it, to ask for it, to turn your back on your troubles and look for it, not wait for Grace to push you and pull you. It had seemed miraculous meeting Oz, but it wasn't, not really. It had only required her to get on a bus, to dance, to hold out her hand from a sofa.

'If I believed in such things,' he'd said, 'I would say you were an angel.'

Was this how an angel experienced the world? She felt powerfully tender towards Oz, and now in St James's Park towards Nerys and Edward and the ducks and the people who stretched out their fingers for the sparrows. Even towards grumpy Harry. There was no possible harm in blessing him too.

At dawn, when she'd asked, 'Do you have everything you came with?' Oz had grinned and said, 'No.' And she'd stood at the window to watch him emerge below and head off towards the rosy-streaked sky. He'd spun around and walked backwards, looking up at the window. And seeing her there, he'd jumped wildly, high off the pavement, again and again, flinging his arms up and out like a lumberjack learning semaphore.

There's no light on at home, and the street's deserted and silent except for a passing train. I slump in the porch, fishing in my pocket for the key.

I'm shivering with cold, but I don't want to go in. I'm angry with Mum but don't want to hear it from Gina. She'll be shocked at Oz's age. She'll say Mum treated everyone badly. Selfish, she'll call her.

I'm inhaling deep through my nose, gathering myself, when I notice there's a light on next door, downstairs back, faintly illuminating the glass in Jane's front door.

Pocketing the key, I step over the low wall and ring the bell for a fraction of a second.

Silence. But I'm sensing Jane's approach along the hall, creeping towards whoever is out here. I've frightened her. I put my mouth to the letterbox. Whisper, 'Hi, Jane. It's me, Mark.'

For a moment we stand, wordless, in her chilly hall that smells of burnt toast. The looking-glass layout's as disconcerting as before. Her eyes are red as though she's been crying. Her hair is all anyhow, and she's wearing her dressing gown. Mum's cat is on the stairs, watching.

'Are you okay?' I say.

She closes her eyes. 'No.'

We're whispering so as not to be heard through the wall. I step forward and put my arms round her, and she holds on to me.

'Are your kids here?' I say.

She nods against my chest and mumbles, 'In bed.' Then lifts her face. 'They played on their bikes with Matilda today. You were visiting your dad, right?'

I let go and back off. 'You saw Gina?'

'What?' Then she gets it. 'Don't worry. It was only mum-talk.'

After a second, she adds, 'You can trust me. I'm not going to rat on you. What are you doing here?'

'Hiding,' I say. 'But what's up? Why aren't you okay?'

She shakes her head. 'Nothing. It's silly.'

'Tell me.'

Pulls a face. 'Really nothing. Just the parents. Christmas, you know. Winding me up.'

I'm watching the dimple in her cheek. I put my arms round her again. 'And Pinter died.'

That startles her into a smile. '*Thank* you. My dad got facetious. He said Pinter wrote meaningless rubbish that I only pretend to like to make myself look clever. He made me so angry.'

'And you told him so, right?'

'Wish I had. No, I stomped out, slammed the door, sulked. A day in their company, and I'm infantile.' She's grinning now. 'But why are you hiding?'

'Being infantile too,' I say. 'I've had a weird day, and I'm not ready to hear Gina's opinion on it. Plus I'm a bit allergic to my mother right now—to her house.'

Jane stands back from me, her hands on my arms. 'Intriguing,' she says. 'Weird day good or bad?'

'Both. Maybe good. I don't know.'

'Do you want someone to listen? I promise to have no opinion.'

She goes into the kitchen, and I follow, closing the door so we can stop whispering. 'Sounds just up my street,' I say.

She laughs. 'That's one thing you can count on.'

'What?'

'My being just up your street.'

She fills the kettle, sets mugs out, drags a comb through her hair. We sit at the table as we did after Asda, sipping coffee and speaking in low voices.

It's well after midnight when I ease open my sticking front door. I creep along the dark hall, but Gina's halfway downstairs. She flicks on the light. Déjà vu. Me. Hall. Woman in dressing gown. Back through the looking glass.

'Where have you been?'

'Brighton—'

'Since Brighton. I've been crazy with worry, Mark. I thought you were lying dead somewhere. I've had the lights off so he wouldn't know we were home.'

'Who? What are you on about?'

'A guy called up here, threatening to kill you.'

'What?'

'Sounded like a black guy. Maybe one of your students? He said, "I know where you live."'

'*What?* Oh my God, is Matty all right?'

'Asleep. I haven't told her.'

I reach for Gina, and she clings to me. I want to smile at the action replay, but my heart's thudding with alarm. 'How long ago?'

'Eight thirty. Your cell was off. I tried Ted, and he said you left hours ago. Then Sally called. Said you'd spoken with her from the train—Mark, where have you been? Why's this guy mad at you?'

'I've no idea. Did you get his name?'

'Nuh-uh.'

'His number?'

'Caller withheld.' Her fingers dig into my arm; her voice wobbles. 'He was shouting and cursing—said you'd been messing with his woman—Oh, right, I get it.' She pulls away from me. 'I'm being an idiot. It's her again, isn't it? You sneak back from Brighton to fool around with that—'

'No. Honestly no. Hand on heart.' I pull her hand to my chest and look her straight in the eye. 'Alison's history.

142

I've been in the pub by the station. You know, the one on the corner? Claims it has the longest bar in the universe or something? It has to have been a wrong number, a wind up, a misunderstanding. I haven't been messing with anyone's woman.'

We stare at each other. The wind wails at the door behind me. Jane's nobody's woman. We only drank coffee.

Gina goes into the kitchen, turning the light on. I follow her shakily. Someone wants to kill me? My family's in danger?

She grabs a scrap of paper from the table. 'Sally asked me to give you this. What are we gonna do, Mark? Should we call the police?'

It's a Bristol address and number. A name: *David Sedley-Jones*. Another name: *Lizzie*. My aunt.

'I don't think the police can help,' I say. 'We don't know who it is.'

'But what are we supposed to do, just wait here?'

I go back to the hall and slide the bolts on the door. I check the living-room sashes; they have solid security locks. The same goes for the kitchen window, and the backdoor has a mortise. 'He'd have to smash a window,' I say. 'We'd have time to dial 999. I'll check upstairs.'

The upper windows are all secure. I tiptoe in and out past Matilda, sound asleep. Back in the kitchen I find Gina tensed on a chair, both hands at her mouth. 'Would a whisky help?' I say, and she nods.

I pour two, put one in her hand, then kneel at her feet as she sips it and shudders. 'Listen, Gina. I'm sorry I didn't come straight home. It was bad of me.'

'Will he come here?' she says.

'I don't know.'

'Maybe it was just talk,' she says.

'Or a mistake,' I say. 'I'm a bad bugger, but I can't believe anyone would go to the trouble of killing me.'

She smiles at last. 'If there were a line, I'd be first in it.'

'How was Matty today?' I ask her.

'Exhausting. It's tough keeping her occupied. How was Ted?'

'Exhausting. I'll tell you tomorrow.'

'But Oz *is* your dad? You didn't make a mistake?'

'He is, and I didn't.'

Her brow furrows. 'Sally said he was seventeen. Is that right?'

When I nod, her frown deepens, her mouth opens, and I seriously don't want to hear her.

'Hey,' I whisper. 'Shall we go on the run from this loony? Do you fancy a trip to Bristol tomorrow?'

Sunday

My aunt's house stands out, cream-painted stucco, on a steep, terraced hill of Victorian red-brick. An elegant Christmas tree glows behind the bay window, and a brass knocker gleams on the glossy red door.

Gina says we shouldn't tell Matilda about Oz until the facts are clearer, so she has taken her to see some film about a mouse and I'm here on my own at Lizzie's. I watch the minicab out of sight, gather my courage, climb the steps, lift the knocker and hold my breath.

Her face comes alive at the sight of me. I'm so sure she's my flesh and blood, I almost embrace her. Hair bleached and grey at the roots, eyes hazel not green, but nonetheless here, in a brown velour tracksuit, is a middle-aged version of Matilda winning at Monopoly.

She throws the door wide, exclaiming, 'Ben!' Then her hand goes to her mouth. 'I'm sorry. I thought...'

It's the smoker's voice I heard when I rang before we set out this morning. She said hello several times and finally, 'Bloody cold-callers,' before hanging up. Her warm, husky annoyance has been replaying all day in my brain.

'You must think I'm daft,' she says now. 'I haven't seen Ben for ages, and you look just like him.'

I hazard a guess—'Your nephew?'—and she says, 'How did you know?'

My brain races. A brother. Somewhere out there, right now, I have a brother called Ben.

'That's why I'm here, Lizzie. I'm not sure how to tell you this, but—'

She interrupts, panicking. 'Is Ben all right?'

Say it. 'I'm your nephew too.'

Her mouth opens. Her hand rises to cover it.

'My name's Mark. May I come in?'

Another moment of staring, then she gestures for me to step into the echoing hall. Thick coir matting, black-and-white tiles, a mixed smell of cigarette smoke and furniture polish. She closes the door, and we gawp at each other. My eyes slide to my reflection in the mirror behind her. 'You didn't know about me?'

She shakes her head, blinking, as realisation dawns. 'Are you saying you're Oz's son?'

I nod.

'Good God.'

'I'm sorry to spring it on you.'

'But I don't understand. Who's your mother?'

'Nancy,' I say.

She looks blank.

'They met here in Bristol in 1978?' I say. 'At a party?'

She steps back. 'Nancy Roberts?'

'Rogers. He lived with her in London that summer.'

'Of course. Oh my God.'

'Where does Ben live?' I ask.

'Australia.'

It's a blow. So far away. I don't know what to do next, so I hold out my hand, and she takes it. 'Well I never.' Then she gestures for me to follow her. 'Come through to the kitchen. Dump your coat on the stairs.'

As I do, I peer up to the landing, wondering if David Sedley-Jones is at home, hoping he isn't.

The kitchen is shiny, immaculate as though it hasn't been cooked in, only photographed by estate agents. She's filling the kettle, opening a cupboard, apologising for having no biscuits. Pointing me to a chair, she lowers herself onto another. 'It's hard to take in.'

I unzip my rucksack and fish out the photographs. 'These may help.'

Her mouth trembles as she examines them; her hand rises to cover it in her habitual gesture. 'Oh heavens, I took these. Just before he left. He and Nancy were in a hired car, heading for Devon. It was their last week together.'

She goes through them again. 'Did he know she was pregnant? Why didn't they tell me? She was lovely, really lovely. He should never have gone.'

The kettle comes to the boil, roars for a second or two and switches itself off.

'Do you have anything stronger than tea?'

She's silent for a moment, still transfixed by the photos. Then, 'Of course. Absolutely.' She jumps up and pulls a bottle of champagne from the rack. 'We should celebrate, shouldn't we? It's not every day I get a new nephew.'

While I pop the cork, she fetches flutes from a cupboard and offers her cigarettes.

'No thanks.'

She lights up and we clink glasses, her eyes fixed all the while on my face. 'What a bombshell. Amazing. How *is* Nancy? And why on earth didn't I know?'

I swallow hard. 'Here's the thing, Lizzie. Mum died five weeks ago. A road accident. I didn't have a clue about Oz myself until I saw these. I found them on Christmas Day. I thought someone else was my father.' My throat is seizing up. 'I don't know why Mum didn't tell me, let alone you. I've been angry.'

Lizzie puts down her glass and holds out her hands. I rise to take them, and she draws me close, hugging me, pinning my arms. Her head's on my chest, but she's in charge here. 'You just lost your mother,' she says in her warm smoker's burr.

I would speak, I want to thank her, but I can't get my voice to work.

She lets go and steps back. 'I liked Nancy enormously. She had so much life. I can't tell you how sorry I am.'

I nod dumbly.

'Let's go through.' She picks up the bottle and leads me to the room with the Christmas tree. Soft carpet swallows my feet. A low-slung sofa invites me to sink into it. I glance around for photographs of relatives, but there are none on display.

'Is your husband here? David, is it?'

She laughs. 'No. I had him for Christmas. The mistress gets him for New Year.'

Her laugh's unreadable, possibly scornful. 'I'm sorry,' I venture.

'Don't be. It works just fine. Really.'

I'm not sure I believe her. She draws me down to the sofa, pours us more champagne and reaches across the coffee table for the ashtray. 'I shouldn't have lost touch with Nancy,' she says. 'I feel bad. I should have made it my business to know about this. Did Oz give you my address? He should have told me you were coming—'

'He doesn't know,' I say. 'At least, I think maybe he knows I'm his son, but not that I'm here.'

Her smile makes me reckless, and in a mixture of telling and answering her questions, out spills the story. Mum's step off the pavement, the mysterious email, the poppies, the cards under the bed, his brush off, what I've learned since. I wind up, 'Now it's your turn. Tell me all about him. He's in Australia, right?'

Something has changed in her face. 'He told you he would rather just leave it?'

'He perhaps doesn't know,' I say quickly, 'doesn't realise...'

'Or maybe he would rather just leave it.'

She's still smiling. Her voice is still kind.

'Even so, you can still tell me about him.'

'I'd love to,' she says, 'but with him saying that... You can see what an awkward position I'm in. I'd need to ask him—'

'I only want to know about my father.'

148

That came out angrily. 'I'm sorry,' I say. 'It's him and Mum I'm angry with, not you.'

She shares out what's left of the champagne. 'I share your frustration. I'd ring him now, but it's the middle of the night there.' She sets the bottle down. 'I'll do it this evening. Can you stay? I'll make up a bed.'

I'm tempted, but it would involve bringing Gina here. I shake my head. 'I have to get back to London.'

'Okay, here's the plan. I'll ring him tonight, square things with him and get him to ring you. Or you and I can talk once I've spoken to him.'

'But can't you talk now? I don't get the big mystery.'

She leans back on the cushions. 'I expect it's Yvonne,' she says, guardedly. 'His wife. He'll be afraid of upsetting her.'

'Of course,' I say, 'his wife—that makes sense, but it doesn't mean you can't tell me stuff. I don't even know why he left Mum.'

She lights a new cigarette, considering. 'Fair enough. That's no secret. He'd been planning it for months before he met Nancy. He and his friend Mike went backpacking in Australia. Mike came back, but Oz didn't. He met Yvonne.'

She pauses. 'Look, I can show you some photos too. I don't see why not. Hold on, I'll get them.'

She's back within a minute, kicking the door shut behind her. She's carrying a bottle of red wine and two fresh glasses, and there's a laptop under her arm. While it boots up, she unscrews the bottle and pours.

'Right,' she says, 'here they are this October. Yvonne, Oz and Ben. And here's one of Ben's wife, Sue, and the kids.'

Her voice hums with affection. Echoes of my face and Matilda's sing out at me, sun-kissed and laughing. Despite his crow's feet, Oz has the same eyes and goofy smile as in 1978. His hair's gingery, greying, no longer burnished but still thick and unkempt as if dumped on his head from a height.

Lizzie's about to log off, but, 'Wait. Please.' I keep staring. Ben Daniels, my doppelganger. Ben's young wife and his two toddling children, robust, substantial, carrying Oz's genes into the future. Yvonne, with small, pretty features, dishing out meat from a barbecue. I touch finger to screen. 'How old is he now?'

'Forty-seven. He should watch the sun with his skin.'

'And Yvonne?'

'Forty-eight.'

Eight years younger than Mum.

Oz's birthday email comes back to me. *Last month we nearly separated.* I turn to Lizzie. 'October, these photos? This October just gone?'

'Yep,' she says. 'Why?'

'Nothing.' I search Oz and Yvonne's faces for signs of disharmony.

'I don't have kids myself,' Lizzie's saying, 'so these feel like my grandchildren.'

I sense sadness. 'I've a daughter. Matilda. Nearly seven.'

I fish out my phone to show her pictures, and she's rapturous. 'What a smashing little girl. My grand-niece! A real character, I can tell. You must bring her to meet me. She looks so like Oz, it's amazing, he'll adore her. All he needs is his big sis to talk some sense into him.'

Her enthusiasm is infectious. 'Matty's never had a proper grandpa,' I say. 'The man I thought was my father, we aren't all that close, and Gina's parents are in America.'

'Gina. Your wife. What a beautiful name, and so is Matilda. I'm so glad you came, Mark.'

She taps another cigarette from the pack and reaches for the lighter. 'Other way round,' I say as the filter tip heads for the flame. 'Whoops.' She rescues it, clicks and inhales. Grabbing my mobile, she stares again at Matilda. 'How amazing.'

'So, Oz is a bus driver,' I fish.

She pulls a face. 'It's his own. Some rusty old coach. I love my brother to bits, but he's got zilch business sense, so what does he do? He sets up in business.' She waves her hands. 'I shouldn't say this,' she says, 'but he's useless. Too nice to make money. Too disorganised. He always slides off the subject when I ask about profit.'

'Driving tourists?' I prompt.

She nods.

I nod too. 'Sydney?' I try.

'Stop it!'

We both laugh, but I can tell that I'm right. Mum was in Sydney a few years back, and now I know why. I get up and go to the tree, where I stare at an encrusted white bauble glistening under a fairy light. I'm struggling to understand the truth of my mother.

It's clear we're pretty much done for today. Lizzie's curled among the sofa cushions with her eyes closed. I dial Gina, speaking low so as not to wake her.

'The movie was good,' Gina says, 'and Matilda's okay so far. We're gonna grab McDonald's. Did you meet with Lizzie?'

'I'm with her now. Tell you later. See you at the station.'

I ring off, all at once exhausted. The trek back to London looms like the ascent of the Eiger.

'So, Lizzie,' I say loudly. 'It's been wonderful meeting you, but I should be making tracks. May I call a cab?'

She blinks awake and makes it to her feet. Her hand's on my sleeve. 'You can't go yet. I haven't fed you.'

She craves company. Her husband is cosy somewhere. 'I'll heat something up,' she says. 'I can do it in no time.'

I'm hungry, and her neediness is endearing. I follow

her into the kitchen. 'I've been wondering,' I say. 'Oz must be short for something. Oswald, or Oliver?'

'Nope, just Oz. And I'm just Lizzie. Our parents must have liked zeds.' She sets the oven and cuts the packaging from a pizza.

'So, are they still alive, your parents? My grandparents?'

'Sorry. No. Gone. My mother died young, Dad five years ago.'

'Another brother or sister?'

'A couple of cousins is all,' she says. 'Dad's brother's kids. They live in Yorkshire.'

How bizarre yet mundane it is, the process of becoming related. While the oven heats I ask about her job, and she tells me she's a legal secretary for a firm that employs and represents women. While the pizza cooks, she asks about mine. Soon I'm chomping gratefully into a pepperoni slice. My phone buzzes, but it isn't Gina; the screen tells me it's Alison.

'Answer it,' Lizzie says. 'Don't mind me.'

'It's no one important.'

I let the call go to voicemail. The idea of Alison deflates me. What the hell can she want? 'So... um... what did your father do for a living?'

Lizzie giggles. 'Nothing exciting. Ran a packaging company. Boxes and bubble wrap, that sort of thing.' Pause. 'And Nancy, what did she do?'

I'm about to answer when my phone bleeps with a text. Alison again.

Ring me u bastard. Student's husband accusing u of inappropriate behaviour.

Suddenly I know who Gina's mad caller is, and I'm up on my feet saying, 'I'm sorry, Lizzie, but this one is urgent. I really must go.'

Monday

The college is deserted. Alison sits behind her desk, straight backed and po-faced, her shirt buttoned to the neck, her blonde hair combed severely behind her ears. She has stopped trying to charm me. We glare at each other.

She taps the yellow file in front of her. 'What have you been playing at, giving one-to-one tuition without clearance?'

'That's bullshit, and you know it,' I say.

'Sit down,' she says.

'No thanks.'

'He says you've been coming on to his wife.'

'Well I haven't. Does Comfort say that I have?'

'I don't know yet. I have to investigate formally.'

'More bullshit. You could have talked him out of it.'

'He was angry, demanding to see you. I took him through the procedures—'

'Exactly. He just wants to sound off, and instead of doing your job, smoothing it over, telling him there's probably nothing to worry about, you take great pleasure in steering him into a formal complaint. You want this, Alison. You're as happy as Larry. By the way, I've a complaint of my own. Did you give him my number?'

'Of course not.' She's indignant.

'Because he's been terrorising Gina.'

She pulls a face. 'I expect your wife is exaggerating. I'm going to have to investigate, Mark, and meanwhile you're suspended.'

'*What?*'

'You heard me.'

'You're saying my job's on the line?'

'I'm not saying anything yet—'

'You vindictive cow.'

She barely flinches. She opens the file up and straightens its pages. 'This has nothing to do with you and me.'

'Like hell it hasn't. You're going to set me up, aren't you?'

'Calm down. Don't be silly, Mark. Would you rather I passed the file to Bernard?'

Christ, no. I don't want her pedantic little bastard of a boss anywhere near this.

'Okay,' she says. 'Let's do things properly. Sit down for a start. I want to hear from you how these sessions came about and what occurred at each one. Then I'll need a written statement from you, ASAP.'

I turn the chair wrong-side round and sit astride it. 'Are you listening to yourself, Ali?'

'Will you stop trying to trade on our personal relationship? It's my duty to take the complaint seriously and look into it without prejudice.'

'You can hardly contain your glee.'

'Not true, and that isn't the issue here. Let's get to the point. Who suggested these private sessions?'

'Not private,' I say. 'In the classroom, working hours, anyone could walk in.'

'Who suggested them?'

'Okay, me—but you know I'd never make a move on a student.'

'Do I? Do I know that? You made a move on *me*.'

'Did I heck! I responded to yours, and now who's being personal?'

She looks stonily at me. 'So why did you suggest this to Comfort?'

'Jesus, Alison. Are you thick? Take a guess.'

She refuses to speak, waits me out.

'Because I want to teach her to read,' I say grimly.

'You may have forgotten, but you're paid to do that in class.'

154

'Yes, Alison. I know, Alison. But the fact is I couldn't.'

'Because?'

'Because the crèche nurse doesn't do what *she's* paid to do. Because the syllabus setters haven't a clue. Because every single one of my students has a different, unique set of problems and—'

'You're saying you can't do your job.'

'I'm saying Comfort couldn't learn in class. She had no chance. I wanted to help. I *am* helping. She's beginning to—'

'Because you fancy her.'

'Bollocks. Because I'm getting to the bottom of what she doesn't understand.'

'Because you fancy her.'

'No!'

'Let's be completely clear about this. You're claiming to have no sexual feelings towards Comfort Owusu?'

'Sex has nothing to do with it.'

'You'd do the same for Lloyd, would you? Or Keith? Or Nazish? This is serious, Mark.'

It takes half an hour to give her the facts. She's unmoved by the 'close' plus 'd' breakthrough and Comfort's assertion that Jesus will bless me. I don't mention the breastfeeding, or the low-cut yellow top, or the manicured fingers touching my hand, or the pleasure of watching Comfort's lips and teeth forming phonemes.

'So, tomorrow night latest,' she says, 'I want all that and anything else you remember in a statement, emailed to me. We can go over it once more—then you come in and sign it. Okay?'

I nod and turn on my heel, head out of her office before I say something actionable. I'm running down the staircase towards the side exit—the front door's closed for the holiday—and I'm out through the door and into the car park, when there he is, right in front of me, tall as I am and wider, neat razor-shaped beard, cornrow hair, big finger jabbing my chest, and I know the name without asking. Kwaku, the husband.

'Mr Jonnson.'

It isn't a question. Alison must have let on I'd be here. Reach for Teacher Guy. Talk straight. Tell the truth. Hold out a hand.

'Mr Owusu. Good to meet you. Let me explain—'

'Stay 'way from my woman,' he growls. 'Y'know what I'm saying?'

'I'm her teacher. Teaching her to read. She's making good progress.'

Then I see them: two hefty black guys climbing out of a beat-up saloon and heading across the car park towards me. I don't wait to chat. I'm running for it, twenty yards to the street and a skidding right turn towards the Tube and the buses. They're following, but carrying weight they've piled on in some gym, and I'm sprinting for my life, plunging through a knot of people blocking the pavement—'Sorry'—and thank heavens here's a 77, closing its doors, and I'm battering the glass, and the driver opens up again. 'Cheers,' I gasp as the doors close behind me, and yes, we're moving, edging towards the traffic lights, past Kwaku's angry face at the window. He's running alongside, waving his arms, but the lights are green, the bus powers through them and we're away free across the junction and picking up speed along Garratt Lane.

I clamber to the upper deck and collapse on a front seat, sucking in air as if I've been rescued from drowning. This isn't the end of it. He has my name, my number. He told Gina he knows where we live.

The house is empty right now, thank heaven. Gina has taken Matilda to a kids' party in Kilburn. I pull out the mobile and call her.

'We're just starting up.' She sounds happy. There are shrieks of laughter in the background and the pop of a balloon.

'So stay as long as you want, eh? Geoff Eliot's been on at me to meet up for a drink. Okay if I do that?'

Her voice freezes over. 'You liar.'

'No, Gina, I swear. The whole truth. Nothing but.'

'How *was* the meeting with Alison?' she says icily.

'Horrendous. I'm suspended while she investigates all sorts of stuff that never happened.'

'Starting by spending the day in bed with you?'

I glance around. The nearest passenger has headphones. I lean close to the window and lower my voice. 'You've got to believe me. Frankly, I'd rather paddle in shit.'

Silence.

'Trust me, the woman is poison. I haven't rung Geoff yet, but I'm going to right now. If he's not free, I'll try the lads. Or have a drink on my own. Scout's honour. No women. Never, ever. Okay?'

'Okay,' she concedes. 'But you better not be lying.'

'On Matty's life,' I say. 'And Gina, listen, because here's the important thing. I just bumped into our stalker and two of his mates.'

'Oh my God. What happened?'

'I legged it. Jumped on this bus I'm on now. I never laid a finger on his wife or even thought of it, but he's not listening. I'm worried he may come to the house. I want you to let me know when you and Matty are on your way home, and I'll wind up with Geoff and meet you at Clapham Junction. Will you do that?'

'Okay.' She sounds spooked.

'It's only a precaution. Don't alarm Matty.'

'I'm not an idiot,' she says. 'I'll call when we're done here. So... okay... say hi to Geoff for me. And take care.'

*

157

Geoff says he's stir crazy, locked away since Christmas with his nearest and dearest. He jumps at the offer.

'How about The Hole in the Wall?' I say.

'Grabbing coat as we speak. First there gets them in.'

The bus is passing the stop above Mum's house, where I'd planned to spend the afternoon Googling *Oz Daniels Sydney bus tours*, maybe emailing him, seeing what Mum's diary has to say about her visit to Sydney. Instead on I ride along Wandsworth Road towards Vauxhall and Waterloo Station.

I arrive first at The Hole in the Wall, get a table by the window in the front bar and furnish it with two pints of real ale and some dry-roasted peanuts. The big screen plus the rumble from the trains overhead will make conversation tricky, but Geoff and I never talk much. The usual deal is a steady slide into oblivion, just what I need. I suck the top third off my pint.

Here he comes, slouching, bespectacled, ambling in. 'Hi, mate. Long time, no booze up!' A hug and a backslap. Ritual enquiries after his wife and kids, ritual responses about Gina and Matilda, a bit of banter about male slavery before we settle into the drinking. I don't share any difficult stuff, just get sucked into the usual mates together. We chew over the credit crunch and the state of the nation, and now he's telling me about the DVD he was watching this morning. I'm barely listening, but it doesn't matter. Mates together is enough, floating on the incoming tide of alcohol, half-reliving some shackle-free teenage binge.

'Same again?'

The trains rumble. The pints slip down. Time falls away from us. Half an eye on the football, we join in with the cheers and groans from the other punters. Drunken Man is taking over my head, and he hasn't a worry that seems worth wasting a thought on. A small voice nags that he's meeting Matilda and Gina, so he checks the mobile to make sure he hasn't missed their call.

'Hey, mate, we should do this more often.'

'Sure thing.'

When the call comes, I take careful pride in not slurring my words. 'Was the party good fun?... That's great... no... yes... about half an hour... the coffee place at Clapham Junction.'

So, mates together are draining their last pints, pulling on coats and fumbling another backslap on the pavement in the freezing, sharp air, and Geoff's heading off for the Tube, and Drunken Man blunders through the traffic in the dark towards the grand flight of steps up to Waterloo Station, and suddenly they're grabbing him, one on each arm, and half-lifting, half-dragging him off to the left where the black cabs come down, and they have him pinned against brick like a moth on a corkboard, and Kwaku's fist heads for his jaw with all the weight of the train that flashes and crashes above.

Drunken Man saves me from serious injury. After mumbling, 'Hang on a mo,' he makes a half-arsed attempt to fight back, but the bastards have his arms pinned and his kicks find thin air. It's too much like hard work. He stops struggling and arguing and sags until they have a job holding him up. He drops chin to chest, the blood drips in his eyes, and when the next punch explodes in his stomach, he crumples, winded and helpless, curling foetal in the road while they boot him.

Numbed by alcohol, he has only a vague sense of what's happening. There's no pain to speak of. Their trainers are smashing into his legs, buttocks and ribs, not his kidneys or head, and no one looks like pulling a knife. He ventures a hand to his face, and it comes away wet. His nose is intact and his teeth seem okay. His mouth's full of blood, but maybe he's bitten his tongue. He hugs his knees and tries for some sound effects: yelps and groans as more kicks land. He must look well worked over. With luck they'll assume the job's done soon and leave him alone.

A fist grabs his sweater, and he's dragged up on one knee, eyeball to eyeball with Kwaku.

'Stay 'way from my woman is what I'm sayin'. D'y'get me this time?'

He gurgles and nods.

'D'y'get me?'

Swallows blood. 'I do, mate. Absolutely.'

A gob of phlegm lands on his nose, and he's dumped back on the ground where he catches one full in the balls. Holy shite. Ow, Jesus, ow, ow. He convulses, head to knees, fingernails scraping the tarmac, sobbing for breath. But they're leaving. He can hear the thud of their fleeing trainers as his stomach goes into spasm and has him spewing a pint of real ale into the gutter.

'Are you okay, pal?'

A black cab has pulled up, the diesel purr of its engine signalling safety. The driver is helping him to his feet, handing him tissues. It's over. It's done. He's survived it.

Vague panic sets in. Where's the rucksack? Huge effort of memory. Didn't bring it today. He's checking his pockets. Finding wallet and phone. Phone not broken.

'Do you want the police?' says the cabbie.

'No thanks.'

'If you're done throwing up and you're not skint, I can give you a ride home. Or to casualty if you'd rather.'

'Do I need stitches?'

'Nah, a few plasters should do it.'

'Home then. Big thanks, mate.'

And Drunken Man has mumbled his address and is slumped on the back seat of a nice, safe taxicab, trying to make sense of the keys on his mobile, trying to explain to Gina what has happened, that he can't meet her as planned, he'll see her back at the house, and he'll be in the bedroom, or if she gets there first can she please get Matty upstairs because he doesn't want to give her a fright.

Tuesday

'No more snacks,' Gina says. 'I'm making beef stew.' She pauses with the tray by the open door. 'By the way, your PM says Obama's extraordinary and they're going to change the world together.'

'Gordon's your PM too,' I correct her. It hurts to speak—my tongue's swollen where I bit it—but I'm smiling.

Her own smile twists to a grimace; then she's gone.

I'm snug and warm, feet up on the bed, my bruised back supported by pillows. The sound of Mozart drifts up from below, together with the aroma of simmering meat.

I've just emailed my statement to Alison, including a full account of Mr Owusu's stalking and violence, supported by digital photographs of my bruises and cuts in close up and full-body long shot. I've suggested she offers the bugger a deal: he drops the complaint, she transfers Comfort to another class and I don't press charges.

Gina's terrified he may come back, and I'm jumpy myself, getting flashes of the knives that could have been pulled on me. It has brought us closer together. Last night, after she had taken the pictures and applied 'Band-Aids' to Drunken Man's face, she set about anointing his bruises with arnica, and one thing led to another until, despite the booze and the sore bollocks, we managed sex for the first time in this house, very gently, Gina on top.

It felt good.

She has stopped cleaning and clearing. She's not catechising me about Mum and Oz. She's been singing along to the Mozart, and now she's letting the stew cook itself while she takes her turn playing Monopoly.

There are three kids today throwing the dice and

amassing subprime mortgages. The two from next door are here while Jane does a shift at Asda. When Jane handed them over, she and Gina chatted in the hall. Their chats make me nervous; I hobbled painfully downstairs, but all seemed to be well. When Jane met my eyes and asked after my injuries, you would never have guessed we were more than acquaintances.

So my problems seem solved, or at least on hold, and I have time at last to find out more about Oz. The clapped-out old Kilburn computer that Gina uses to email her American buddies is on the table across the room. On my knee is Mum's laptop, which I'm systematically searching for mentions of Sydney. Turns out her trip was 2001, and of course I remember. It was the winter after Gina and I got married.

There are diary entries in January about being keyed up to go. But then, hang on, there's a gap. We've jumped forward to March, and she's waxing lyrical about the spring weather in London and how she's determined to put the Muswell Hill flat behind her and move to a house with a garden. Nothing in between, not a word. I scroll up and down, but there's barely a reference to Australia and not a squeak about Oz.

Look again, scan more carefully, keep going, and yes, wait, okay, here's something—second of April.

Down under was amazing, but I'm not going to write about it. I couldn't do it justice, just as the camera snaps don't come near. I won't try—it can stay in my head, where I'll mislay bits and embroider others no doubt, but that's fine—let memory do its imperfect thing. There is one moment I must never lose, though. Cremorne Point. Just naming it makes me smile and will stop me forgetting. Now... on with the move! I've found a smashing little terraced house in Battersea. Fingers crossed they'll accept my offer.

Cremorne Point? I consult Wikipedia.

... a harbour-side suburb on the lower North Shore of Sydney... between Shell Cove and Mosman Bay... one of the few

Sydney Harbour peninsulas with a public waterfront park.

I try to imagine Mum and Oz meeting there. Embracing, exclaiming, gazing at one another.

I've heard nothing from Lizzie. It's time to track him down myself and persuade him to speak to me. I tap in 'Daniels bus tours Sydney', click on 'I'm feeling lucky', and bingo—

Daniels Days Out Down Under. My name is Oz Daniels and I've been doing small Group bus tours from Sydney for 10 years. My Deluxe coach has Air-conditioning and comfortable seats. A day out with a difference with Lunch ($89) or without ($79). Offering the best Blue Mountains Experience at a Budget Price with Expert commentary. Wentworth Falls, Echo Point, Three Sisters, Katoomba Railway. Hotel pick up. Wildlife park. A Parramatta river Cruise back to Darling Harbour or Circular Quay.

He gives a mobile number but no address, so next I'm into *White Pages Australia*, and—hell, this is too easy. There's only one 'Daniels, O' in Sydney and I'm looking at his address.

I lean back on the pillows, feeling a buzz of excitement. Then my fingers are moving again. Google maps serves up a satellite picture of a suburb close-packed with streets. Zoom in to street view, scan the house numbers and yes! here it is: bungalow plus carport, with a few trees out front. Almost no gap to the neighbours either side.

I know where you live, Dad.

I stare at the image, try different views, zoom in and out. This is where Lizzie's barbecue pictures were taken, on this patch of scorched grass round the back.

Someone leans heavily on the doorbell below. A short pause, then again. Jesus, it's Kwaku! I rocket from the bed, yelping as my ribs jab with pain, and lurch to the landing. Gina's halfway upstairs, her face blank with alarm.

She and the three children gather behind me as I peer through the front-door glass at the black face. But it's a woman, I realise, and then recognition dawns. Jesus H Christ, it's Comfort, although she barely looks like herself.

I open the door, blocking the way with my body. Her lip's swollen, and one of her eyes is bloodshot. The sumptuous braids are gone, replaced by a short, shiny wig with a heavy fringe.

'Bloody hell. Did he do this to you? Does he know you're here?'

'No, Mr Jonnson, no, no.' She's jabbering, nineteen to the dozen. 'He beat me—look, my face—look, my arm—the children are crying, bad crying—the neighbour, he bang on the door, he call police—the police come, the police take him—'

Her false nails, digging into my wrist, are broken. Her tears are real now, not delicately shed to persuade me. Her words flood on. 'He not want me to learn—my father, grandfather, no one want me to learn—Kwaku say you don't teach me, but you *must* teach me, please, Mr Jonnson, God bless you, I want you to teach me—'

She's pleading with Teacher Guy. It breaks my heart to refuse her. I point to my own face. 'How can I? Look what he did.'

Gina eases the door from my fingers. 'Come on in,' she says.

'I'm sorry. I'm sorry,' Comfort wails along the hall. The children try to follow us into the kitchen, but Gina steers them back to the front room and shuts the door firmly. She puts a mug of tea into Comfort's hand. 'Here. I just made it. Would you like sugar?'

'How did you find us?' I'm asking. 'Has he followed you here?'

'No, no, he gone now, I swear it. He say your address —people point me the way—'

165

Gina interrupts. 'Are the police helping you? You need protection.'

'They don't let him come near—but Mr Jonnson, please teach me—sweet Jesus will help you all your life and bless you—'

'Comfort,' I say, 'My family... I can't teach you alone any more.'

She bursts out in sobs. 'Please, Mr Jonnson. *Mrs* Jonnson.'

Gina offers a chair. When Comfort plants her broad backside on it, I realise there's no blue-and-gold wrapper round her middle, no baby to hamper her. 'Where's Matthew?' I say. 'Who's looking after your children?'

'My cousin, she help me. Mr Jonnson, I not want Kwaku. The police keep him away—please, I want to learn—'

'Listen, Comfort,' I say. 'Listen to me. In January, when term starts, come to the college and ask for Alison Finlow. Tell her you want her or one of the other women teachers to—'

'No! *You* my teacher. In my life you the only person who help me learn. I work hard. Please. Jesus bless you. I want my children to learn. I want a good job.'

Gina squats beside her, close to her swollen face, her bloodshot eyes. 'You will,' she soothes, frowning at me not to speak. 'It will work out,' she repeats. 'There's time. You need to see first what happens. If Kwaku doesn't come back—'

'I don't want him round me—'

'Well, that sounds to be the best decision, and when it's settled, your husband will calm down. He'll get on with his life. He can't stop you from going to college. It's the vacation. You don't have to resolve this today.'

Gradually Comfort is calmed. 'He not my husband,' she says. 'We not married.'

'That's good,' Gina says, patting her hand. 'It'll make

it easier to be free of him.'

'Ah-*huhn*.'

'Except he's the children's dad,' I say.

Bellows of rage erupt from the front room. The door bursts open and Christopher runs in, face scarlet, streaming with tears, hiccupping his outrage that Josie and Matilda won't let him play Monopoly.

'Go home to your kids now, okay?' I tell Comfort. 'We'll sort this out next term, I promise.'

When she's gone, Gina dishes up stew and I answer the children's curious questions. Josie's perplexed to hear that Comfort is illiterate. 'All grownups can read,' she says.

'They can't,' Matilda proclaims with pride. 'That's my Daddy's job. They didn't go to school, or they were naughty and didn't listen, so my Daddy has to show them how to read.'

'Or maybe they're aliens,' says Josie.

'What?' I say.

'Gloopy monsters,' says Matilda. She does an illustrative mime, collapsing bonelessly in her chair and dribbling gravy.

Gina wipes Matilda's chin with a tissue. 'Sit up straight now.'

'Maggie Simpson's an alien,' says Josie. 'She grew lots of legs, and dribbled disgusting long streams of snot, and walked on the ceiling.'

Matilda throws her arms about and pulls faces. '*Are* there aliens, Daddy?'

'Nope,' I say.

She pleads. 'Never ever ever?'

'Not around here,' I say. 'Maybe a zillion miles away, on some planet out in the stars, but no one has found them yet.'

Gina scrapes her chair back from the table. 'Some people believe there are aliens here.' She sounds angry.

She's been very quiet through the meal.

'But they're bonkers,' I say, trying to catch her eye with a smile. She gets up and takes a plate to the sink.

'Like there's no Santa?' says Matilda.

'Exactly,' I say. 'Just stories people want to believe in.'

I'm still smiling at Gina, but she isn't paying attention. She looks without seeing, as if she's doing arithmetic in her head. She takes the kids into the front room. I'm clearing the rest of the plates and running hot water, trying to imagine Comfort's life with that man and three children, and unable to read—what huge obstacles lie in her way—but my ribs are aching, and mostly I want to lie down. I'm thinking about the bed upstairs and Gina's ministrations last night. I'll wash these pots, put the stew pan to soak, then drag my bones up there, and later, when Matilda's asleep—

The doorbell goes, and I run to the hall, hands dripping suds, but it's fine, only Jane. Gina is opening the door to her, and she's saying how she won't come in, she'll get out of our hair. She's thanking us for having the children.

'No trouble at all,' Gina tells her. 'They're great kids.'

After some protests about an unfinished game of Uno, Jane and her children are gone, and I'm back in the kitchen, finishing up at the sink, wiping my hands on a tea towel and planning on giving Gina a big, sloppy hug. She's in the living room trying to persuade Matilda to clear up the mess. Matilda leaps into my arms.

'Ouch. Mind my bruises.'

'I'm an alien,' she shouts.

'The very first one,' I say. 'And you know the odd thing about aliens? They like helping their mommies put toys away.'

And I'm grinning at Gina, but she's frowning and busy, and I'm sensing the shutters are back down. When the tidying's done, she announces, 'Bedtime,' Matilda protests and threatens meltdown, and soon they're upstairs, reading *The Wizard of Oz*, which Gina has dangled as a bribe, and it seems I'll be lucky to get two words out of my moody wife.

I slam around, doing the drying and the putting away, scraping the waterlogged gunge off the pan, washing it up. Then I limp into the living room, switch on the TV and surf channels. There's nothing worth watching. I turn it off and head back to the kitchen, where I finger the cap of the whisky bottle and manage to resist unscrewing it. Go to bed, I tell myself. Ignore bloody Gina.

But here she is, coming down, her hand on the banister rail. She looks stunning. She has looked stunning all day in that big, baggy sweater over her skinny jeans. Her hair's loose on her shoulders. Her eyes meet mine. I grin and hold out a hand.

She takes the hand and looks down at it. 'Mark, I've made a decision,' she says. 'I'm sorry, but this isn't gonna work out. I thought, with more space, with more money... but in a way that has just made it plainer. I'm sorry, I've tried—'

'But— '

'Please don't argue. There's no point, no use.'

I'm gripping her fingers, frantic. 'Was it something Comfort said?'

'Not really. She had me seeing there's no point in postponement, is all.'

'You'd already *decided?*

'Kind of. Not really. Look, I've tried hard, Mark, and I know I've been snippy so it looks like I haven't tried, but in all truth I feel trapped here.'

Her eyes fill with tears. I try to hold her, but she's tense in my arms.

'Trying's no good any more. I'm done emotionally with the UK and with us, that's what I've realised. I've thought about it and thought about it. It's not gonna work out.'

'But last night?'

'Yeah. I know.'

Her eyes soften. I'm willing her to relent. She's smiling and shaking her head, looking up at me. 'I do like you, Mark. I don't hate you, and last night I was relaxing because I could feel I was solving it. Because the reality is we both made a mistake here, and I have to go home. I'm sorry, but Matilda and I, we have to go to Connecticut.'

New Year's Eve

We're at an LSE reunion party where Gina's hugging one old friend after another and saying goodbye. She looks wonderful. She's gloriously relaxed. She radiates relief and happiness like a storm-tossed landlubber who has glimpsed the harbour lights. I never realised how homesick she was. 'I need to be in the States,' I hear her repeating.

It's twenty-five minutes to midnight, and I'm skulking by the wall, weary of answering questions about my beaten-up face. I'm not drunk, or not very, because I can't afford a moment's befuddlement. I have to find a way to change Gina's mind. I don't want the new year to begin.

'We don't have to split,' I protested this morning. 'I'll sell up and come too, get a green card. There must be heaps of literacy jobs in New York.'

'I don't believe that's such a good plan, Mark,' she said. 'I would rather you didn't tag along after us. You would drag me down. You would drag yourself down. We both need to make a new start.'

'We can make one in America. That's what I'm saying.'

'Are you for real?'

'Of course.' I was eager. 'It's my turn to be uprooted. I accept that absolutely, okay?'

'Not okay, Mark, because we're through, you and me.'

How the hell do I turn this around? My brain boils with what ifs. What if I hadn't slept with Alison, hadn't bolted when Mum died, hadn't shown Gina the door at the funeral? And then, when I had the situation half clawed back, what an idiot I've been. I should have been working at my marriage, not chasing off after Dad and

Lizzie.

Matilda doesn't know yet she's going to Connecticut. I've barely been with her since Christmas. I didn't want to leave her tonight. I begrudge every second, but she was practically running up the walls with excitement at the prospect of a sleepover next door.

'We're having a midnight feast, Daddy, with mince pies and strawberry milk.'

'If they can stay awake.' Jane winked at me as Matilda hurtled past into her hallway.

'How about you?' I asked Jane. 'Do you have company tonight?'

When she smiled and shook her head, I was tempted to say, 'Hey, my wife's leaving me anyway, so why don't I see the year in with you and Matty?'

But it would hardly have fitted with my pleading to Gina. 'Everything has changed,' I've told her earnestly. 'I'm your husband, and I love you, I mean it. I'm not playing around ever again. Come on, Gina, you've got the whole thing wrong in your head. Your place is with me and Matty in this "neat little house" cocooned by our inheritance. It makes no sense to break up before we've given it a real go.'

Do I love her? It scarcely matters. I love Matty, and Gina is her mother. I've invested these three treacherous words with all the heart and belief I can muster, but her only reply is, 'I'm sorry, Mark. We've run out of road.'

In the taxi she's laughing, excited by the boozy goodbyes. She tells me, 'Please be quiet, Mark. You're not saying anything new. Just accept it, okay?'

I glare out at the delicate, glimmering tracery of Albert Bridge as we sweep south over Battersea Bridge towards home. I'm remembering a year ago, how different it was. There was no taxi home from that party: we couldn't afford one. We took a night bus and walked the rest of the way through Kilburn, our arms linked, exchanging greetings with strangers, making doomed promises about behaving better to each other. There in the wretched flat over the bookie's were Mum, watching telly, and Matilda, asleep in our bed. It was Mum who took the taxi, from Kilburn to Battersea, who watched the Albert Bridge glide by, thinking of her own new year ahead, not knowing she wouldn't see it out.

'I'm gonna call Dad when we get home,' Gina says. 'He said he'd pay for the flights.'

I don't answer.

'I figure there's no point in hanging around,' she says.

I lean my forehead on the cold window-glass. On Latchmere Road, the taxi swings under the railway bridge then up again, slowing to turn left. I tell the driver the house number and fish for my wallet.

Inside I climb the stairs dumbly, feeling my bruised bones, wishing Matilda were here, not next door. Gina's picking up the hall phone and dialling Connecticut, where 2008 holds on by the skin of its teeth.

'Hi, Daddy! Happy New Year!'

I slam the bedroom door shut and lean against it. I can still hear her, not her words but her excitement and pleasure. Snapping on the light, I cross to the bed, collapse onto it and cover my ears with my hands.

Then I'm up again, emptying my pockets. My mobile's been off all day, and I find there's a voice message on it.

'Hello, Mark? Happy New Year. It's Lizzie. Well...' She pauses. 'Well, I've spoken to Oz, and I'm afraid it's not good news. He's known about you all along, it seems. Nancy told him she was pregnant. He understands that of course you'll be curious, but he'd rather leave things as they are. I said he should speak to you himself, but he wouldn't budge, I'm so sorry. I asked why he didn't stay here and marry Nancy, but that got him stammering badly—did I tell you he stammers? The gist was he didn't want to talk about it. I'm going to bed now, but give me a ring in the morning. You know I'd love to see more of you. Bring Matilda to stay soon. I can't wait to meet her. Bye bye now. I'm sorry. Happy New Year.'

Another brick wall. Too much. I can't breathe. I don't know how to take the next breath. I battle the air with my fists, wanting something to punch or to wrestle, to break the knot in my chest. The phone by the bed dings as Gina hangs up downstairs. On the table across the room is the scrap of paper I scribbled on yesterday. Oz's mobile number.

Damn it, you don't get to choose this, Oz. You're going to speak to me, now.

I'm making the call, finding my breath, hearing the phone ring in that bungalow with the carport in Sydney, or maybe in his coach out on the road somewhere, and then there's a click and he's answering with a chirpy smile in his voice. 'Happy new year. Daniels Days Out. How can I help?'

What a question. He's my father, for Christ's sake. 'Why don't you want to know us? I'm your son, and Matty's your granddaughter.' I'm shouting. My eyes are squeezed shut.

There isn't an answer. He's killed the call.

'You bastard!' I yell. 'You selfish bastard!'

When I open my eyes, there's Matilda stalled in the bedroom doorway in her pyjamas.

Her first sleepover made her anxious. She pestered Jane to let her come home. It's half past two in the morning, and Matilda and I are huddled on the bed with the photographs of Oz while Gina paces around us. Gina tried to pack Matilda straight off to sleep, but she made a commotion, insisting on knowing why Daddy was shouting at Grandpa. Gina said, 'Be quiet. You'll wake the whole street.' I said, 'Sod the whole street. We're not going to tidy this away any more. We're going to tell her right now.' And Gina was too tipsy and too pleased with herself to argue the point.

This room is too warm—Gina has put on the heating—I'm sweating and shaking, clenching and unclenching my fists. I'll be alone on this bed soon, with no option but to fly back and forth to Connecticut. I stare at Matilda, trying to commit every hair, every eyelash, every freckle to memory.

She's enthralled by the photographs, especially the full-face portrait of Oz. She holds it close to her nose, examines every detail, stares as if by refusing to blink she can bring him alive.

'He's a whole lot older now, honey,' Gina says.

'But that's how he was then,' I snap back.

When Matilda finally puts down the picture, she flings herself onto my bruises.

'Ouch. Bloody hell, Mat.' I hold her tight and glare at Gina.

'But isn't Grandpa Jonnson my grandpa?'

Sure he is,' Gina says smoothly, sliding herself onto the bed with us, 'and he loves you very much, kiddo. But it was the man in the picture—'

'Oz,' I growl.

'—who put Daddy in Granny Jonnson's tummy before she met Grandpa Jonnson.'

There's an unearthly bark from the street. Matilda jumps, her eyes wide.

'It's only a fox, Little,' I say, pulling her close.

'Is Grandpa Franklin my grandpa?'

'Of course,' Gina coos. 'So you have three grandpas, isn't that great?'

'Like Josie has three?' says Matilda.

'Yeah, just like Josie.' Gina drifts into her soft, story-telling voice. 'Only yours are one in England, one in America, one in Australia—'

'With red hair like me.' Matilda wriggles away to snatch up the photograph.

'Exactly like you, Matty,' I say.

'Where's Australia? Can we go there?'

I sit bolt upright. It's an idea. A way to buy time.

'It's too far away, baby,' says Gina. 'You know how the world is a ginormous great ball? Well, Australia's on the other side of the ball, a long, long way away. Oz is walking around upside down, but it looks the right way up to him.'

Matilda has swallowed stuff like this before, but now she is sceptical. 'That's just a story, like Santa and aliens.'

I turn her to face me. 'Believe it or not, the story of Australia is true, Matty, and when you and I get out of the aeroplane, we'll be walking upside down too, although we won't know it.'

'I want to do that,' she says, making me grin. 'Can we do that?'

I take a breath. 'Yes. We. Can.'

I see Gina catch on. 'Not really, hon.' She holds out her arms, but Matilda stays with me. 'I've an idea,' Gina says brightly. 'Let's go see Grandma and Grandpa Franklin? We can do that real soon.'

'*If* I sign the consent form.'

Her eyes harden. 'What are you saying?'

I lean forward, speak low and clenched. 'I'm saying I'll sign the form when Matty and I get back from Australia. If you still want me to sign it.'

'Stralia! We're going to Stralia!' Matilda's up on her feet, jumping on the mattress.

Gina clutches the headboard. 'It's out of the question. Completely impractical, plus it's cheap of you to—'

'Please, Mommy.' Leaping high, crashing down. I

reach to rescue the photographs flying off the bed.

'The subject's closed, Matilda. We'll discuss it tomorrow.'

I catch Matilda mid-flight. 'The subject's closed, Gina. We're going to Australia.'

'You don't do this in front of her.'

'I've done it.'

'Yes, in front of me!'

'A few weeks, out of your hair, Gina. Mum's money. You can decamp to Connecticut with my child and your bloody form afterwards.'

'You're out of order, Mark. You have to discuss this with me first.'

'Bullshit. You decide about Connecticut without discussion.'

'There's no way she can go to Australia. It's her birthday in two weeks' time—'

'Fifteen sleeps,' shouts Matilda.

'Grandma Franklin will give you a party.'

'Don't want one!'

'She'll bake a cake with seven candles.'

'Don't care!'

'And invite lots of children.'

'I want to go to Stralia!'

And I'm bellowing so Jane and the whole street can hear. 'I'm going to do this, Gina. Because where is the problem? She's my daughter, this man is my father, and if you're leaving me then I'll be having joint custody, and at some point I'll be taking Matty to see him.'

I'm up off the bed, heading for the computer. 'I'm booking the tickets right now.'

OZ

Sydney. She was going at last.

Beyond the big, first-floor sash-window, Muswell Hill drizzled and gloomed while Nancy imagined the sun. 'February's a lovely month,' her Aussie dentist had said last week as he forced floss between her molars. Good heavens, what an upside-down notion. In only four days, she would be airborne. In five she would be there, starved of sleep and chock full of adrenaline. She could barely imagine it. Calm down, she kept telling herself. You're forty-eight, for heaven's sake. She felt unquenchably twenty-five, as though the years hadn't passed. She turned away from the window to the suitcase on the bed and began to find things to put into it. Sunglasses, a beach towel, yellow shorts. But she shouldn't be packing. She was only distracting herself. She should be telling Oz she was coming.

She was a coward to leave it so late. She had her tickets, visa and passport. The hotel was expecting her. The Social Security Bill she'd been drafting was signed off, final version with the printers. Commons committee stage wasn't scheduled until late March. Her assistant, Nigel, could field any questions that came up at second reading, or in emergencies get hold of her in Sydney. Mog was booked into the cattery. Mark had promised to drop by at least twice in the next four weeks to water the plants. But she hadn't told Oz she was coming.

She'd even at last drawn up a will and had it witnessed by Harry and his secretary.

'Don't be daft. You won't crash,' Harry had said. 'You'd better come back, or I'm not letting you go.'

'It's just a precaution,' she'd told him. 'Mark wouldn't thank me if I bowed out intestate.'

Harry had a point though. The departure was

developing an odd flavour of finality; it did feel like a kind of goodbye. To old ways of thinking, maybe. To this big, cluttered Muswell Hill flat that she no longer needed now that Mark was so suddenly married. She renewed her resolution to be out of it by the year end, making a fresh start somewhere different. She would set about house-hunting as soon as she was back.

She pulled open a drawer and began sorting through underwear. Paused. Leant her head on her hands. Come on, she told herself. Stop procrastinating. Get it done.

Before Christmas when Oz had rung for a chat, the words had been there in her mind. She should have said them straight out: I'll be in Sydney in February. But he'd been making her smile as ever, and they'd been talking easily, back and forth, as if it weren't six months since their last conversation and twenty-two years since they'd been face to face. He'd been so relaxed, barely stammering except when she'd asked after Yvonne, and the words had stayed unspoken.

Afterwards she had kicked herself. What an idiot. When better to tell him, when he could hear that she offered no threat to his marriage? It would seem horribly sudden now.

She must do it. She lifted her head.

She had the mobile number for his bus tours. He'd said it was okay to use it. But the custom was for him to phone her. He rang when he felt moved to, at unpredictable intervals, sometimes of a year or more. A call from her—I'll be there in five days—would seem urgent. Alarming.

She went through to Mark's bedroom—she must stop calling it that—to her 'study' and switched on the PC. You have nothing to fear, Oz. Never from me. She opened a blank email and fingered the keys. Maybe she should start by just hinting.

Hello again, dearest Oz. It was lovely to chat to you at

Christmas. Hearing your voice always makes me happy. I'm glad things are going okay for you. This is to let you know my next email may be from Sydney. What do you think about that? Much love, Nancy

Only a draft. Nothing final. She leant back on her chair, looking at it. She deleted *What do you think about that?*, considered for a few more seconds and clicked send.

Even that might alarm him. How silly. But what would he answer? Would he answer at all? She never got a conversation going with him by email. She wasn't sure how often he checked his inbox.

Five days from now she would touch down in his world. Somehow she would let him know. And then what? Would he be pleased? Of course he would, she had no reason to doubt it, and somewhere safely away from Yvonne they would meet. After all this time she'd be seeing his madcap smile.

In Singapore she tried not to think about time. It was afternoon here, morning in London, but most importantly already evening in Sydney, which was still a long flight away. Friday was lost, she decided. It hadn't begun when she left, and it would have vanished by the time she arrived. Perhaps she would find it again on her way back.

Changi airport, cavernously vast and hi-tech, supported the illusion of limbo. There was daylight beyond the glass walls, but nothing to see except one plane after another taking off, graceful and silent, through grey sheets of equatorial rain. Inside, soft music slowed the pace, quietened the voices, and the staff were so gentle in explaining things they could have been angels in heaven's waiting room.

After buying a fresh T-shirt and putting it on, Nancy checked her emails. Still no word from Oz, but she was too spaced out to worry or plan. Next she mooched through an indoor garden smothered in climbing orchids, pausing a while to watch giant koi, orange and black, nose their way round a pool. She had no more purpose than they did.

Later, slumped in the Quiet Lounge, her mouth found a slow smile and tears prickled her eyes. For two decades she'd been dreaming of this journey, and here she was making it. The dream wasn't about Oz exactly. Perhaps it never had been. It was about flying free. The idea was corny but felt true nonetheless.

She was even forgetting to feel anxious about Mark. She hauled herself upright and went in search of a telephone. There was no need to worry about him and Gina. Time resolved everything, and maybe there wasn't a problem. She should have a little faith in young love. She just wished that Gina could find more in England to like. She hoped they would give themselves time to settle, not have babies too soon.

'Hello love, yes, it's me... Singapore. So far, so good... Fine. Asleep on my feet... I don't think I did—too much noise, too excited... Yes, I remembered—walked the aisle, got in everyone's way—How are you, though? And Gina? Good. Good.'

Drifting back from the phone, she noticed a door through the glass wall to a couple of benches outside. When she stepped through, she was drenched with heat and the roar of jet engines. The torrents of rain had let up, and the fat sun smouldered behind a heavy, grey sky. She sat a while, inhaling the steam that rose from the ground and nibbling the last Muswell Hill sandwich. Ants began harvesting the crumbs at her feet, and a starling-like bird with red on its beak hopped around hopefully. There was sweat on her neck, on her forehead. She pushed back her damp hair and smiled at the sun.

*

After churning for hours over endless, daunting miles of red desert she expected another huge, modern airport, but Sydney was so disarmingly informal and haphazard, it felt more like a bus station. The intense daylight had her blinking, reaching for her sunglasses. The dry heat enveloped her. The sky was piercingly blue, and the pick-up area was fringed with tropical vegetation, ringing with birdcalls and crowded with cheerful people in crumpled baggy shorts and shirts.

'D'you need help, Miss?' The twang of the accent was startling, thicker than she expected. The Aussies she knew in London must have had the antipodean corners rubbed off them.

'A bus to the centre?'

'Best is the taxi-bus. Over there.'

Three minibuses stood by the kerb. The driver of the nearest listened before cheerfully stating his terms. 'Seven dollars to any hotel, love, and we leave when I'm full.'

The drivers agreed among themselves who would take whom, eight in each bus. 'Okay. You're with me,' he said, lifting her case aboard. 'Do you want to sit up front, see the sights?'

'Please. And no hurry. Take me the longest route you like.'

A woman jumped in beside her. 'You from London? A month? I'm so jealous. I'm over from Auckland for three days. I've been meaning to come all my life. When I saw the Olympics in September, I said that's it, I'm not putting it off any longer.'

The woman quietened as the city began to roll by. Nancy strained forward against the seatbelt, staring right and left, overwhelmed by a sense of wonderful otherness. Okay, a city. A patchwork of brick and concrete, brightly painted stucco and glass-sculpted high-rise. But unlike any city she knew. Sometimes she glimpsed a resemblance, but blink and it vanished. Paris, Italy, New York, suburban London, small town America, the Kent of her childhood—each took brief shape and evaporated until she stopped looking for reference points. All she was seeing was Sydney: another world, crammed full of otherworldly trees, plants and animals, and drenched in unimaginable light, where she was going to have the time of her life.

The driver pulled into a hotel forecourt, not her own yet, and leapt out to help people with their bags. A man wearing khaki shorts and pale-pink rubber gloves was collecting fallen leaves into a bucket. He straightened up by the minibus window, and his weather-beaten face split in a grin. 'How's it going? Have you come far?'

'From Auckland.'

'From England.'

'Welcome to Sydney.'

Before long the woman beside Nancy had gone. Couple by couple the other passengers were delivered until she was alone with the driver, who began diligently naming sights to her. 'Darling Harbour. The AMP Tower.'

'But where are the bridge and the Opera House?'

He pointed. 'Down there a few blocks.'

She craned her neck but saw only buildings and traffic. Crowds of pedestrians on wide, sun-blasted pavements. She wanted the smell of salt water, but her nose filled with exhaust fumes.

The radio crackled with a woman's competent, harassed voice. 'Come in, number fifteen.'

'Here I am.'

'How long will you be?'

'Five minutes.'

He drove calmly on beneath Monopoly-board street signs—Liverpool Street, Oxford Street—before turning right. 'This is your road. Look, you have a shopping mall right opposite. Have a great stay.' He accepted her three-dollar tip affably and waved as he drove off.

Her room was still occupied. It would need to be cleaned. Would she mind waiting in the lobby? Finally she understood what the time was. She'd been awake thirty-six hours, travelling for twenty-five, but the hotel's day was only just starting. The lobby chairs were upright, not a sofa in sight. She badly needed a wash. She headed for the Ladies.

Lifting her wet face from the basin, her shining eyes in the mirror caught her off guard. She'd done it. She'd arrived. She jumped on the spot, telling herself aloud, 'You're in Sydney.' She was daft. She was crazy. She got so much out of this one little life of hers, but still it kept coming, and very soon she would see Oz again.

Back in the lobby, she watched last night's guests check out. The older and more veined their legs, the less self-conscious they seemed of their unisex uniform of loose shorts and shirt. She stared at her own swollen ankles. She stank of exhaustion. She fell asleep and nearly slid from her chair to the floor. Came awake. Had the desk clerk changed?

'Is my room ready yet?'

The new clerk looked shame-faced, but all Nancy felt was relief. The waiting was over. She was going up eleven floors in a lift. A door was being opened, then closed behind her. And here she was, alone in a room with a view. She ran forward, slid the door, and from the balcony at last saw, beyond a mass of treetops, a shining line of blue water and the white shells of the Opera House. Stupendous. Her brain offered the word but then let it go because, stumbling backwards, all she could think of was the enormous, flat, empty, soft bed.

She awoke to the night sounds of a city drifting in through the still-open balcony door. Glittering and murmuring below in the warm dark was a tract of Sydney, south of Hyde Park. An unidentified bird sat cheekily on the rail, above the drop to the street. Shouldn't it be roosting by now?

Nancy opened her arms, tipped her face to the ceiling and rotated. What bliss to have slept and awoken, free of fellow passengers, of slender Singaporean beauties offering hot flannels and refreshments, of decisions about where to put her feet and how often to go walkabout, of anyone's presence constraining her from being herself.

She had no thought beyond ringing room service. 'A chicken sandwich, please, and a can of Fosters.'

'You don't want to drink that piss, love,' the man laughed. 'I'll send up a Toohey's New.'

'Okay.' She laughed too.

She planned much, much more sleep. Unpacking could wait. Oz could wait. She was here for a month. She felt no urgency to see him. She opened cupboards, pulled out a few drawers and came across Gideon's bible. Good heavens, did they have these in Sydney? She stuck in her thumbs and opened at random, finding Psalm 147. *He heals the broken-hearted and binds up their wounds.*

January 2009, Saturday

'I'm not sleepy. Can I draw in my book?'

I fight my way up from unconsciousness. Sydney. Matilda. Jetlag. I peer through the dark. She stands between the twin beds, balancing on one leg, holding her other toe, starting to topple.

I throw myself forward to catch her. 'Do you need the loo?'

'Nah.'

'Or a drink.'

She shakes her head, dumps herself on the floor and sticks her pyjama-clad legs in the air. 'I'm dizzy being upside down,' she complains, 'and I want to draw all the upside-down things before I forget them.'

'Remember what we promised, Matty. Best to leave the light off.' I try to pull her from the floor. 'Come into my bed. Close your eyes. Try to sleep. Your body thinks it's...'

I flick the lamp on and off to see the time on my watch, then attempt to subtract eleven from three. My brain spins out of gear, forgetting why it needs to compute, sidetracked into the idea of elevenses—

'Dad-*dee*.'

I come awake again. There's a weight on my arm. Matilda is sitting on it, kicking her feet high so as better to slam her heels against the side of my bed.

'Aw, come on Matty. Stop waking me up.'

'How many sleeps till my birthday?'

For pity's sake. 'I'm not sure,' I say. 'I think we lost one in Bangkok. We'll work it out tomorrow.' I pull my arm free. 'Listen. This is a sleep now. We should be sleeping.'

She squirms and whinges, 'You're so stinky. I'm bored. I want to draw. Can we find some kangaroos soon?'

My eyelids are drooping. This is fine, I'm telling myself. She's not tearful or homesick. The websites said most children manage jetlag okay, because they can sleep when they're tired, day or night. This child is not tired. I'm the one who's tired.

'All right. I give in.'

I stumble grumpily upright, set her up with the desk light, and she launches into drawing flamboyant orange and green trees.

'I don't like the noise,' she announces.

I find the air-conditioning unit and fumble the off switch. The silence is good, but already I can sense the atmosphere beginning to heat and coagulate. If I open the balcony door she could fall to the street while I sleep. I keep it shut, angling the slats above to try for a breeze. No chance. The night is sludge hot.

'Can we go to Bondi Beach soon?'

She's been bleating on about Bondi Beach for the last twenty-four hours. She's heard of it somehow and thinks it's the next best thing to Disneyland.

'Maybe. We'll see. Let me sleep.'

'Look, Daddy. I'm drawing a kangaroo.'

I can't summon any interest. I hunt through the stuff on the floor for her books—*Matilda*, *Harry Potter*—and dump them in front of her. We got to the end of *The Wizard of Oz* on the plane. *Oh, Aunt Em! I'm so glad to be at home again!*

I've run out of gumption. I want darkness and slumber. Here's the eye mask the airline gave me. 'Try to sleep when you're done, Little,' I mumble. I slump horizontal. I'm gone.

Screams. Matilda is screaming. 'What? What?' I'm off the bed ready to kill her attacker. Blind—I clutch at my eyes, find the mask, rip it off. By dawn light there she is, huddled on the desk, terrified. The chair's kicked over, and her book and crayons are scattered across the floor. She stares beyond them at... what? I see nothing.

'A beastie,' she whimpers.

'A spider?' Visions of redbacks and funnel-webs.

'No, a beastie.'

'Where?'

'Under the chair.' She points frantically.

'Maybe he's gone.'

'No. No.' Her hysteria rises a notch. 'He's there. He's hiding. He'll come back and get me.'

I drop to my hands and knees and peer beneath the armchair. 'How big?'

'This big.' Her fingers are inches apart.

'I can't see him.' I tip the chair backwards.

'Shit!' I leap three feet in the air as the creature makes a dash for it, across into the pile of clothes. A huge, dark-brown cockroach, a superfast mover. Matilda shrieks hysterically.

'Hush, Little. I'll get him. I promise.'

I pick up a heavy glass ashtray and start gingerly dismantling the pile.

It's ahead of me. Out it darts, across, behind the TV stand—breathless pause—out again towards my bed. It stalls midway in a stretch of open carpet. It has brains of a sort, but this is a bad decision. I approach with the ashtray.

My nerves are jangling. I don't fancy hearing the crunch. I don't want to risk only maiming it. I drop the ashtray concave-side down, trapping it inside, where it panics, hurtling round and round as though in a spin drier.

Matilda clambers down from the desk and has a look. 'Is it poisonous?'

'No, it can't hurt you.' Spiders were what the internet warned about, no mention of this critter.

A knock on the door has me lurching to my feet. I'm in cotton boxers, unshaven, smelling like rancid pork scratchings. I grab a shirt off the pile.

'Hello. Open up.' A man's voice.

Put your T-shirt on, Matty.'

'Why?'

'Because.'

'But I'm hot.'

'Open up, please.'

No time to argue. Buttoning the shirt with one hand, I unlock with the other and peer into the corridor at an old guy and his missus, both in white towelling robes. She's clutching his sleeve as he attempts to look fierce through his leather wrinkles.

'No offence, mate, but we heard a kiddie scream.'

Yikes, they think I'm a paedophile.

'I'm her dad,' I say, smiling gormlessly, trying to look harmless. 'She was spooked by a bug.'

The missus stares at the paedophile's fading black eye. 'May we see her?'

'Of course. Sorry. Come in.'

The couple edge into the room, their eyes taking in the chaos, the half-naked little girl, the rumpled twin beds.

'Here she is,' I enthuse. 'Say hello, Matty—and here... look... the culprit.'

Matilda points gleefully. 'Daddy caught him. A beastie.'

She crouches over the ashtray, displaying the crack of her bum above her pyjamas, but the couple are beaming with relief. 'Ah,' the old guy says heartily. 'It's just a roach, sweetheart, mad as a cut snake by the looks of him. Won't hurt you. You'll need to give him the flick out the window.'

'I don't like him,' she says.

'It's a beaut,' says the old guy, digging himself deeper

into rampant Strine. 'Flew by looking for tucker, I reckon. Are you going to Queensland? They're much bigger there. Sorry, mate. No worries,' he says, looking the paedophile in the eye. 'The old lady had to check, you know.'

'No worries at all,' I agree as I usher them out.

The bug has stopped looping the loop. It waits for my next move. I slide a laminated page from the hotel's information pack under the ashtray, and it flattens itself trying to wriggle to freedom. 'Ugh! Ugh!' screeches Matilda. 'Don't let him out, Daddy!'

'For goodness' sake hush. They'll be back if you make so much noise.'

I'm shunting card and ashtray across the carpet towards the balcony. Lots of insect panic, round and round.

Stand up. Slide open the screen door and the window. Bend, take hold, prepare myself—one, two— whip card and ashtray up, squish him halfway out, leap across, shake him free—

Shit! No! He's sprinting down the balcony wall, back towards the room. He's under the door sill. I race inside, slam the window across and lock it. Close the slats.

'Has he gone, Daddy?'

'All gone. Far away.'

It's full daylight, no more sleep to be had. I start mindlessly picking stuff off the floor, putting Matty's clothes in drawers, hanging shirts in the cupboard, stacking *Germinal*, *A Farewell to Arms* and *The Rough Guide to Sydney* by my bed.

Matilda gathers up her crayons. 'I'm going to do a picture of him,' she says. 'His name's Alexander.'

'Fine. Okay.'

She starts reciting A. A. Milne at full volume. Shit, can't she shut up for five minutes?

I pick up the plastic freezer-container and look

around for somewhere dignified to put it. The internet assured me there was no rule against bringing Mum's ashes as hand luggage. She's here on a last minute whim. Maybe her heart is in Sydney. Maybe she would like to be scattered here. But even if she goes back to Battersea with us, it feels right that she's along for the ride.

Maybe she'll be my ticket to an audience with Oz.

I blunder into the bathroom, strip off and step into the shower. The water beats on my head, helping me focus. I can't tackle Oz right now, I decide. I have to get through the exhaustion. Matilda wants kangaroos and Bondi Beach. I want breakfast. We must follow the jetlag-busting rules: take exercise in daylight, drink lots of water, no alcohol, eat healthy food.

'I'm too hot. I want Mommy. I want to go home.'

'Hey, cheer up. Look at the baby chimp.'

We found kangaroos here in Taronga Zoo after a spectacular ferry-ride across the Harbour that thrilled Matilda no end. She ran from one side of the ferry deck to the other, hooting with joy and telling anyone who would listen about Alexander Beetle. The view back to Circular Quay looked a bit like the City of London with the Victorian churches dotted in amongst the glass, steel and concrete, but the Harbour itself, wide blue water churning with steam, sail and jet ski, was pure Australia.

Who am I kidding though, pretending to look at the sights like a tourist? Truth is I'm procrastinating.

Since we disembarked at the zoo, Matilda has wilted, and now she's grizzling like a four-year-old. She stands in my shadow and whinges.

Please God, let her not have a tantrum. I don't think I could cope.

'Come on, Matty,' I say. 'Cheer up.'

The kangaroos didn't do much, and now the chimps aren't doing much either. They seem out of sorts, swatting at flies and looking grumpily at us. We squint at them through our headaches and sunglasses and inhale the stench of hot animal poo, while the zoo's cable cars glide overhead in an incandescent white sky. The keeper tosses fruit to the chimps while he tells us about them. Their grand old dame, Fifi, made it to sixty before dying two years ago. They have politics and personalities, and some of them have sexier bums. The dominant male lies on his back and waits for someone to bring him a melon.

People frown and edge out of earshot as Matilda redoubles the volume. 'I'm hot, I'm hot, it's too hot, I don't like it here, I want Mommy.'

'Hush. Drink some water,' I urge her.

'It's yucky. It's warm.'

I should have put juice in it.

Jesus, it's way too hot to be only ten-thirty. I should be having a tantrum myself. Oven temperature. The wind burns the skin on my forearms. The sun hammers my head through my hat until I can almost feel my blood start to boil. Sweat runs in my eyes, and my T-shirt feels oppressively heavy. People wear loose cotton here for a reason. I've smothered Matilda in sunblock, but I must get us better hats. I lean over, trying to shelter and shush her. Some of the women carry silver reflecting umbrellas. Maybe we should have one of those. There's no shade. I'm desperately looking around for some. The patch under that withered gum tree is crowded with people.

I'm unsure of everything suddenly. It's all coming and going in my head. Sleep's what I need. I dread another night without it.

Matilda bellyaches, 'My head hurts,' and tries to burrow under my T-shirt. I stoop over, rocking her —'Hush, Little, poor Little'—shielding her from the blinding light, buckling beneath a weight of despair. This is useless; the whole trip is useless.

Headaches? Something I read online. Sunstroke.

Salty snacks. Sod the rest of the zoo tour.

'Hey, Matty,' I say. 'Shall we get some crisps? Have another ride on the boat?'

'Are we going to see my new grandpa now?' she demands on the ferry, as the motion breeze cools us.

'Best not call him "grandpa", not yet,' I say. 'If he isn't nice to us, we'll forget all about him and have a great holi—'

'But when are we going to see him?'

'Tomorrow, I hope.' I'm half-mesmerised, inhaling the sea spray, watching the white shells of the Opera House approach and expand into giant origami. 'I want to see him on his own first, in case he's—'

'Can't you do that today?'

I try to focus.

'I want to see him,' she says.

'Me too, but it's tricky.'

'Why is it?'

She wallops me until I look at her properly. I squat down, my back to the ferry rail. She stands between my knees, bashing me on the shoulders to get some sense out of me.

I do my best to supply reasons. 'You saw what happened when I rang him from London. He wouldn't talk. He hung up. He would do the same again.'

She sighs as though I'm dense. 'But that's why we've come, so we can go to his house and tell him he's *got* to talk to us.'

'Yes,' I agree.

'So let's go,' says Matilda.

How to explain this? 'The thing is, his wife will be there, and she'll see my red hair and your red hair and—'

'Is her hair red?'

I shake my head. 'She might be upset—'

'Because she doesn't have red hair?'

196

I smile. 'Because we do. Because she'll see we're related to Oz. I don't think she knows about us. I don't think he wants her to know. Suppose I were to tell you I had another little girl—'

'A *sister?*' She leaps at me, nearly head-butting me. '*Do* I have one?'

I shake my head, flummoxed. 'No... no, you don't, but...'

Images of Ben's two little kids flash in my mind. These are her cousins, but I mustn't get her hopes up.

'Okay, Matty, listen.'

I pause. Maybe it's wrong to mention this, but she needs some idea of what we're up against here. 'The thing is Granny Jonnson was Oz's very special girlfriend. His wife isn't going to be happy about that.'

Matty's brow puckers. She leans away from me, dodging my eyes. 'Like that blonde lady is *your* special girlfriend?'

'Who?' I say, hoping that she doesn't mean—

'Alison,' she says. 'At the party.'

'She isn't my girlfriend, Matty, cross my heart. But Mommy thought that she was. And do you remember how mad Mommy got?'

Matilda screws up her face, staring past my shoulder at the mammoth white shells gliding by. Her voice shrinks. 'Mommy wanted to go to America.'

'Exactly,' I say miserably. 'And that's what the problem is here. Maybe Oz's wife will get mad if she knows Granny was his girlfriend. If she realises that Oz is my dad and your grandpa.'

Matilda stands on one leg, massaging my knee with the flat of her hand, twisting her face every which way like play-dough, considering her new role as outsider, intruder, rogue comet in someone else's solar system. 'Poor Daddy,' she says.

I pull her in, give her a hug. 'Thank you, Little. So,

let's think. He won't answer my emails or talk on the phone. We can't knock on the door. So, how are we going to see him? Any ideas?'

She sucks her lips in, leans her head sideways and considers. 'I know,' she says, lurching upright. 'We'll sit outside his house in a car like on television. When he comes out we'll duck down really, really quickly and then follow him.'

'An excellent plan,' I say. 'Or we could go to the Blue Mountains in his bus. Which do you think is best?'

'The Blue Mountains! The Blue Mountains!' She breaks from my arms and bounces across the ferry deck —'Yes! Yes! Yes!'—making the other passengers laugh. Then she shouts, 'Oh Daddy, look, look!' as a butterfly the size of my hand, splotched black on white, flutters past us and over the rail like a torn page in the wind.

A surge of capability seizes me. 'Okay, that's decided.'

I root in the rucksack before remembering that the mobile won't work. I need to get an Australian SIM card. We called Gina on the hotel landline this morning.

'We'll find an upside-down phone,' I say, 'and we'll ring him and book a trip on the bus. How about we go to the Aquarium? There'll be a phone there, it'll be nice and cool and they'll have sharks and seals.'

'Yes! Yes!' she hollers, pirouetting with her arms outstretched, so I have to leap up and rescue her from collisions.

Matilda is deeply in love with Little Penguins. From Australia's southern seas, barely a foot tall and coloured iridescent sloe-blue, they're as entertaining as meerkats. She spent at least half an hour in front of their enclosure, pressing her nose to the glass, above and below water level, laughing and jumping and clapping her hands.

But now we've seen every sea creature there is, and I can no longer put off ringing Oz. While she tucks into chicken schnitzel and cola in the aquarium café and chatters to the stuffed Little Penguin we bought in the gift shop, I gather my courage. Only glass separates us from Darling Harbour, where there's a payphone in view.

'Will you be all right to stay here while I call him?'

'I want to come with you.'

'I'll only be gone a minute. You can watch me through the window.'

She starts wailing, 'I want to come. I want to talk to him.'

Shit. I can't risk it. She'll give us away. 'Please don't do this.'

Her distress grows in volume. 'I want Mommy.'

People are staring. 'Be quiet, Matty, please.' An idea hits me. 'Bondi Beach,' I offer.

She shuts up and listens.

'If you're extra specially good and let me phone Oz on my own, I'll take you to Bondi Beach on your birthday.'

I'm ready to up the offer to include Luna Park, a funfair we've seen from the ferry. Its entrance is a colossal face you have to pass under, through leering red lips and white tombstone teeth. I would rather stick needles in my eyes than go anywhere near the place, and luckily Bondi Beach does the trick.

So I'm outside again in the furnace, keeping an eye on her through the window, ready to run back if she starts crying or talking to strangers or wanders off from the table. I'm finding coins, feeling my stomach tighten, dialling his number.

'G'day. Daniels Days Out. How can I help?'

I lower the register to find a voice not quite my own. 'Ah. Yes. Hello. I came across your bus tours online. Do you have two seats for tomorrow?'

My heart pounds. I half expect him to hang up.

'Sorry, but there's n-no tour on a Sunday. Would M-Monday be okay?'

It's done in half a minute. I give my name as Geoff Eliot. I say I'll pay cash when I see him. He'll be outside the hotel ten to eight Monday morning.

'Great. Thanks,' he says. 'It's a white coach with our n-name on the side.'

When I hang up I'm shaking. Not with anger or anxiety, but from hearing the stammer and warmth of my father. From realising I don't want to hurt him. He may be forty-seven, but he sounds nearer seventeen.

Monday

We're wearing state-of-the-art, UV-protective, micro-fibre hats, which cover our hair and obscure our faces. Mine is floppy-brimmed khaki. Matilda's is a candy-pink bucket. I got her to stand still long enough for me to squash her hair into a rubber band on top of her head so scarcely a wisp can be seen. Our sunglasses are inscrutably dark. I'm Geoff Eliot, and Matilda has chosen to be Josie. She's hyper with anticipation but has promised not to blow our cover before I give the word. We're on the pavement outside the hotel to head him off from shouting for Geoff in the lobby. I've a hundred and seventy-eight dollars in cash clenched in my fist, ready to hand over fast, head down, and get on the bus. The plan is to stay incognito until I can get him alone.

Matilda slips my grip and starts jumping and making high-pitched squeaks. Passersby turn to look. I'm afraid her hat will fall off.

'Please,' I implore her. 'Be a grown up today. This is important, Little. We don't want him to see who we are and run away.'

'Are the mountains really blue?' she shouts.

'I don't know. Maybe a bit. When he comes, don't look up at him. Pretend you're one of those sulky girls who only look at their feet.'

Could be I'm overdoing the cloak and dagger, but Mum may have sent him photographs, or Lizzie may have described us to him, listing the features that match his own, and sure as hell I will be on his mind.

Matilda grabs my hand, the one that isn't full of damp money, with hers, the one that isn't clamped around Little Penguin. 'We'll be all right, Daddy. Don't worry.'

It's not just the heat that's making me sweat. I'm

tense as if treading a high wire. I scan the street right and left in search of a white bus. All the tour buses are white. Some rusty old coach, Lizzie said.

Matilda was up for the adventure of disguise because she's excited by the idea of leaping out saying, 'It's us! Here we are!' I spent a long time last night explaining why we have to wait and go carefully. 'He may be angry or scared. He may turf us off the bus.'

'But I'm not in the least bit scary.' She demonstrated demurely, giving me her sweet, gap-toothed grin.

Oh my God. Here it is, drawing in to the kerb. A nice little bus, one step up from a minibus, shining and polished, with DANIELS DAYS OUT emblazoned across the front and DANIELS DAYS OUT DOWN UNDER along the side. The driver's a shape behind the windscreen. I wave, averting my face.

He parks and turns off the engine. The door halfway along the bus hisses out and slides open. He's out of his seat, coming to greet us.

'Don't look up at him, Matty.'

'Don't look up at him, Daddy.'

I adjust my sunspecs, pull at my hat brim and stare at Oz's feet on the steps of the bus. Desert boots, socks, cotton trousers. He's as sun-shy as we are. I brandish the money and feel it pass into his hand as I choke out, 'Hi. I'm Geoff. This is Josie. You'll find it's all there.'

'Hi, Geoff,' he says. 'Hi there, Josie. Looks set to be another scorcher.'

I dare to glance up. Catch a glimpse of the big grin from the photos. He's stuffing the dollars, uncounted, into his leather bum-bag and waving us aboard. The door slides shut behind us, and Matilda and I are standing right next to him in the cool, air-conditioned aisle between the seats. It's impossible to hide now because he's shorter than I am. I mask my chin and push the sunglasses up my slippery nose. His hand is outstretched;

I drop mine to take it, and that is some weird kind of a moment, palm on palm with my father, his grip firm but not too firm, no stammer in it. He lets go before I do.

His mobile erupts into *Money, money, money*. He pulls it from his pocket, saying—'I wish'—getting a ripple of laughter from his passengers.

'G'day. Daniels Days Out. How can I help?'

I need to find a seat fast before Matilda gives us away or he starts looking too closely. The forward places are taken by assorted couples, so I steer us towards the rear. Matilda slides in next to the window. I take the aisle seat beside her and dare to peer along the bus.

After fielding his call, Oz returns to the wheel. I can see the back of his head, his rough-cut, ginger-grey hair. He's pulling away from the kerb. We're rolling. He lifts a hand and pulls a microphone to his mouth.

'Welcome aboard, Geoff and Josie. We have two m-more pickups to make, folks, before we head out of Sydney.' His accent hovers between English and Aussie. 'First stop on today's tour will be a wildlife park, where we'll see koalas and sheep shearing and a real m-m-mean saltwater croc.'

Matilda jiggles with excitement, 'A crocodile,' then leans in for a whisper. 'Is that him?'

I nod and mime zipping my lips.

'He looks different.'

'Just thirty years older,' I tell her.

He's rattling on with his 'expert commentary', telling us what to look at, explaining what we're seeing. The stammer's there, but it's endearing; his passengers smile at it. 'He's lovely, isn't he?' says the woman across the aisle, and I nod, warm with the knowledge that this is my father. He doesn't avoid the troublesome sounds. He seems aware of the charm of his hesitant speech and of the sprinkle of adopted Aussie phrases he's treating us to. Halting and repetitious, he bumbles along as he did in his emails to Mum, winning his listeners' affection. Cruising the motorway, giving us his chat, there's no risk he'll run out of words.

'Hello, Josie.'

The woman across the aisle flutters her fingers at Matilda. The accent is English, the face is burned red and the large nose thrust towards us is blistered and peeling. Her equally sun-challenged husband is doing a word-search puzzle.

Matilda takes no notice, but the woman persists. 'You can take her hat off on the bus. I expect her mother's not well today?'

I'm about to explain, but Matilda sighs and leans across me towards her. 'Mommy's in Battersea, and I like wearing my hat.'

I could kiss her, but now's not the time. 'Law unto herself,' I say, craning to see Oz's face in the rear-view mirror.

'I expect your mummy's with your brothers and sisters?'

God, we don't need this busybody. Matilda is quick on the draw. 'I'm an only child, actually,' she announces at top volume, 'and Mommy's in the bookshop.'

I hoist my rucksack to my knee and start rummaging in it to disrupt communication between them.

'We're from London, too,' says Mrs Busybody and pauses for me to reply.

I grunt into the rucksack.

She continues, 'Turnham Green. My husband retired before Christmas, didn't you, Jim? So we thought, chance of a lifetime, always wanted to travel the world. We've had four days in Thailand, then Singapore and Bali, but my daughter's in Melbourne, so we're...'

She's deep into monologue about herself and her stolidly word-searching mate. Matilda loses interest and looks out of the window, nattering secrets and admonitions under her breath to Little Penguin, whom she holds close to her face. I'm contributing nods and 'uh huh's to Mrs B while locating the juice bottle. Sheltered by the flap of the rucksack, I twist to give it to Matilda and whisper under the brim of her hat, 'Don't tell.'

'Course I won't,' she says, rolling her eyes at me. 'I'm not a baby, Daddy.'

'You won't what, dear?' chips in Mrs B, quick as a squirrel.

'Be sick on the bus,' says Matilda, and smiles very sweetly.

By the time we arrive at the wildlife park, Matilda's fidgeting with her hat and beginning to whinge. Any minute she'll pull it off, or Mrs B will, and even if it stays on Oz will be curious if we keep our hats on for lunch, which is the next stop after this one. I have to get him alone here, and the chances look good because he's staying with the coach. 'See you back in forty-five m-minutes,' he tells us. But Matilda drags me onto the cinders and away through the ferocious, animal-smelling heat towards the arrow nailed to a post. She's keen to see the mean crocodile.

She wants the toilet too, which is just round the corner. I'm planning to double back to the bus afterwards, but she's jumping with impatience, insisting, 'Come *on*, Daddy,' and I've zilch chance of dissuading her because a bronzed youth is welcoming us to the Little Penguins' feeding time. She breaks into a run. Hell, this is impossible. I jog after her, glancing over my shoulder, but the coach and car park have vanished behind eucalyptus scrub.

The penguins are in an open-air enclosure, where they dive and splash in a small lake, chasing and catching the fish being lobbed to them. The keepers play for laughs. They're laid-back young guys ready with anecdotes and quips that have Matilda by turns gobsmacked and in stitches. All good stuff, but I'm fidgeting, anxious. Maybe I can leave her with the others for a few minutes, ask someone to watch her.

Not yet though because next comes the crocodile. Armoured, gigantic, unsettling, it basks half-submerged in a fetid soup of green mud, returning my gaze like Hannibal Lecter. Matilda clings to my leg, and I don't blame her. I'm certainly not abandoning her here.

Now we're offered the shade of a tent, where two burly lads announce a sheepshearing demo. We file in past a pen of baaing wool. One of the two guys sits splay-legged on a raised platform above a line of assorted chairs. The other manhandles a ewe towards him.

Here's my chance. 'I need the loo,' I whisper. 'Are you okay to stay here?'

I make favour-requesting eyes at the young Japanese couple sitting along from us, but Mrs B cuts in from the row behind. 'Need a comfort break, Geoff? I'll keep an eye on Josie for you.'

Matilda's attention is riveted by the panicked animal and the buzzing electric clippers. She has no interest in spilling our business. I stand up, 'Okay, thanks,' and I run.

We've been walking in a circle, and there are only kangaroos and koalas to go, so it's no distance to the coach. I arrive, panting from heat and nerves, at the end of the path, and start across the cinders, trying to steady my breathing. Oz must hear the crunch of my feet, but he doesn't turn to look. He's standing in the dust on the shady side of the coach, leaning against it, bush hat in hand, swigging from a can of cola and humming to himself.

I press a fist to my chest to stop my heart

hammering. I'm a few paces away when he glances in my direction, cracks his big, toothy smile and says, 'Hot enough for you, Geoff?'

My mouth is on autopilot—'Plenty, thanks.' I'm seeing the glisten of sweat on his flushed forehead, the trail of larger brown freckles across his nose and right cheek, the ginger stubble on his chin and throat, his hand with bitten fingernails gripping the cola can. Now's the moment to announce myself. There won't be a better one.

'Do you miss England?' I say.

He's unfazed. 'Well spotted. The Aussies kn-know I'm a pom, but the poms mo-mostly assume I'm an Aussie.' He tips his head back and drains the can, crushes it and takes aim at a nearby waste bin.

What's the worst that can happen? He'll probably just give me my damp dollars back and say find your own way home.

The can sails through the air and lands plumb in the bin. 'That's a first,' he says, grinning.

'Look,' I say. 'Don't freak out, Oz, but there's no easy way to spring this on you.'

Uncertainty dawns in his eyes.

'I'm not going to mess anything up for you. I'd just like a chat, no big deal. So, I'm sorry,' I pull off my hat and my sunglasses, 'but I'm here.'

I'm blinking in the glare, bracing myself for anything he'll throw at me, but whatever I expected it wasn't this. I have my sunglasses on again, and I'm seeing a man disintegrate in front of me. He shrinks as if trying to pull himself into a shell, and although his lips move he says nothing.

'Hey,' I say. 'I'm not here to do anything bad, Oz. I'm not angry, and I won't tell your family. Okay, I was pissed off when I rang you from London, but believe me, it had been a bad day...'

I laugh, groping for humour to unite us and put the bones back in his body. He's cowering against the side of the bus, shaking his head without force or conviction.

'What's so terrible?' I say. 'I get it you don't want to know me, but why?'

'Let's g... let's ge-ge... let's ge-ge-ge-ge...'

It's painful to watch him. I want to help, but I don't know where he's going with this. New Year's Eve makes sudden sense to me. He didn't hang up on me coldly. He simply couldn't speak.

He makes a supreme effort. 'L-let's ge-get on the b-b-b—'

'On the bus! Yes, of course. It's too hot to think straight. Except, sorry,' I'm all at once anxious, 'Oz, the thing is, I have to run back to Matty. I'm sure she's okay, but...'

He nods helplessly.

'Look, I'm sorry I ambushed you, but I didn't know what else to do.'

I pause, but it's no use. He's not going to say anything.

'So, you're working—you've got to look after these people. I'll keep shtum, and then later, when they go back down the river, we'll stay behind, okay? We'll find Matty a milkshake, and you and I can have a beer. You'll see I'm no threat, not at all.'

It's like coaxing a child, and like a child he has no ultimate means to deny me. I grab his shoulder and squeeze it, and the contact reverberates up my arm to my brain. He nods again, and I turn and head off at a run to where Matilda, held aloft by an Aussie hunk and cheered on by Mrs B, is tickling the ear of a koala.

'Your hat's come off, Daddy.' She pulls hers off too. 'My head itches.' The rubber band breaks, and her hair falls down.

'What beautiful curls,' says Mrs B.

'Daddy, did you know,' shouts Matilda, 'if you whirl a billycan round your head, the tea leaves go to the bottom?' She whirls Little Penguin, clouting the Aussie hunk in the face as he lets her slither to the ground. 'Have you told him?' she asks me.

'Told who what, dear?' says Mrs B.

'My grandpa!' She doesn't wait for an answer. Her feet touch the ground, and she's off, sprinting towards the car park.

'Matty, stop!' I scoop the pink hat from the ground and race after her. I glance back to see Mrs B hot on our heels, her scarlet face running with sweat, and behind her the whole group is strolling this way.

By the time my feet hit the cinders, Matilda has reached Oz where he stands by the open door of the coach. 'Hello. You're my grandpa!' She flaps her arms and twirls to display herself from every angle. 'I've got red hair like you in the picture, and green eyes, look!' She takes off her sunglasses and pushes her face up at him.

I skid to a halt, watching him look at her.

'Oh my goodness. What a sweet story,' Mrs B announces to the growing crowd.

'Mind your own bloody business,' I say.

I don't believe it. Oz is turning from Matilda to the bus. He hasn't spoken or reacted. I'm hurtling forward. 'Wait. At least smile at her. She's just a little girl.'

He takes no notice. He's disappearing into the bus. I lift Matilda from the ground, hug her tightly to me and follow.

'Doesn't he like me?' she says.

I leap up the steps. He's in the driver's seat, looking ahead. He sets the engine running. He doesn't even glance round.

'You shit,' I yell at his head. The passengers are coming aboard. Matilda clamps my ribs with her arms and legs like a koala and stares, her eyes wide, threatening tears.

'Don't cry. Let's sit down. I'll explain,' I tell her.

'You owe my wife an apology,' says Mrs B's husband.

'Your wife can get stuffed.' I'm on the edge of shoving him aside and punching Oz's lights out, but I have to look after Matilda.

I grab a seat well away from the Busybodies, near the front, behind the Japanese couple. The people who sat here before tut and fuss when they see us, but, 'Sorry,' I say, 'she gets travel-sick at the back.'

I clutch her head to my chest. 'Is he cross with me?' she whimpers.

'No, you've done nothing wrong.' I clamp down on my rage so hard that my teeth hurt.

With everyone on board, he has to stand up and count us. He does it fast, avoiding my eyes. Sliding into his seat, he puts the engine in gear and takes off, steering out of the car park to the road, while I hold tight to Matilda, battling fury and shame. I shouldn't have brought her here, shouldn't have exposed her to this, shouldn't be snapping at her.

'Listen, Matty, he wouldn't speak to me either. He's a silly little boy. You're much more grown up than he is, and I love you to bits.'

She looks up. She's not crying. 'Will he say hello to me on his microphone?'

'I don't think so. He's pretending we're not here.'

'That's *very* silly,' she says loudly, 'because we *are* here.'

'Quite right.'

What indeed will he say through his microphone? Will he be able to speak? Speeding west across the scorched brown terrain, he's silent. Some of the passengers are curious, peering at us and at him. My chest is paralysed, waiting, until eventually there comes the tap of the mike and his intake of breath. I gulp air and hold it. Matilda straightens in the crook of my arm, straining to see him between the heads of the Japanese couple.

'Welcome back, everyone... I hope you enjoyed seeing the ani... the animals.'

You coward, I want to shout. You can talk to strangers, but you can't say hello to a child?

'We'll be on the road for about thirty m-minutes, starting to climb higher. Then we'll stop at a n-nice place for tucker.'

He's back on form, doing his job.

For a while I do nothing but hug Matilda to me and stare through a red mist at the back of his head. Gradually my pulse slows, allowing me to gather my thoughts about what to do next.

I plant a kiss on Matty's head. 'I'll need to talk to him again later, Little. Will you be okay with that?'

She nods solemnly.

'When the others go on the boat, we'll stay behind.'

Her face puckers. She wheedles, 'I want to go on the boat.'

'We'll go on some good boats tomorrow, I promise. We'll sail to Cremorne Point, the place Granny Jonnson likes. But tonight we'll come back with Oz on the bus. If we don't, we won't see him again.'

She pulls a face, but she nods, wriggling free to look through the window.

'And we won't get upset if he still won't talk to us,' I say.

'Because he's silly silly silly,' she says loudly.

'Exactly,' I say, 'and until the boat we'll pretend we don't know him, okay?'

'Well, I don't know him, *actually*,' she announces for the whole bus to hear.

She's quiet for a while, before, 'Daddy?' she whispers.

211

'Yes, Little?'

'The water at Grandpa Jonnson's at Brighton is properly salty, isn't it?'

'Yes, it is. Properly salty.'

'So, do they have a saltwater crocodile there?'

It's getting late, and the bus is approaching Parramatta ferry. The atmosphere's tense. Mrs B has been whispering to anyone who'll listen, and I've been getting curious looks.

Matilda, oblivious, has had a whale of a time. Through the long, blistering afternoon, she's discovered the Blue Mountains' rainforests. She's squinted in the sun's glare at craggy views above them, hung suspended in a cable car peering at the undulating green sea of them, gawped at long, silver cascades of water plummeting into them, ridden the 'Sceniscender' two hundred metres down into the deep, steamy heat of them, and clutched my hand on a path winding through them, declaiming stridently to keep away the unimaginable creatures that lurk in them.

All the while, all I've been seeing is a man crumpled against the side of a bus unable to say the simplest thing. I've been remembering Lizzie's words. They've taken on new significance. *He slides off the subject. Did I tell you he stammers? The gist was he didn't want to talk about it.* Lizzie does no better than I do.

It's some time since he last spoke into his microphone, and I'm peering forward to see him. I must stay close to him at the ferry, give him no opportunity to cut and run. Matilda has absorbed my anxiety and is whispering soothing words to Little Penguin.

Two hours ago, deep in the rainforest, out of sight of the Sceniscender and other people, I sat on my heels and turned her to face me, my hands on her shoulders. 'Hey, Little, you've heard how Oz has a bit of trouble with his m's and his n's?'

She craned backwards, staring up at the sun filtering through the canopy.

'It's called a stammer or a stutter. He can't help it. When he realised who I was, he couldn't speak. The words wouldn't come out at all. It may happen again when I talk to him later.'

Matilda stood in the steam bath of dappled light and loud insects, wearing her hat to keep the ticks from her hair, and stared off into the forest. 'There's a girl at my school,' she said. 'Sometimes they make her cry. The teacher says *she* can't help it. She sits on her own at playtime.'

'Do *you* make her cry?'

She shook her head evasively.

'Do you ever sit with her?'

She screwed up her mouth and put her head on one side. 'Not really. Cos she never *says* anything. Can we ring Mommy tonight?'

The ferry pulls out from the jetty. Mrs B shoots me a last glare and waves to Matilda, who wags one of Little Penguin's flippers at her until the boat disappears around the next bend. Suddenly the place is isolated and wild, a road ending at a wide, green river, a few modern buildings but no people in sight. The sun descends towards to the horizon upstream, still throbbing its unbearable heat.

I've been watching Oz from the corner of my eye, poised to rugby-tackle him if needs be, but he makes no sudden move. He lingers by the jetty, where he's shaken hands with the passengers and accepted their tips. He faces up to us approaching him.

Unwanted son holds out a hand, guarded, cautious.

He blinks.

'So. I'm Mark, and this is Matilda.'

Matilda hangs on so tightly to the pocket of my shorts that I fear she will rip it. I curl my fingers around her shoulder, ready to comfort or calm her.

He takes the hand awkwardly, releases it quickly. I can see he is gathering himself.

'You're both so like m-me,' he manages. 'I wish you looked a bit m... a bit m-more like Na-Na-Nancy.'

At this, Matilda leaps from my grasp, bounds forward and throws her arms around his hips. 'I've come to see you,' she announces, 'because you won't talk on the phone. Daddy's very cross with you because you're a silly little boy.'

He looks at me. I shake my head.

'Daddy is silly sometimes,' she says. 'And so am I, though I'm *very* grown up.'

'Ah,' he says. 'Perhaps n-not so different from,' he takes a breath, 'from your grandma after all.'

Matilda leaps high on the spot. 'We've brought her to see you. She's at the hotel.'

I'm about to explain, but I'm transfixed by Oz. His eyes shine, the years drop away, and I'm seeing the boy in the photograph.

Matilda rattles on. 'She decided to come because she likes boats and Little Penguins, but Daddy says her best bit is Come On Point. We're going there tomorrow on a *boat*. You can come too if you like. It's three sleeps to my birthday. We're going swimming on Bondi Beach for my birthday treat.'

Oz's eyes search mine, wanting confirmation that Mum isn't dead. She's waiting for us to deliver him to the hotel like a trophy. All talk of funerals and flowers has been an elaborate practical joke.

He reads the truth in my face, and his hopes crash. 'Her ashes,' I say. 'I thought she might like them scattered in Sydney. She said something about Cremorne Point in her diary. Perhaps you met her there?'

He stares at me.

'Eight years ago?' I prompt. '2001?'

Still nothing.

'She was here for a month,' I say.

'She was?' he says. 'Here in Sydney?' His face loses focus.

'I'm hungry. Can we go home?' says Matilda.

She stretches out her arms and twirls towards the open bus door. The sun's starting to slide behind a low hill. The fire of the day is easing. The cicadas and birds are racketing away in the bush.

'Look,' I say. 'Do you mind?'

He half turns towards me.

I hardly know if I mean this, but I step forward and hug him, briefly, as Matilda did. He doesn't resist or shrink away. He doesn't return the hug.

'We need to talk on our own,' I say. 'Can I buy you dinner?'

'I'd rather just drop you at the hotel.'

I freeze. Take a step back. 'Only a meal,' I say. 'No strings attached.'

He shakes his head. 'I've a family. I really can't d-do this.'

'You'll stay for a drink, at least?'

'I can't,' he says. 'M-mustn't. Really. It's best we leave it.'

That dead phrase. Matilda's out of sight, inside the bus. A weight of hopelessness descends on my shoulders.

'Sod you,' I snap. 'Have it your way. Is there somewhere here I can call a cab?'

Nancy was at a phone booth, but she still wasn't dialling. Instead she was watching the aboriginal man who was dressed neck to toe as a gorilla.

On this western edge of Circular Quay, under The Rocks, before you reached the white bulk, like a felled skyscraper, of the berthed QE2, a line of entertainers waited in freeze-frame for passersby to drop coins in their begging-bowls and bring them to life. Silhouetted on his plinth against the dazzling noonday traffic of ferries and water-taxis, the youth in the Tin Man suit was jerking robotically, lifting an arm to salute a child who stared from his mother's arms at the silver hair and face paint. Ten yards further on the gorilla waited motionless.

Four days in Sydney and Nancy hadn't rung Oz. Each morning, each evening, she'd picked the hotel phone from its cradle, sometimes started to dial but then always hung up. He still hadn't replied to her email. The only messages in the internet café had been from London: from Mark, Harry, her girlfriends in Muswell Hill.

She should have been plainer; Oz couldn't have realised what her email meant. Or he hadn't yet read it. Or maybe he preferred to let her visit go by. She wished he would just say so. It irritated her suddenly, the elusiveness she'd acquiesced in for so many years. She lifted the receiver now. Of course she should ring him. It would be perverse to be in Sydney and leave again without making sure that he knew. Nonsense to stand here, not dialling, thinking instead about the aboriginal man.

Was the gorilla suit consciously ironic, or was he innocent of irony, which she was shamed for imagining?

Why shouldn't he dress as a gorilla?

In the basement of the New South Wales Art Gallery two days ago, a mixed-race man in blue jeans and green singlet, with white ochre paint on his skin, had chatted easily to his audience as he demonstrated the didgeridoo. Yesterday on a baking-hot city bus she'd exchanged smiles with an aboriginal family—mum, dad and baby—across the aisle from her. The dad, in a light-cotton suit, had looked like an office worker. When the baby sneezed, the mum had said, 'Bless you.' But these encounters were the exception. Mostly it seemed impossible even to make eye contact with aboriginal people. An invisible curtain divided the multi-ethnic crowds Nancy mingled with from the native Australians who sprawled, growling, spitting and shouting, in the squares of Kings Cross, or swilled spirits wrapped in brown-paper bags outside bottle shops. The etiquette seemed to be that the two worlds ignored each other.

Framed on his pedestal against the blue of the Harbour, the gorilla confronted the etiquette. Come on, he seemed to say, drop a dollar in my hat. Let me dance for you. Let me take the shine off your prejudice. What *is* your problem? I'm not drunk. Does my jutting brow put you off, or my scowl?

The Tin Man was doing good business, rarely still for half a minute before being summoned into action by another small child, but the crowds flowed past the gorilla, chatting and eating their ice creams as if he were not there. You make it too hard for us, Nancy thought. It's not irony you intend; it's anger.

She turned away. Focused again on the phone. Held her breath and made herself dial Oz's number right through to the end. It began to ring. She leant forward, staring at a fly crawling up the dusty Perspex of the booth. She gathered herself to say, 'Hello. It's me, yes. I'm here—here in Sydney. Did you get my email?'

She willed him to be pleased. Maybe they could meet, she would say. Just for a drink and a chat after all these years. How about this Friday evening? It's the Mardi Gras launch in the Opera House forecourt.

The pause told her she was through to voicemail. 'G'day. Thanks for calling Daniels Days Out. We're away until Monday the twenty-sixth of February. Please leave a message or call again. We offer great-value tours. Enjoy your stay in Sydney.'

Not a syllable of hesitancy. He must have practised and recorded until it was smooth. She replaced the receiver and leant her forehead on it. What an idiot she was. How ridiculous to come without checking dates, to be here twenty-eight days of which he would be here only two.

We, he'd said. *We're away*. He, Yvonne and Ben.

She lifted her head. The gorilla loomed dark against the bright water and the distant, snowy wings of the Opera House. She crossed the quay to stand close in front of him. He gazed sullenly over her head, as impassive as a mounted sentry in Whitehall. He must be horribly hot in that costume.

She took out her wallet and dropped a ten-dollar note in his hat.

Slowly he juddered into motion, turning his scowling face to look first one way then the other, bringing his fists up to pummel his chest and parting his black lips in a silent, white snarl. She watched his eyes, waiting for them to meet hers, to meet anybody's, but he stared above the heads of the parents and children who were gathering around her. Finally he halted, one arm in a strong-man pose against the sky, the other loose at his side, his expression empty, unfocused.

She couldn't bear it. She stepped forward, near enough to smell his heat, and reached to take hold of his big, naked fist, dangling from the sleeve of the suit. She wriggled her fingers into his palm, feeling the calloused skin. Absurdly she held on, squeezing his thumb, willing him to react somehow, a smile or a growl. But still he refused, pulling away, lifting his hand out of her reach.

Her vision swam; blood rushed to her cheeks. 'Are you all right, love?' someone said. She set off, walking fast, almost running, back along the quay towards the ferry stations, escaping the onlookers' stares.

2009

Oz wouldn't let me call a cab, insisted on driving us back. I'm in the front seat across from him as he steers through the city suburbs towards the hotel. Matilda is asleep on the first double seat behind me, the seatbelt secured across her middle and under an arm, padded with Little Penguin so it doesn't cut into her.

All I can see through the dark is his profile. He's been smiling nervously, his cheek creasing into a deep, jovial crow's foot, but in his ineffectual way he won't budge. His bitten finger-ends grip the wheel tightly. He won't even glance across, so I carry on staring as if he's an inanimate object. It's my first, probably last, opportunity to have a good look at him.

Towards the city centre the traffic grows thicker and the street lights brighter. Even on a Monday night Sydney is festive; milling teenagers crowd the entrances to clubs and a multiplex cinema. Oz brakes to let a group of shouting girls cross in front of us. They wave and pull faces.

He pulls up at a stop light, turning his face to me, but I've nothing to ask him or tell him. The signal is green, and the bus is moving again. The last few hundred yards are rolling beneath us. This is it. I've no mother, no father, and soon I'll have no child.

When he pulls in at the kerb, he keeps the engine running. He puts on the aisle lights and presses the door release. He looks at me. I look at him. I start to gather up our things.

'If Mum were here,' I say sourly, 'you'd be racing me into the hotel.'

He has the grace to look sheepish.

'Daddy?' Matilda sits up, her eyes blank with sleep. 'Are we there?'

'Yes, Little. Shall I carry you?'

I disentangle her from the seatbelt and manoeuvre her awkward weight to my shoulder. Her head lolls against my neck.

Oz half rises, says nothing.

'Okay then. Goodbye,' I say.

I get myself, child and bags along the aisle and into the street, where the heat envelops us. My skin's clammy before I'm across the pavement. The doors to the hotel's cool interior slide open. As they close behind us, I hear the bus driving away.

Fifteen minutes later, I'm drinking mini-bar whisky, watching Matilda sleep, feeling tragic and bloody, when the desk clerk rings up. 'There's a visitor for you.'

He stands in the lobby, his bush hat in his hand.

'What is it?' I say coldly. 'What do you want?'

'I'm sorry. You're right,' he says. 'I can't do the long-lost-family thing, but I suppose we could talk about Na-Nancy.'

In a pub garden balmy with late summer warmth Nancy raised her glass to shield her eyes from the noon sun and leant lazily against Oz as Lizzie kept clicking the camera shutter. Autumn was coming. In a week it would be September and Oz would be the other side of the world. His arm slid round her waist and squeezed her against him. 'Cheese,' he said.

They were in Bristol again, on their way to the West Country. Dave, Lizzie's bloke, and Mike, Oz's friend with the glasses and the bad complexion, were inside the pub, playing pool. Oz could be playing pool too, but he'd opted to stay here, sharing this bench with her, stroking her hip. He wanted so much of her. It should feel oppressive, but it didn't, not at all, and he would be gone soon.

'It's a great camera, Oz,' Lizzie said. 'Dead simple to focus.'

She stepped nearer, shoving the lens at his face, adjusting the dial. 'I can get in ever so close. Give us a grin.'

Lizzie had put the swanky new camera, a leather case and six rolls of colour film into Oz's hands when they'd arrived at her place an hour ago. 'From Dad for your Australian trip.'

He'd accepted the gift without smiling.

'Go on,' Lizzie said. 'Enjoy it. Dad's guilty offering.'

'Why guilty?' said Nancy.

'Never m-mind,' Oz said quickly.

'Haven't you told her?' said Lizzie.

'Told me what?'

'Tell you later,' said Oz.

She knew almost nothing about his parents. He spoke of his childhood offhandedly as though it hardly mattered, across the pillow, or in the chaos of spilt sugar and smeared butter as he attempted to make the puddings he remembered from boarding school. He said he didn't believe childhood affected you: all that Freudian stuff was ridiculous. He'd let drop that he'd been bullied at school, and she'd seen him withdraw into himself at the memory, but all he would add was, 'They bullied M-Mike too, because of his acne.' He'd clammed up until she changed the subject.

'One more. Lift your glasses,' said Lizzie.

It was good to see Lizzie again. She radiated sisterly warmth and seemed relaxed about Oz being cradle-snatched. Dave was as saturnine and silent as he'd been at the party. Mike was okay, witty, making her laugh, although Nancy wished he would shut up about Australia. It was the last thing she wanted to think about. On Friday Oz and Mike were due to fly from Heathrow. They'd be gone for three months at least, maybe six. 'I'll be back by Christmas,' Oz kept insisting. 'I'm not risking leaving you alone any longer. You'll meet someone else.'

She shook her head, grinning. 'So might you. We're both free.'

A shadow passed over him when she said things like this. He wanted forever; he wanted a promise. 'I don't have to go,' he kept telling her.

'It's an adventure,' she said. 'You shouldn't turn down adventures.'

'Being with you is a bigger adventure.'

'Than Australia? Come off it. Anyway you can have both. I'm not going anywhere. I'll be here, getting up, going to work, coming home, not meeting anybody, not *looking* for anybody, I promise.'

It wasn't enough. 'Come with us,' he insisted.

'I'd love to, but I can't quit my job.'

'Yes, you can.'

'My job means a lot to me.'

He hugged her as if she might vanish. 'I shouldn't go. I shouldn't leave you.'

'Trust me,' she said. 'I'll be here. You can't let Mike down.'

The truth was that a little corner of her was looking forward to being without him. She needed to catch her breath and get some perspective. For eight weeks Oz had been sharing her space and her air and her bed and her brain. She was off her feet, spinning and flying. She'd scarcely had time to blink, let alone to ask herself how, and how hard, they would land.

He'd turned up at Maida Vale with no warning a week after Sally's party. He'd been waiting outside when she got home from work, sitting halfway down the area steps, his head level with the pavement, wearing his lumberjack shirt and with his backpack beside him.

Her heart had sunk and leapt simultaneously. He hadn't seen her yet, and she'd paused, watching without saying his name. He'd looked bored, almost depressed, chewing on a finger, staring vacantly at his feet in their laced walking-boots. When his eyes lifted and he noticed her standing above him, his face broke into its intoxicating smile. He sprang up the steps, his arms closed around her and his mouth landed on hers, knocking the breath from her.

This was insane, she'd tried telling herself ever since. Daft to get swept up in a teenager's fantasy. Also she wasn't used to being needed by someone. It felt awkward; she didn't quite believe it or know how to respond. Might she grow tired of it? There was more chance she would hurt Oz than vice versa: that was the danger. But she'd clung to the thought that what was to come didn't matter. It was good now, and now was enough; let the future take care of itself. The whirlwind would blow itself out, but wherever it deposited her why paint the beginning as laughable or bad?

'I want us to go away together somewhere,' he'd said suddenly two days ago, and she'd immediately agreed, wanting it too. August Bank Holiday wasn't the most sensible time to be looking for bed and breakfast in Devon, but what the hell, they would manage. With no hesitation she'd booked a car for the week and thrown a few things into her duffle bag.

It would have been of little use to refuse. Whenever she resisted his ideas, he smiled and repeated until her protests felt foolish or selfish or snobbish. He led her along paths she wouldn't have thought to explore. 'We'll go to jive classes,' he said. 'There's no such thing,' she objected, but he hunted one down, only a five-minute bus ride from her flat, where they learned the names of the steps—simple, back, rotating base, spot turn, underarm turn—and how to put them together until they were real dancers and their knees didn't collide any more.

Dave stuck his head out of the pub door. 'Another round, folks?'

'I'd better not,' she said. 'One of us needs to stay sober.'

'We'll share the driving,' she'd said to Oz when she booked the car.

'Celebrate me passing my test.'

'Good God. You're seventeen. What *am* I doing?'

'Come to bed,' he said.

'But we only just got up.'

'Marry me,' he said.

'No,' she laughed.

'Seriously. M-marry me.'

He wanted sex constantly. It should have annoyed her. She should have said, 'Give me some space.' But he was so beguilingly happy to see her wake each morning, so eager to greet her each evening, leading her straight from the door to the bed, peeling off her black suit. The hand he held out was easy to take and the sex strangely

225

effortless; she never got tired of it. Sometimes—when she was hungry for him too—they went at it furiously, panting and sweating, but more often they would gently join up without haste or preamble and lie almost motionless for a while, face to face, her leg curled around his thigh, his eyes smiling into hers, not a word. All idea of resistance or of wanting food or a drink or a shower fell away. She hadn't experienced sex quite like this before. She could scarcely be bothered to do anything these days but lie naked and smiling, merged with her lover and gazing into his eyes.

It couldn't possibly last. He was bound to move on, to meet a girl his own age. She wished she could bottle the surfeit, not live it all now, keep some for the months he was away.

'Maybe,' she said when he pressed her to marry him. 'Give it time. Go to Australia. Live a little. See what you think when you come back.'

'I love you,' he said. 'That's n-not going to change.'

They drove on towards Devon along the back roads through a landscape of woods and hills. They wound down the car windows and inhaled the hot breeze and the smells of the farmyards. The journey itself was the holiday. There was no destination. The shadows cast by the western sun were long fingers drawing them on away from Heathrow. They didn't have to go back, Nancy thought idly. Nothing compelled them. He didn't have to leave. Or she could go with him. It wasn't too late.

'What did Lizzie mean about your dad feeling guilty?' she said.

He didn't answer immediately. She took her eyes from the road for a moment to look at him.

'He's n-n-n...' He stopped, took a breath. 'From the start he d-didn't ever mu-mu-much like me,' he said.

The stammer startled her. It had afflicted him so

slightly until now. 'Are you okay?'

When he didn't answer, she glanced at him anxiously. 'I'm fine,' he said.

'We have that in common,' she found herself telling him. 'My father doesn't like me very much either, and I don't like him at all.'

She could feel how her colour was rising. Her voice was obstructed by emotion. She'd never told anyone this. 'My mother's not much bothered either. You've probably noticed I haven't heard from them or phoned them. Birthdays they send me money. Christmas I go home for two days, and we're polite to each other. That's it really. It's been that way for so long I don't mind. I've decided they're just two people I happen to know. I can do fine without them. I can look after myself.'

Oz slid his hand along her shoulder, stroked the back of her neck. She tried to calm herself. 'Of course, sometimes I mind,' she said, clearing her throat, 'but not often. It would feel awkward, I think, if they made any effort to change, if they bothered to feel guilty.'

'Awkward. Exactly,' he said. 'You understand everything.'

The road rolled ahead west. She had the warm rushing wind on her elbow, the sun in her eyes. She lowered the sun visor and smiled.

Oz was saying something.

'What? I can't hear you.'

'The real p-problem my dad has is that... well... um... my m-m-m...'

She glanced at him. He was looking at his hands.

'Your mother?'

'Yes... well... she d-died. And it was sort of my f-f—'

'Your father?'

He shook his head savagely, fighting to get the word out. 'Fault.'

'Your fault your mother died?'

227

'Yes,' he said.

'How?'

'Look,' he said, 'could we stop for a while?'

'Okay.' She scanned the hedgerow for a place to pull in. Here would do. A five-barred gate to a field of tall grass and poppies. She eased the nose of the car to the gate till it bumped and the tail was clear of the road. She killed the engine, put on the handbrake and twisted to face him.

He told it in stuttering snatches. It started from the day he was born. His mother was depressed, and no one understood quite how bad it was. She swallowed sleeping pills and booze, and she died.

'That wasn't your fault,' Nancy said.

'But my dad blamed m-me.'

His dad would have nothing to do with him, had just focused on Lizzie. He was fostered as a baby; then when he came home he was looked after by nannies. From age seven he was at boarding school.

'Where they bullied you.'

'Yup.'

So now he'd left school and moved in with Lizzie because his dad still didn't want to know. He'd been getting under Lizzie's feet quite a bit. They were fine, little brother, big sister, but no, Lizzie wouldn't miss him. Lizzie had Dave. It was Lizzie who'd suggested he should take a look at Australia, his dad who was financing the trip. They would neither of them mind if he didn't come back.

Would Oz get under her feet too, Nancy wondered. That was the thought in her mind. She must have looked worried because, 'It's okay,' he said, breaking into his easy, beautiful grin, 'I *am* coming back, because n-now I've found you.' He seized hold of her hand. 'I'm fine. I'm not at school any longer. I'm free of the bullies. I don't have to tiptoe around Dad.'

Australia would change him, she thought, widen his horizons. Things would work out one way or another. She kissed him, pulled the key from the ignition and said, 'Shall we go for a walk?'

They climbed over the gate. There was a trodden path along the inside of the hedge, and she started to follow it, but he said, 'Through the flowers,' and set off into the field. The sun was low, ahead of them, softly blinding her as they waded towards it, waist high in grass and poppies. The world grew quiet as they pushed on, away from the wind-tossed trees of the lane. The ground sloped down at first but then rose before them towards the crest of a hill. At the lowest point Oz paused and looked at her mischievously, sweeping his hand in an invitational arc.

'Here?' she said.

'Please.'

His smile was too big to refuse. Silently he was telling her that his past was of no consequence, had no hold over him, any more than her cold father and mother had hold over her. All hurts could be healed by the kiss of their bodies, now, in this meadow.

He was spreading his tartan shirt on the ground and unzipping his jeans. She was unbuttoning her blouse, stepping out of her jeans and knickers. It was simple. They lay face to face, their hips on his shirt, her leg hooked over his thigh, eyes locked, arms entwined, their heads in a hushed thicket of green stalks. She could hear a bumblebee humming above them. She hugged Oz tighter, drew him into her deeper and rolled him over above her, so all she could see were his green eyes, his shaggy red hair and the scattered crimson of the poppies dancing against the deep blue of the sky.

'Are you driving a tour tomorrow?' I say.

I set down a third round of draught Tooheys New in the hotel bar. The place is empty apart from one other bloke who's engrossed in watching cricket highlights with the barman.

The alcohol and the memory of his summer with Mum have freed Oz's tongue. The first pint got soaked up by the steak and chips I ordered for him. His stammer more or less disappeared two-thirds the way down the second, when he began to talk about Devon. He has fond memories of a poppy field that Mum and he got it together in. Awkward to listen to. It's why he sent poppies, he says.

My question about tomorrow startles him from his reverie. He straightens his back, shifts to the edge of his seat and reaches for the new pint as though he would like to glug it in one and head off.

'No pressure,' I say quickly. 'It's just I was thinking of scattering her ashes at Cremorne Point. She said in her diary the place made her happy. It's the only thing she mentioned about her trip here.'

His shoulders droop, and he shakes his head mournfully. 'How could I have missed her?' he says to his beer.

'So, I was thinking,' I say, 'you might want to come along with Matilda and me. Help us to give Mum a send-off.'

Before he got started on Devon, after his rosy recollections of the bedsit in Maida Vale, he phoned home to tell Yvonne that he'd bumped into an old friend from England. Not altogether a lie, but his stammer worsened and he went through a mini-version of his shrinking act, trying to disappear into his chair. I had the impression this was his normal mode with his wife, that he was uncomfortable asserting his plans above hers.

'Anyway, you'd be welcome,' I repeat, and he smiles vaguely and nods.

I'm not sure if it's a yes or a no. There's no point in sweating it. I sit back, close my eyes and think of Mum, young and in love. Desolation takes hold of me. It's not right that she's dead.

Nancy climbed the four flights of stairs slowly and let herself in.

Emptiness. Absence.

A faint sound of music came from Laura's bedsit next door, something classical, but she couldn't face Laura, couldn't speak to anyone right now.

More than once she had seen disdain flicker across Laura's face at something Oz said. All Laura saw was a boy. 'Easy come, easy go,' she would say.

Not easy. Unbearably painful.

Nancy dropped the keys on the draining board, crossed to the bed and crawled beneath the duvet in search of his warmth and his smell.

It had happened too fast, too abruptly. She hadn't been able to slow time hurtling forward, only last night arriving back here from Devon, falling into deep sleep, dragging themselves from bed in the half-darkness this morning, grabbing the rucksack and hand luggage that she'd helped him pack a week earlier, and heading off for Heathrow on the new Piccadilly Underground link.

His body bumping against hers on the escalator.

It was fine to cry at Heathrow. No one took any notice. Three times he'd kissed her and set off towards the departure gate. Mike went through the first time, but Oz shied away and came back. The second time he got only halfway there before swivelling on his heel and near running at her, streaming with tears.

'Go,' she'd said.

Part of her had willed it. Part of her had craved the time and the silence that would open up with his absence. She would take care to have things arranged for when he came back so she wouldn't be so overwhelmed. He would be calmer then. He'd get a job, have other interests, wouldn't be around her all the time. They could get a flat with more than one room.

'I can't leave you.'

'Go,' she'd said. 'Go.'

And he had obeyed her. He had passed through the barrier. But still she could see him. Still he was there.

His eyes. His tears.

He'd raised his hand, waved and turned to the right.

He was gone.

She'd stared, hoping to see him again.

Gone from the escalator. Gone from the Underground. Gone from this room and this bed. Here was the time and the silence. There was no one to see these tears, no remedy in hugging a pillow.

She sat up. Looked around her. It would be okay, she told herself; in just a few months he'd be back. Meanwhile this ache would ease and she'd think things through sensibly. She hadn't known how shocking absence could be, that someone so there could be so abruptly not there. The silence was terrible. She reached for the radio.

It was then that she noticed them. Her pills lying by the radio on the table beside the bed where she'd left them a week ago, forgetting to pack them in her haste to be on the road west, away from Heathrow.

When I open my eyes, I find Oz is staring at me.

'What?' I say hoarsely. 'What?'

'I don't know. It's just... I still can't get my head around you turning up here. Lizzie said you seemed troubled.'

I'm cheered by the memory of Lizzie. Her warm, throaty voice, the hug in her kitchen. 'I *was* troubled,' I say with feeling. 'I still am.'

I wait for him to ask why, but he glances at his watch, frowning.

Then I get it. 'For Christ's sake,' I say. 'You think I'm some kind of a stalker? Get over yourself. I didn't come just to find you. Not even mainly for that.' He has offloaded his grief onto me. Now he can hear mine. 'I'm your son, and I'm troubled. Does that count for nothing?'

His glance flickers to the barman and his customer, who are watching us. I lean forward, grab his shoulder.

'I'm losing my child, goddammit. That's what matters. My marriage is belly-up. My wife's going back to the States, taking Matty with her, any day now, and there's nothing I can do. Or okay, there are things I can do, but not fairly—I would have to drag it through the courts, and for what? Do you think they would give her to me, huh? Do you think so?'

He shakes his head helplessly.

'On my own? No support?' I lean closer. 'Not even a pathetic excuse for a dad in Australia. Whereas Gina has her mother itching to take over as parent-in-chief and a whole network of friends and relations. I've begged her to stay, but she won't. New Year's Eve, when I called you and shouted at you, the idea came to me. I said, "Hang on. I'm taking Matty to Sydney first." *That's* why I'm here.'

I fling myself back on the seat and suck hard at my pint. I give the man at the bar two fingers, and he turns back to the cricket. The barman turns up the sound.

'Hiding,' says Oz.

I look up, and there it is, the thing I've needed: a look of understanding in my father's eyes. A roar of applause bursts from the TV.

'Buying time,' I say, breathing more easily. 'But Jesus, it's so bloody hard.' I sit forward again. 'Tougher by the minute. I've never been with her twenty-four-seven like this. I can't bear it to end. I can't move to Connecticut—Gina will divorce me, and I won't get a green card. I'll have to fly back and forth, spend time with Matty in motels and rented apartments. I detest Connecticut, but what choice do I have?'

Oz drops his gaze and runs a finger round the rim of his glass before looking up again. 'Children steal your life,' he says.

'What?'

He's looking straight at me with Matilda's astonishing green eyes. 'I m-m-mean it absolutely,' he stammers. 'That's what they do.'

I stare at him.

'She got p-p-pregnant on purpose,' he says.

Shit. That's enough. 'You just took off, you bastard.'

He has his hand on my arm, trying to speak.

I won't let him. 'A few lousy cards, a few slushy emails, guilty valentines—oh dear, what a trial for you. While she had to marry poor old Ted.'

The barman and his customer are staring again.

'And she couldn't even do that right. She hoarded your miserable messages, and—'

'Listen,' he's saying. 'Listen. It wasn't Na-Na-Na...'

'Spit it out, for God's sake.'

'It wasn't Tigger who got pregnant on purpose. It

was Yvonne.'

'Yvonne?'

'Pregnant with Ben. You happened by accident. Tigger forgot her pills. Forgot to take them to Devon.'

'Tigger?' I'm staring.

'Your m—'

'My mother is Tigger?'

His face flushes pink. 'Just privately, between her and me. It was easier to say. And she was very b-bouncy.' He ventures a smile. 'She was wonderful.'

I snort, trying to stay furious. 'Bloody hell. And I supposed she called you Pooh?'

'N-n-no,' he says, blushing scarlet. 'Sillier than that. I was P-piglet.'

For a split second, I don't take it in. Then I do.

'Shit.'

At last I know who to be angry with.

But she doesn't deserve it.

I can't control the emotion. Oz has his hand on mine, and I'm throwing it off, lurching up and away from the table and heading for the Gents, which is empty, thank goodness. And I'm looking at my nonsensical face in the mirror, flushed with drink, yellow round the eyes with fast-fading bruises, and I'm watching my mouth contort with the grief that claws its way out of me, for my bouncy mum who used to infuriate Ted by calling Oz's child Piglet.

Nancy looked out across the swollen, black Thames at the lights of the Royal Festival Hall. Behind her the Underground entrance sucked in commuters. Beside her Harry was hesitating, forming diplomatic words. She'd hoped for understanding, expected mockery, but what she sensed was suspicion, a drawing away.

Why the hell had she told him? He was watching the home-going crowd stream past as though waiting for a chance to dive into it.

Finally he took her hand in its knitted grey glove from the Embankment wall and planted a kiss in its woolly palm. 'Does Oz know?' he said.

She shook her head. 'There's no rush to tell him.'

She hadn't told anyone. She hadn't been to a doctor. She hadn't confessed to her parents. They would only start haranguing her and ordering her about. Then this afternoon she and Harry had been alone in the office, and though she'd kept her eyes down she had sensed him watching her, lolling back on his chair behind his big wooden desk, and when finally she'd looked up he'd been kind, not flirtatious. He'd said, 'Are you all right?' and her need to tell someone, anyone, even clever-dick Harry, had overwhelmed her.

'Are you sure?' he said now. 'He may not stand by you. He may do the dirty.'

She turned to face him, detaching her hand. 'Of course. But it won't be the dirty. He has a perfect right to opt out.'

'Very noble of you. Very modern.'

'It's not his fault I forgot my pills.'

'But still—'

'And he's only seventeen.'

'Seventeen?' Harry rocked on his heels. 'Are you

serious? What in hell are you playing at, Nancy?'

'I know it sounds odd—'

'More than odd. He's a baby himself—'

'He isn't. That's—'

'Did his mother know he was out?'

'She's dead.'

'Cue the violins. So you're his mother now, are you?'

'Not at all. Nothing like that.'

'He's a teenager, Nancy. You're an adult.'

'Look, shut up. At least I'm not *married*.'

Harry's mouth hung open. The heads of a few passersby turned, mildly interested in what must look like a standard boss-secretary, end-of-affair tiff.

She tried to explain. 'He's seventeen, but not seventeen. I didn't take him seriously at first. He came out of the blue at me, and he wouldn't leave off, and I found I didn't mind. It began to seem normal. I can't explain it. I can't figure it out or decide to believe in it, but when I was with him it was different, the age gap didn't matter, I felt...'

She stopped. Harry's expression was relentlessly sceptical. 'Love?' he said.

'In a way. Much, much more complicated, but yes.'

He snorted. 'It's a fantasy, Nancy. He's a spotty kid, and you're an idiot.'

'No spots,' she said, grinning. 'Not a single spot anywhere.'

Harry pulled a face. 'Which makes him a fully fledged grownup? Does he have a job to come back to?'

She shook her head. Angry.

'Any qualifications?'

'Harry, leave off. I'm not Oz's mother, and you're not my father, okay? I don't need this. I told you because I wanted to share it with somebody, but I'm wishing I hadn't.'

'You told me because you're terrified.'

'I'm happy and excited,' she lied furiously. 'This is something I've decided to do for myself.'

'Of course you're bloody terrified.' His eyes followed the crowds hurrying past. 'And you should tell the poor little sod and make him bloody terrified too.'

'But that's it, don't you see?' she insisted. 'That's exactly why I'm not telling him.'

'Australia is wonderful, but I m-miss you,' Oz had said only last night on the phone. His infrequent calls were hurried and tense, stammered against the countdown of seconds he'd so expensively prepaid. He'd been to Melbourne and Sydney, to Alice Springs and Ayers Rock. He was back in Sydney now, hanging out with some friends he'd made there. He couldn't wait to see her. It was very hot. Mike would be there soon, and they would fly home. Mike had gone north to Brisbane and maybe the Barrier Reef. How was she? Did she miss him? Would she marry him? Had she met someone else?

She didn't say she was pregnant. She kept promising herself she wouldn't say it, not on the phone. She wasn't going to alarm him or derail his adventure. It would be wrong to interrupt his three minutes of rushed speech with her own garbled announcement.

But more importantly, every time she imagined telling him, that was when she became terrified. She would say the word 'pregnant' or 'baby' and hear Oz's silence or hesitancy. And whatever he said next they would have no way of knowing, ever again, what they meant to each other. She didn't know if she loved him enough to marry him. She didn't know if he loved her enough to take on a baby. She didn't want to end up like her mother, bound by duty and habit to a grudging man. She would rather be alone for the rest of her life. She wouldn't be alone. She would have the baby.

She had to find a way to say all this to Oz and show him how completely she meant it. She imagined and re-imagined it many times. He would come home when he was ready to come home. She would meet him at the Heathrow arrivals gate. He would be tired and ecstatic. She would wear a big chunky sweater, so he couldn't see. They would ride the Underground to Maida Vale and climb the four floors to the flat, she ahead, he behind. If they bumped into Laura, she would smile warningly. The boy is back; mind your manners. Once inside, he would grin and hold out his hand. He would start peeling her clothes off. But before he could see her breasts or her tummy-bump, she would say the words she kept rehearsing, revising. They weren't right yet, but they would be, because they had to be right.

'Listen, Oz. I've something important to tell you. Please don't speak until I've said everything. There's no one but you, no one at all, and I love you. I forgot my pills when we went to Devon, that's all, so I'm having a baby.'

It would be there in his eyes at that moment. He wouldn't be able to hide it. Would his face shut down, as her father's would do if he knew, as Harry's had done five minutes ago, or would he be eagerly interrupting her, rushing to lay his life at her feet?

'Listen, please listen,' she would interrupt back. 'We barely know each other. We need time, and the baby doesn't change that in the slightest. I want us both to choose freely. I want *you* to choose freely.'

'I'll tell him when he gets back,' she said now to Harry, 'when I can see in his eyes if he's poor sod or lucky sod. If it's poor sod, he can go, I won't stop him. I'll *make* him.'

Harry shook his head impatiently. 'But meanwhile your own choices are leaking away.'

Her gaze was drawn back to the river. The water was almost still, on the turn, glassily reflecting the lights of Hungerford bridge. 'My choices are fine,' she said. 'This is entirely my choice.'

'Look. Nancy.' He spoke close to her ear. 'You have to understand this. I'm sorry, but I need to say it as plainly as I can, while there's still time. I'm not going to leave Cathy.'

For a moment or two she couldn't speak, the words in her mouth were so violent.

She couldn't get past them. They had to come out. 'Shit, Harry. Fuck you. Fuck off. You just don't get it, do you? This isn't about you!'

And she was running across the road, furious and tearful, into the path of a bus that blared its horn at her. Up the steps to the station, weaving in among the commuters, pushing through the barrier and down past the people clogging the escalator. Impatient to ride the Underground home to Maida Vale and climb the four floors, where she would tiptoe past Laura's door and pause inside her own, spreading her fingers across her stomach, calming herself, imagining her baby growing safely, untainted by the world's assumptions and judgements, in need of no one's understanding but hers.

As the spasm of grief passes, I'm seized by the conviction that Oz will take this chance to leave. I hurry back across the lobby. The desk clerk is in the bar doorway with her back to me. She turns. 'Mr Jonnson?'

Beyond I see Matilda in her pyjama bottoms and T-shirt, standing beside Oz. Her hair's sleep-flattened on one side. I leap towards her. 'What's happened?'

'My fault,' says the clerk. 'I woke her. I called your room with the message. Your wife said it was urgent.'

'What message?'

'And your kiddie came down. I tried to tell her no, but—'

'Can I talk to Mommy?'

'Your wife sounded fine,' the desk clerk assures me. 'It sounded like good news. But she asks will you please call her back.'

Good news? Has she decided to stay after all? I draw Matilda close with one hand, reach for my pint with the other. 'Okay, thank y—'

Oz's mobile erupts into *Money, money, money*. He jumps up, pulling it from his pocket. 'G'day. Daniels Days Out. How can I—Oh hi, Yvonne.' He drops into his chair and half-turns away from us, hunched over the phone. He does his trick of losing several sizes. 'N-no... I'm still with m-m-my friend from England.'

'I want Mommy,' Matilda whinges.

'I couldn't stop her coming down,' says the clerk.

'Ssh, please, I need to listen.'

'Ma-Ma-Mark Jonnson,' Oz says.

After a pause, he names the hotel, bending forward, his eyes fixed on his shoes. 'But I'm too p-pissed to dr-drive to the... Yes... N-n-no, but—'

For a while he keeps listening, chewing a fingernail.

He's shaking his head. 'B-but Yvonne, it isn't worth getting a cab. I'll stay here and take the coach to the garage tomo-mo-mo—'

He holds the phone from his ear, lifting his face to mine while her voice carries on. He looks helpless. I nod and point at the ceiling. 'Stay with us,' I say.

He brings the phone to his mouth. 'So, Yvonne... Yvonne... So I'll see you tomo-mo—'

She's still arguing the odds. He hits the off button and winces. His freckled face is bright crimson.

'Okay if my dad stays in our room tonight?' I say to the desk clerk.

'Sure. No worries,' she says. 'Least we can do after giving you such a fright.'

'I want to talk to Mommy. Can I talk to Mommy? *Please* can I?'

I stoop to lift her. 'Of course. Absolutely. First thing in the morning.'

The clerk says, 'But—'

'Thank you, I know,' I say. 'I'll be down soon to deal with that.'

I rock Matilda in my arms. 'How clever of you to find me, Little. Really clever, so clever. So let's go up in the lift, shall we, with Grandpa Oz? Get you safe in bed. Ring Mommy the minute you wake.'

Twenty minutes later I'm back in the lobby dialling London while the clerk pretends not to eavesdrop.

It rings through to voicemail. 'Hello. This is Nancy Jonnson's number. So sorry I can't come to the phone right now. Please leave a message.'

I hang up, moaning softly, resting my head on the wall.

Time passes. I have to ring Gina. Pick up. Dial again. Brace myself to hear Mum, but this time Gina answers. 'Hi,' she says.

I can't speak. All I can think is that her voice is not Mum's.

'Hello?' she repeats.

'I never thought to change it,' I whisper.

'Pardon me? Is that you, Mark?'

'Mum's voicemail message. You must have heard it when you called me from Kilburn. You should have told me.'

'Sure. Sorry. I'll erase it today,' she says. 'So have you met with your dad?'

'No, please don't erase it.' I'm still reeling. 'Do you know what time it is here?'

'Have you met with him?'

'We spent today on his bus—'

'So you're done in Australia, right?'

She isn't interested in Oz. She sounds excited, expectant.

'Well, no, we're not done,' I say. 'We've only just started to—'

'Because I'm sorry, Mark, but something has come up. We have to be in the States. I'm not kidding. I need Matilda here on the first flight.'

The floor tilts, the lobby quadruples in width, the clerk recedes through the thickening air. Powerless to interrupt or protest, I sense Gina's words forming like lead shot.

'Because I have a job, Mark. It's awesome, a real break for me. An internship has come up with a congressman my old Vassar professor knows. The guy's a real hotshot in health care reform. Plus there'll be some pay, so I won't just be freeloading off Dad and there could be a serious job at the end of it. I emailed my résumé, and I'm way older than he had in mind of course, but we talked on the phone, and he says the Vassar reference is impressive, and—what do you know? —if I can get there by yesterday, the job's mine!'

My mouth's dry. 'That's great, Gina,' I say. 'Well done, but—'

'I've gotta start right away, Mark. He can't wait. So I'm sorry, but what I need is Matilda here on the next plane, okay?'

I clutch at the wall and try to speak with authority. 'Not okay, Gina. We just got here. We only met Oz a few hours ago. He's with us now, and—'

'Listen,' she says, 'I could lose this job. How much time do you want with some guy you don't even know who knocked up your mother?'

'For pity's sake, Gina, we still have jetlag—'

'Big deal.'

'Okay... right... but Matty,' grabbing at straws, 'it's her birthday on Thursday. I've promised her Bondi Beach not Bangkok airport. She needs until Friday.'

Silence.

'You won't lose the job, Gina. He wants you. A couple more days is all. I'll book a flight for Friday. We gain a day flying back—we'll be there Saturday morning.'

'Okay,' she concedes, 'but call me with the flight number as soon as you know it. I'll book us straight through to Hartford. Gotta go now. Lots of stuff to sort, packing to do—'

'Hang on,' I say. 'When Matty calls you, don't tell her about this, okay? I'll sit her down, choose the right moment, maybe after her birthday—'

'Yeah,' she says. 'Okay. Thank you, that's best. Oh, and by the way, Mark, something else. I don't know if you should tell her this too, but Mog died yesterday. I paid the vet bill for Jane. He stopped eating. Had a tumour or something.'

She pauses, but I can't find any words.

'Speak soon, Mark,' she says. 'I'll let you get back to your dad, but make sure to ring me with the flight number. Bye.' And she's killed the call.

Tuesday

'Out of road,' Gina says. 'We've run out of road.'

I'm trying to sleep, but I can't get past a waking dream of a road winding downhill through a rainforest swarming with predatory life. I have hold of Matilda's hand, but my fingers slip with sweat, and she's wriggling, trying to escape me, saying, 'Mommy. Where's Mommy?' We turn another corner and the road abruptly runs out. A man stands by a jetty, his back to us, looking out across the sluggish green water to where a giant crocodile stares into my eyes. When the man turns and sees us, he starts to shrivel until he's a wizened Munchkin smaller than Matilda and still shrinking. I jump forward, trying to catch him before he disappears. 'You're not Nancy,' he says.

I groan and turn over in search of a weightless position, geeing myself to dive in and wrestle the crocodile, but I look down and my feet are sinking in mud, and Matilda's escaping me and running, not to the river and her grandfather but back towards Battersea. 'Not yet, Matty,' I plead. 'Stay with me,' but the words are a whisper, straining against the parched roof of my mouth.

Sirens howl far away in the city. I snap my eyes open and sit bolt upright, tense from head to toe, ready to fight for her. The sun blasts in across a room littered with crumpled, stale clothes and unconscious bodies. Oz sprawls on his stomach across the divan base of Matilda's bed. She's flat out on her back on the mattress on the floor. There's the morning-after stink of the hard drinking that Oz and I got into last night.

Oz cannot help me.

I disentangle myself from the sweat-sodden sheet. My head swims, and my legs threaten to buckle. I lurch to the basin, pull a glass of water from the tap, down it, refill it and reach for the wall switch. Cooled air begins to waft over us.

Oz is spark out, softly snoring, his hand trailing the carpet, his face squashed against the mattress. His mouth hangs open, and the sideways droop of his stubbled cheeks shows his age. Freckled back, green boxers, pale legs. Like father, like son, and what miserable messes we've both made of our lives. We talked for hours on the balcony after Matilda fell asleep. We carried on until the sky began to lighten, knocking back whisky miniatures. I shared my wretchedness, then in fits and starts he blurted his own.

He first met Yvonne at some backpackers' knees up. She and her flatmate took him and Mike in, free billet, so when they came back from Ayers Rock, they dropped by again. Yvonne knew he had a girlfriend in England, he was just passing through. He should have gone to Brisbane with Mike, but he didn't. He was a sucker for sex.

And then Yvonne was pregnant, and when he told her, 'I said all along I'm with Nancy,' she began crying and arguing. And her parents came round with the local vicar in tow, lecturing him about his responsibilities. They wouldn't listen; he had trouble explaining himself; he wasn't sure what was right. They were going ahead, fixing a date for the wedding.

He rang Mum and spilled it all out, wanting her to save him, to insist that he come back to England for her, to give him the backbone to tell Yvonne no. But all Mum would say was, 'It's your choice.' She asked him was he sure what he wanted. Was it Yvonne or her, or maybe it was neither? 'We barely know each other,' she told him. 'What do *you* want to do?'

He thought Mum didn't want him. Yvonne wanted him; he knew that. Yvonne was crying and pregnant. He very much needed the crying and shouting to stop.

At this point in the story I was confused. 'But Mum was pregnant too. Didn't she tell you? You told Lizzie you knew.'

I'm watching him sleep now, remembering how he moaned and squeezed his eyes shut before answering. 'She said it made no difference—I was still free to choose. I should only go back to her if I was sure that I wanted to. I cried for a day.'

He was almost crying last night. He gripped the balcony wall and stared out across the city, his voice thick with drink. 'Hitched a lift out of Sydney, headed for the outback. Couldn't talk to the driver. Couldn't see the road.'

'She wanted you to choose her,' I told him, but he shook his head.

'How can I know that? I never could work out what she wanted.'

Yeah, I thought. Yeah, Mum, that was always your problem. What the hell did you want from any of us?

'Ted told me she wanted you.'

As I said this, I realised Ted was guessing: all he knew for certain was that Mum didn't want him.

'One reason for never much contact,' Oz was saying, 'the cards and the valentines, it was emo-motionally too hard. Why would I put myself back in that turmoil?'

Through the blur of alcohol I was seeing how near Mum and Oz had come, how different the whole thing could have been. She should have confided in Sally or someone else impartial who could have sussed out what she wanted and told her to speak plainly to Oz.

He slid to the balcony floor, hunching a shoulder to wipe his eyes on his shirt. We looked at each other.

'I still don't get why she kept it secret, the fact you were my dad.'

'Her parents,' he said. 'Didn't want her parents to

248

know.'

'But why lie to *me?*'

'Why unsettle you? You had Ted.'

'Except I didn't, did I? Had him down as a shit, a deserter. Poor sod didn't deserve it. How could she not care about that?'

'Dunno.' He was slurring. 'Maybe didn't know you were angry.'

Then, loud in my face, Oz's vehemence came out of nowhere. 'You were fine. You had *her.*' He sounded unlike himself. Bitter. More like Ted, in fact.

'Are you still that hacked off?'

He slumped back. 'Suppose.'

'She should have told you she loved you, right? She should have made you go back to her?'

But, 'No,' he was insisting. 'Not with Nancy. Never hacked off with Nancy. One I'm hacked off with is Yvonne. No more kids.'

It took me a second or two to compute. 'Yvonne said no to more kids?'

'Me. I said no to more kids, and then she went frigid on me.'

'Other way round with us,' I mumbled. 'It was Gina said no, me who went frigid.'

For a minute I was silent, then, 'Your last email to Mum. You said you nearly separated. Why don't you?'

'What?'

'Yvonne. You're still with her.'

'Mmn.' Shrugging helplessly.

'Why?'

No answer.

'Something must keep you.'

He was staring with glazed eyes at the night sky. 'Suppose it's fine most of the time.'

I followed his gaze. 'With no sex?'

'Sex sometimes.'

'And you've had affairs, right?'

The sky began to rotate. I closed my eyes, and the balcony span out of control. When I opened them again, the deceleration nearly wrenched my brain from my skull. Oz was still mumbling on.

'... so not really. Women on the bus sometimes. Now and again. Well, rarely again.' Laughing. 'Stay behind at the ferry. Day trippers.'

I tried to focus, to find something matey to say, but he beat me to it, mildly triumphant. 'Come to think of it, cheers. This is probably first time I've stopped out all night.'

What a pathetic achievement. I leave him sleeping now, slide the window open and step onto the balcony, stooping to pick up the bottles. I vaguely notice the city sirens are louder, heading north to the Harbour, but I'm not paying attention. I'm five years old, miserable behind Ted's sofa, picking at the hole in the tweed. Arms reach for me. 'Come along, Piglet.'

I abandon the balcony, slip the bottles in the bin, then kneel beside Oz and nudge him awake. 'You idiot,' I say. 'You should have gone back to her. You should have taken the chance.'

He blinks and stares. 'But I'm still pissed,' he says in a clogged voice.

I give him a moment to focus. 'Or when I was five,' I say. 'When she split from Ted. When Yvonne had iced over. Why didn't you go back to Mum then?'

He sits up on an elbow. 'Be-Ben was five too. And I still wasn't sure she wanted me. I nev-never was sure.'

'Of course she bloody wanted you,' I say, willing it to be true.

'She never once said it. She always said I was free.'

'But you weren't free, were you?' It's my turn to shout. 'She was showing you how. She was giving it to you, and you weren't understanding.'

He shows no recognition. This loser has never been free in his life.

'Daddy,' Matilda says, rolling off her mattress and rubbing her eyes. 'Daddy, I'm hungry.'

Christ, I can't bear it. Who am I to judge Oz? I'm the bigger loser by far. He didn't know me, I didn't know him, but I've been this little girl's father and now, however often I fly back and forth to Connecticut, I'll have messed up on that.

Sydney's on fire. We turned on the TV, and it's all over the news. A suburb called Killara is having water dumped on it from a giant helicopter. They're evacuating people from their homes and want everyone to check their back yards. The blaze is well north of here, beyond the great fire-barrier of the Harbour, but it's fuelling my edginess, adding to my misery and guilt. Ashes to ashes: I picked an apt day to throw Mum to the antipodean winds.

'So, do you want to come with us?' I say to Oz as we finish our room-service brunch.

'I'd like that.' He glances around. 'Where is she?'

Matilda says, 'Here,' and bounds across to the desk. She runs back with the freezer container and plonks it in his hands. He stares at it.

'Take a look inside if you like,' I say.

He pops the lid and peels it back.

'It doesn't get you any nearer to her,' I say. 'At least I haven't found that it does.'

Matilda peers in as well, joggling Oz's knee.

'Take care, Matty,' I say. 'We don't want to spill it till we're at Cremorne Point.'

There's a soft knock: room service wanting the tray. Matilda dashes to open the door, and a woman steps in.

Holy shit, it's Yvonne. I leap to my feet. Small, tanned, middle aged, I recognise her from the photographs on Lizzie's laptop, and my first, fleeting thought in the rush of panic is that she looks a little like Mum. A hint in the shape of the face.

I find my voice, hold out a hand. 'Yvonne. Come in. Hello. Good to meet you.'

'Hello,' shouts Matilda.

We're dressed and decent, thank goodness, but the place is a tip. Yvonne closes the door and leans against it, staring at us. She has small features, short, fluffy, brown hair, large brown eyes. Frown lines where her nose meets her eyebrows.

'So, what's going on here?'

I look at Oz, but he's speechless, still holding the ashes. I rescue them from him, pick the lid off the floor, reseal the container and put it back on the desk. All the while Yvonne's staring, and I'm feeling instinctive dislike. I take conscious breaths, trying to calm myself.

She steps towards Oz. 'You're this man's dad, they told me downstairs. I said they were wrong, but they weren't, were they?'

Oz tries to speak, 'He's—'

'An old friend from England? D'you think I'm fresh off the boat?' Her voice is soft-edged but insistent. She turns back to me. 'Mark Jonnson. That your real name?'

I nod.

'And it's true, you're his son?'

I look to Oz, but he's busy shrinking to nothing. Matilda has retreated behind me. I reach for her hand.

'I'll take that as a yes,' Yvonne says.

'He is,' admits Oz, 'bu-but—'

'And your mother is...?'

'Nancy,' I say.

Her eyes widen.

I step forward, touch her arm. 'It's a helluva shock. I was shocked too. I only found out myself at Christmas. Here, sit.'

I lead her to the armchair. Matilda hangs back, but I

252

draw her forward to be introduced, while I squat on eye-level with both of them. 'It isn't bad news, Yvonne,' I say. 'Not when you get used to it. Your Ben has a brother. His kids have a cousin—Matilda.'

'Who's Ben?' says Matilda.

'When were you born?' Yvonne asks me.

'Seventy-nine.'

She blinks. 'What month?'

'June,' I say. 'England. Nine months after Oz left.'

She twists to look at her husband, who hovers white-faced by the window as though he would like to jump out of it.

'Why bullshit me?' she asks him.

He can't speak.

'Last night. On the phone. Why tell lies?'

He looks physically ill.

She doesn't have to know everything, I'm thinking. She doesn't need to know they were in touch.

Matilda leans heavily against me, shunting Uno cards around on the floor with her big toe. Oz opens his mouth to say I don't know what.

I jump in. 'Because it was a helluva shock to him too, Yvonne, us turning up yesterday out of the blue. It knocked the wind out of him. I came because Mum died in November. She never told a soul about Oz, not even me. Going through her things I found out. Managed to trace him.'

'Nancy's dead?' Yvonne says.

I'm rocked by her directness. Her face relaxes, there's a glimmer of triumph, and that's it: I loathe her.

We're not off the hook yet. There's no softening. For a few seconds she says nothing, just looks at me, and despite the petite features I'm seeing the crocodile.

What's the worst she can do? I offer my hand again. 'So, it's good to meet you.'

'Who's Ben?' repeats Matilda.

'Oz and Yvonne's son,' I say softly. 'He's a grownup like me.'

Yvonne gets to her feet, looking past me at Oz, who shifts from one foot to the other, chewing on a finger, his gaze flitting uneasily. Is she going to call him to order and march him out of our lives?

Her face finds a stiff smile. She accepts my hand briefly and drops it.

'And you're in Sydney for how long?'

'Until Friday.'

'Going where after?'

'Back to London,' I say miserably.

'Ah.'

The worry's gone from her voice. It's the answer she wants.

'My mother died in November,' I repeat, but she's turning away.

'So say again, why take the piss, Oz?'

I smile encouragement at him.

'I d-d-didn't want to upset you,' he says.

'Exactly right,' I say. 'He wasn't expecting us. I ambushed him mid-tour, held him hostage at the ferry, insisted he spend the evening with me, plied him with drink.'

Oz grins. My eyes lock with the crocodile's. 'So... a drink, Yvonne? A coffee? A beer?'

'No thanks.'

There's a short silence while she marshals herself. She's no fool, this woman. I give her a smile that says I'm no fool either. Oz still looks edgy, scared probably about punishments in store, but she's his problem not mine. What's bothering me is Matilda. She's too quiet, all her noise and energy in hiding. She leans against me and fiddles with my watch strap, her eyes fixed on Yvonne.

'Hey, are you all right, Little?'

'What do you mean, I'm a cousin?' she whispers.

'Is it okay to tell her?' I check.

'Up to you,' Yvonne says coldly.

'Well, Matty,' I say. 'Ben's my half-brother, and he has two little children, a boy and a girl, younger than you. They're your cousins.'

She's immediately back to her rumbustious self. 'Can I *meet* them? Can I *meet* them?'

Yvonne shakes her head, smiling tightly. I shake mine too. But, 'They can come to my party,' she pleads.

Which has me thinking, why not? Why shouldn't these little kids meet each other?

'Bondi Beach,' I say. 'It's her birthday on Thursday. You'd be very welcome. How about it? Oz?'

He starts, glances nervously at Yvonne and mumbles, 'I've a tour tomorrow, but I'm free Thursday, so...' He leaves the sentence hanging. 'Bondi's not the nicest beach.' He tries to rescue himself. 'You'd like Manly better.'

'Bondi Beach, Bondi Beach,' chants Matilda, bouncing back with a vengeance.

'Say yes, Yvonne, eh?' I give her my warmest smile. 'Bring Ben and the kids to meet us.'

'Please,' says Matilda.

She's going to say no.

'We're flying on Friday,' I remind her. 'We'll be out of your hair.'

Her lips tighten.

Try blackmail. I keep smiling, remembering to crinkle my eyes. 'Ben would be disappointed to hear that he missed us.'

I can see her computing this.

'But never mind, I can find him on Facebook,' I say.

It's working. She's wavering. I reach out, touch her shoulder. 'There's absolutely no harm in us, Yvonne. Mum's dead. We're your relatives. We only want to say hi.'

'Okay, I'll ask him,' she says.

I contain my excitement, nod soberly. 'If we're out, leave a message. Whereabouts on the beach, what time. We'll be there.'

Yvonne's at the door. 'Are you coming, Oz?'

He gets up and follows her.

'Cremorne Point?' I say as he passes.

He jumps, 'Oh,' and spins on his heel to face me. Yvonne's through the door and moving off along the corridor without a backward glance.

'Granny wants you to come,' says Matilda.

His face can't find an expression. The grin it settles on is so awkward it's more of a grimace. 'I'm sorry.' He's backing away, reaching for the door handle.

And then the door's closed, and he's gone.

The hot breeze carries a trace of something, maybe the smell of burning. The Killara fire's under control, they say, but the ferry passengers swap worried remarks about threatened homes, too many years without decent rain, global warming. I lean my back on the rail, half listening, clutching rucksack to chest, feeling the shape of the plastic container inside. Behind me Cremorne Point draws nearer.

I can't stop watching Matilda. She's dashing from one side of the deck to the other, thrilled to be afloat again. 'Look, Daddy,' she calls, pointing at the grotesque, grinning gate of Luna Park. 'They have a wild mouse ride.'

'Not a chance,' I say.

She waves up at the bridge before running to have another look at the Opera House. The view feels illusory, like a film backdrop. The only real place left is Heathrow, where in four days' time Gina will meet us before marching Matilda straight through another departure gate.

'Have a heart. She'll need a break from flying,' I tried

to insist, but Gina was adamant. 'He can't keep on holding this job for me, Mark. What's another eight hours? She can sleep on the plane.'

I'll have to ride the Tube home from Heathrow alone. One moment my daughter, solid, substantial, arms, legs, hair, eyes, gapped teeth, noise and nattering, unpredictable worry and loveliness. The next moment vanished.

I can't stand it. I'm desperately racking my brains for some way to prevent it. I need to take Matty home with me to Mum's little two-up, two-down house, with Jane's kids running in and out as they please. I need lazy days with Matilda in Hove, showing Ted that my resentment is a thing of the past. A weekend in Bristol getting to know Lizzie. A whole new life with my daughter. I would drop her at her new school on my way in to work, pick her up on my way back, stroll home with her via Asda. I would work with new energy, nag the college to provide one-to-one teaching, teach better myself. I wonder how Comfort's getting on.

The heat gains intensity as the ferry slows to dock. We're here. They're tying up, releasing the passengers, and I'm stumbling down the ramp, feeling Matilda's fingers curl and uncurl in my sweaty palm. Turn right, it's a stone's throw from here to the waterfront park. I'm worried that someone may tell us we can't scatter Mum here. Ash is inert, but there are probably rules that we're breaking.

'Does it hurt when they burn you?' Matilda asks.

'Absolutely not.' I halt and crouch down beside her. 'Granny didn't feel the bus hit her or anything after that.'

Matilda nods violently to convince herself. 'She's in heaven, where everyone's happy.'

My face gives me away.

'Isn't she?'

'What I think, Little,' I say, 'is that heaven's just a

story to make us feel better. I think Granny's completely gone. But she wasn't hurt; she's not hurting.'

Matilda's expression hovers on the brink of something.

'Some people believe in it,' I say. 'In heaven, God, angels. Maybe your Mommy does sometimes, and your Grandma and Grandpa in Connecticut definitely do. I won't mind if you decide you believe in it too.'

She squints through the sun at me, her head on one side. 'A story like Santa?'

'Exactly.'

'And aliens?'

'You've got it,' I say.

I straighten up, and we carry on walking.

'There's a bit of Granny inside the box,' she says firmly.

'And lots more in our memories.'

Here we are in a small public park, approaching the end of the point. It seems nothing much, but my mood's colouring everything. More gum trees buzzing with cicadas. A slope down to another nice view of the Harbour. No one here to savour the haze in the sky, the smell of fire on the wind.

No one here to tell us we can't.

'So, where shall we scatter Granny?' I say. 'In the sea, or up here?'

'In the sea,' says Matilda.

The dinky white lighthouse would be fun if it weren't ruined by the grey-steel security gate on the little walkway that goes out to it. There are steps down to rocks, then a crumbling iron ladder to the walkway. I go first, helping Matilda to climb down behind me. We walk out above the water as far as the gate, which bristles with spikes, left, right and skyward. The sea swell slops and pulses below us.

Matilda complains loudly. 'I want to go to the

lighthouse. Why can't we?'

I don't answer. I prise the lid off the container and hold it low so she can reach in. I dip my fingers in the ashes, feeling their slippery grain. It's not Mum, but it's the nearest I can come to her now. I grab a fistful and cast it in an arc over the water.

Should I say something formal, I wonder. Words were useless at the crematorium.

'Your turn,' I say. 'Keep your back to the wind so the ash blows away.'

She takes a handful and flings it. 'Bye bye, Granny. We love you,' she says.

'Yes,' I mumble, 'we do.'

Perhaps it's all that needs saying.

We take turns to chuck handfuls into the water and up at the sky.

'Love you, Granny.'

'Love you, Mum.'

I'm biting my lips, smiling, tears in my eyes.

I shake the dregs to a corner, meaning to pour them into my palm, but Matilda grabs the box from my hands. She whacks it hard against the gate, so the last of the ash falls on the boards beyond, and the wind gathers a trace and bears it up past the lighthouse and on.

It had struck her immediately, and it wasn't a fluke; it persisted. Even now, two weeks into her stay, except to the drunks in Kings Cross and the angry man on his plinth, she wasn't invisible.

In other cities—Florence, New York, Madrid—she'd sensed herself fade and lose colour. Tourists moved in sight-seeing bubbles, but their company with one another kept their egos strong. Sight-seeing alone in those cities, Nancy had fallen silent, almost forgetting who she was. For a while she had relished drifting like a ghost through their streets and metro stations, gazing unseen at their art treasures, eating with a paperback propped beside her and only a waiter's impersonal attention, but before long a near-desperate need had seized her to be back among colleagues and friends, feeling her substance return. She had headed home with relief, fearing more solitude would unbalance her, reduce her to muttering to herself like a bag lady.

Sometimes she'd gone out at night in those other cities, dressed in her best, not to be seen but to melt unobserved into the crowds. To the opera in Madrid. To a dubbed American movie in Florence. To peer into Tiffany's window in New York. But mostly she'd dined early and retreated to her hotel room to commune with English newspapers and novels and to check in the mirror that she still existed.

Sydney could not be more different. Here she was unassailably substantial. It had been a huge, foolish letdown to find that Oz was away, but it was impossible to mope long in this place. After a brief wobble, the turning point had come on her posh night out at the opera, the night of the Mardi Gras launch, when Circular Quay had been jam-packed with wildly celebrating gay men and lesbian women. Clutching her glass of sparkling wine, she had joined the more conventional crowd on the Opera House balcony, looking where they were pointing, sharing their excitement.

Shore to shore, the Harbour had been a pale, translucent blue in the twilight, and easing out against the grand backdrop of the bridge the QE2 had been heading their way. Nancy had whooped and waved madly with the rest. The massive liner was sliding by, smoke belching from its funnel, its decks crackling with tiny, bright flashes as dozens of its eighteen hundred passengers took her photograph. Dwarfed by it, the replica of the Bounty was keeping pace, and on the Harbourside below the Mardi Gras crowd scrambled for vantage points, cheering and aiming cameras. She'd added her voice to the cheers.

The ship had grown small, pushing on past the next headland towards Watson's Bay and the Pacific. Behind the crowd on the balcony, through the Tannoy a girl's voice had been announcing the opera—'Please take your seats now for Cossy Fan Tooty'—'cossy' rhyming with 'flossy' and 'tooty' with 'booty'—as Nancy grinned into another stranger's eyes and said, 'Wow.'

She felt her existence here if anything more keenly than in London. It would be magic to see Oz before she left, but then a wrench to part from him again and from the wonder of this city, its acceptance and helpfulness, its easy humour. 'Well done,' joked a café waiter today when she signed his MasterCard chitty. 'Forged very nicely.' 'Yes,' she said. 'I'm getting good at it.' Sometimes in the heat, she felt nostalgia for English drizzle, but as often as not the next morning she would step out to discover it was drizzling here too, as if to say, 'Is this what you want, love? We can do it.'

Most evenings she was drawn back to Circular Quay. She fell into step with the crowds that processed up and down. She waited for the moment when the setting sun ceased to illumine the objects of the earth and instead lit up the sky above the quietening Harbour. The polished pink stone of the broadwalk behind the Opera House was deep with reflections of trees, of lamps not yet lit, of the handful of people who waited with her for the city to slip into the warm, festive dark.

When the night had deepened and she could at last tear herself away, she would stroll back to the hotel, the same route each night. Up Macquarie Street past the Botanic Gardens, where the notices said, 'Please walk on the grass.' Through Hyde Park, where the vault of the gum trees was an avenue of fairy lights and the flying foxes flapped by. Last night a Chinese couple, the bride in flowing white silk and veil, had posed for their wedding snaps against the floodlit fountain, while nearby the tramps had been stretching themselves out for another night on the benches. If it weren't for Mark, she'd realised, she would be seriously thinking of trying to move to this wonderful place.

She was addicted to Sydney Ferries. She used her Rover ticket at least once a day, for no other reason than to stand at the rail transfixed by sights of the busy, blue Harbour. Today's first crossing deposited her at Neutral Bay on the North Shore, a millionaires' paradise of waterfront homes and yachts. The map offered plenty of options for picking up a return ferry, so she set off walking east towards the Pacific, past leafy, secluded mansions, following the ins and outs, ups and downs of the Harbour coastline. Quite accidentally she wandered into the park at Cremorne Point.

There were people here, but not many, and they were oddly quiet. It was the first clue to the specialness of the place. It made her pay attention. The day was hot, and the sound was the usual, unceasing racket of the cicadas. Beyond the trees she glimpsed yet another view of Sydney to die for. The wide water. The huge sky. Over there beside Circular Quay lay a newly arrived cruise ship, bigger even than the QE2. This one, Aurora, had the television presenters excited: the first ever to be too big to get under the bridge.

Her feet were still moving, carrying her towards the view. Out across the water some kind of yachting event was in progress. At least a hundred small boats flitted across the waves like mayflies: giant, fragile wings levitating tiny cores of life. The path ran out, and she followed stone steps down to rocks where a couple stood apart with their dog, taking no notice of her. Beyond was the slap of the waves against a miniature Victorian lighthouse. Arches below, screened by mesh. A lookout platform above. An ornate metal dome. All painted as white as a wedding cake.

From the rocks a ladder went down to a narrow bridge leading out to the lighthouse. A handrail on one side, open on the other, it was splashed wet, but no notice announced, 'This far and no further.' She clambered down the ladder and took off her shoes.

A dozen paces out above the water and there she was, at the lighthouse, planting her feet squarely on the boards, gripping the railing and seized by inexpressible joy. Clouds by MGM blossomed from an Opera House vanishing point. Yachts raced past from left to right, while almost within touching distance a ferry called Friendship chugged by in the other direction. In its wake, another boat—Vagabond Cruises—steamed past even closer, its passengers dancing to gypsy music and waving to her, 'Hi, hello.'

The immensity of water and sky lifted and expanded her. For minute after minute she stayed, rising from her heels to her toes, ready to fly.

It seemed impossible to let go and turn back. It seemed this joy was the truest thing she could feel. She struggled to memorise every detail. The salt smell of the wind, the exact angle of each white sail, the vast, glorious, three-hundred-and-sixty-degree moment. From now on, she promised herself, if ever her happiness faltered, if ever her life seemed dark, heavy or empty, she would think of this place, of this moment, and if the memory failed to make her smile, she would come running by plane, ferry and foot, to be here again.

2009, Thursday

So, here we are on the steps to the beach, deafened by the deluge of rain that threatens to break the umbrella I bought for Matilda to use as a sunshade. Despite the rain, the heat is oppressive. Sweat springs all over my body, dripping into my eyes, rolling down my back.

The pink colonnade of the Pavilion behind us is crowded with people sheltering from the downpour. Groups of boys, groups of girls, a little, ancient, tottering Chinese couple, a Muslim family, the wife in head-to-toe black, a troupe of Japanese tourists aiming their lenses at rain and gulls. Kids in trunks and bikinis shriek as they scramble up past us from the steaming, pockmarked sand.

Matilda is drenched. She keeps darting away to cavort like a pixie in a power shower before bouncing back yipping with excitement. She's in her swimsuit and impatient to be down at the ocean, which is pregnant with heavy swell and littered with tiny figures sitting on, riding and falling off boards. 'You mustn't go in without me,' I keep telling her.

I'm worried about giving her a good birthday. She's had bead necklaces, a digital watch, sparkly flip-flops, a card, a book about Little Penguins, a jigsaw of the Harbour and a large stuffed crocodile, but what she needs is a party. I hope her new family rises to the occasion.

The message via the hotel desk was inscrutable. 'Mr Daniels says two o'clock Thursday, Pavilion steps, Bondi Beach.' Surely Ben will come too. His mother won't be able to douse his curiosity. Though I wouldn't put it past her not to have told him at all. They're late.

I look at my watch, the second hand ticking, my time running out. Tomorrow there'll be nothing left but the droning, recycled air of the flight. A reprieve in Bangkok, where I'll be watching Matilda desperately, refusing to let myself doze for even a minute, imagining making a run for it, begging for sanctuary. No escape possible. No option but to shepherd her onto the plane that will deliver us to Heathrow.

I reminded Gina not to mention Connecticut when we rang her this morning. 'Don't unsettle her on her birthday,' I said. 'I promise to tell her before we see you.'

Tonight it will have to be. I'll have to smile and console her, tell her America will be a big, shiny adventure like Australia. Maybe she won't be upset, will take the news in her stride, will leave me without a backward glance.

A woman hurries past us, a child on her hip, another led by the hand. She reminds me of Jane and her two, of the drizzle, the grey, the downbeat Englishness of Battersea; but bucketing, pelting, pouring, the Australian rain thunders down, and—'Hey, Matty,' I say, 'here they are.'

Six of them, four adults, two children, are splashing towards us. They're shielded from the torrent by a huge beach umbrella and carry armloads of clobber, including a surfboard. Oz in his long trousers and bush hat shoots me an uneasy smile. Yvonne in shorts and shirt, hefting a giant beach bag, nods coolly.

Matilda grabs my hand, and for a few moments we all of us stare. Ben's wearing a fluorescent surf vest and shorts. His wife is tanned and curvy in a bikini and a rain-sodden dress. As if on cue the rain eases and stops. A cheer goes up from the Pavilion.

I hold out a hand. 'Hi, Ben. I'm Mark. I'm your brother.'

'Hi,' he says. 'Nice little sprinkle there, hey?'

I laugh uncertainly. His handshake's a bit limp. I expected to be face to face with the doppelganger I saw on Lizzie's laptop, but in the flesh he's a lot shorter and slighter than I am, and there's something else not the same. I can't pin it down, but this feels nothing like meeting a twin.

'This is Matilda,' I say. 'A bit soggy, I'm afraid. It's her birthday today. She's seven.'

'Hi,' says the wife. 'I'm Sue. Happy birthday, Matilda.'

I want Matty to charge forward, announcing herself and chattering on about stuff, but she doesn't.

'Good to meet you, Sue,' I say. 'So, Matty, say hello to your cousins.'

The children stare at each other.

'Say hi, Tom and Ella,' prompts Sue.

'Hi,' they whisper.

Yvonne gives Ben a nudge—'Let's get set up'—and we start to move down the steps and across the wet sand towards the ocean's bilious green. The sky broods heavily, pendulous and grey, a bushfire blanket with attitude. I can see columns of rain still battering the headland, where the rollers are thickly dotted with surfers. The air's loud with the cries of gulls who've taken off from the groups they were huddled in and now swoop low over our heads. Matilda holds my hand tightly as I fall in beside Ben.

He walks sideways, staring up at me, falling over his feet. 'We got a space,' he says. 'That's a first. We usually have to cart the stuff a few klicks. The women hate Bondi, but the surfing here's ace.'

His skin glows. His whitened teeth flash. His fingernails are unbitten. He looks as healthy as I feel unhealthy. 'It's bizarre meeting you,' I say. 'Weird having a brother I didn't know about.'

'Too right. Blimey. Could be looking in a mirror.'

'So what do you do, Ben?'

'Oh, you know,' he says, 'teach.' Laughs. 'Phys ed and

geography. And you?'

'I teach too—'

'Over here, Ben,' Yvonne calls, and he sets off towards her. An elderly couple are in process of packing up, and the sand beneath their umbrella is dry. Yvonne plants her massive, striped brolly like a flag on Everest and sets down the beach bag.

Oz smiles vaguely and looks out to sea. Ben's helping Sue to spread towels and smear Tom and Ella with sunscreen. The children stare at Matilda with round eyes.

'You're my cousins,' she tells them, too loudly, so that Tom sways with surprise and sits down hard in the sand.

A lifeguard strides by, his arse muscles rippling the emblazoned white 'Bondi' on his navy trunks. Loud doof-doof music surges and recedes as a gang of kids dash past, recolonising the beach. '... like, you know... omigod... like, I *know*... aw, you're such a dipshit...'

Matilda's eyes follow them as they head for the water. She tugs at me, wanting to swim, wanting to know, 'Daddy, are there crocodiles here?'

'Don't think so.' I size up the waves bobbing with swimmers. Hard to think in this steam bath.

Yvonne straightens from unpacking, her mouth like a cat's arse. 'Of course not,' she says in her softly grating voice. 'There's a shark net, and swimming here's safe, whatever Pommie stories you've heard.'

'But don't go in without me,' I say. 'Let's get to know Tom and Ella first, eh? Hi, kids.'

They're still gawping at her. Matilda jumps at them again. 'Have you brought me presents?'

'It's bad manners to ask, Matty,' I say.

'I'm sorry,' says Sue. 'We didn't know it was your birthday. Let's sing happy birthday, kids.'

She leads a chorus that only Ben and I sing along with, the children mouthing silently.

'We'll build a birthday castle,' says Sue. 'The sand's nice and wet.'

'Thanks, Sue,' I say.

'Well, catch you later,' says Ben.

'What?' I say, swinging round.

'How big are those waves?' he says. 'Too good to miss. You'll still be here, yeah?'

He's holding his hand out, so I take it, and we shake again, his palm dry, mine slipping with sweat. He's bending to pick up the surfboard.

'Hang on,' I say, but it's no use. He has the board under his arm and is already jogging away south towards the headland, weaving between the bodies that are beginning to pile up on the beach.

'Sorry,' says Oz. 'He's a bit of a surfie. Just shooting through.'

'Shit,' I say. 'Unbelievable. How long will he be?'

Yvonne shoots me a smirk. 'Couple of hours. Maybe longer.'

This is no game of happy families. Oz sits on a towel with his arms round his knees, radiating anxiety, his eyes flicking between Yvonne and me. Sue's busy with the children and the sandcastle.

I don't feel like letting it drop. 'Did you prime him to do that?' I challenge Yvonne.

She doesn't answer, goes on rooting stuff from her beach bag.

I step closer. 'Or did you bring him up to be a dick naturally?'

She straightens to face me, and as I glance back at Matilda I see Sue's startled expression.

'I'm wise to your agenda,' says Yvonne.

'What agenda? I'm his brother, and we're leaving tomorrow.' I appeal to Sue. 'Does Ben *know* we're leaving tomorrow?'

All I get from Sue is a cold stare. She goes back to

digging.

I'm the dick, and I've blown it. The heat's crushing; I can't get my head together. I flop on the towel next to Oz, defeated. Take a swig from my water bottle. Try to figure out what the hell Matty and I are doing here anyway.

Slowly I refocus. The castle is sprouting turrets with the aid of a castellated bucket. Matilda's helping Sue to engineer moats and bridges, while Tom and Ella fetch and carry. The kids seem to be getting along fine. That's good, I think forlornly. That has to be worth something. I sit up, wind my arms around my knees, mirroring Oz beside me, and wait to catch Matty's eyes and smile at her.

Yvonne sits apart, observing Oz and me. 'What do you reckon to a walk, Sue?' she says. 'We could go to the headland.'

The children pay no attention, but I see Sue's eyes lock with Yvonne's.

Yvonne stands and goes over to Sue. 'It's a bad idea to let them get too attached,' she says silkily. 'It could upset them as now we hear Matilda is leaving tomorrow.'

'You knew that on Tuesday,' I say.

Silence.

'They can keep in touch on the internet,' I say.

No one responds. The two women are circling the children. 'Ella, Tom, come on,' says Sue. 'Let's go see your Dad surf.'

'Can we paddle?' says Tom.

'All the way,' Yvonne says with a big, jolly smile.

'Do you want to go too, Little?'

Yvonne opens her mouth to deny me, but Matilda saves her the trouble. 'No,' she proclaims. 'I don't like paddling. I like swimming *properly* with my Daddy.'

Yvonne smiles sweetly. 'Check your bag, Sue? Do you have some drink for the kids?'

Matilda kicks sand. 'You're mean,' she tells Yvonne, but Yvonne ignores her. 'Look after my bag for me, Oz. Okay, kids, let's go.'

They need no coaxing. Dumping their spades, they set off running and shrieking towards the ocean. The women call after them. 'Tom, Ella, be careful. Wait for us.'

Their voices fade, and that's it. Oz, Matilda and I are alone again, with a beach umbrella, a whole heap of stuff to guard and a half-finished sandcastle.

'Yvonne certainly gets what she wants,' I say, almost admiringly.

'Yup,' says Oz.

What a coward. He could have told Sue it was Matty's birthday. He could have made sure Ben knew we were leaving tomorrow. We sit watching the women and the two little children receding, leaping and splashing in the waves that race up the sand.

'She's not bad at heart,' Oz says. 'She's insecure.'

Matilda picks up the bucket. 'I'm going to get some water,' she says.

'Wait. I'll come with you.'

We go down to the ocean. Yvonne, Sue and the kids are minuscule figures now, hard to spot through the crowd. We fill the bucket and come back with it.

'The water won't stay in the moat,' I say. 'It'll drain away.'

She nods, tongue between teeth, intent on not spilling the brimming bucket. She's carrying it past the sandcastle towards Oz on his towel. For a moment I think she means to drench him, and I'm throwing myself forward to stop her, but too late. Before either of us can prevent it she's poured the whole lot with force into Yvonne's beach bag.

Oz yelps, 'Oh shit,' and lurches to his feet, grabbing the bag and upending it. A tumble of wet stuff falls on the sand: a towel, keys, sopping tissues, assorted items of clothing, some plastic toys and a dripping copy of *The da Vinci Code*.

I'm trying not to laugh as he fusses, shaking things, spreading them to dry. I would be sweeping Matilda off her feet in a victory dance if the pain of being about to lose her hadn't just redoubled. I'm unable to say anything sensible to Oz, so instead I say, 'Okay, let's go swimming.' I strip down to trunks and T-shirt, dump my watch on a towel and take Matty's hand. Halfway to the waves, I fall on my knees in the sand and tell her, 'That was a hell of a naughty thing to do, and I love you to bits forever for doing it.'

What a relief to be in the sea. It's calming me, cheering me, clearing my head. Some breakers I dive through, some I bodysurf, some I allow to tumble me towards the beach. *Bondi* means the sound of crashing water, says the guidebook.

I can't strike out on my own because Matilda splashes beside me—'Look at me, Daddy'—and I need to stay close. Her doggy paddle has developed into a clumsy crawl. I grab hold of her, shout, 'Hold your breath, Little,' and plunge us through the next wave. She emerges the other side, flinging her arms to the sky, yelling, 'Again, Daddy. Do it again.' So I do, holding her tight, hoping she'll remember this day.

We thrash, spin and float for what seems like a long time. Occasionally I wipe the spray from my eyes and peer up the beach to where Oz sits, a lonely figure with nothing to do but mind the gear. The rest of them can go to hell, but I'm still in two minds about Oz. It's my last day with him too. I should be re-forging the bond we made in the small hours of Tuesday.

Matilda tugs me towards the next wave.

'One more,' I say, grabbing her. Our ears and eyes fill

with white, frothing noise before we break into air again. 'Matty, listen. I want to have a chat with Oz. We'll swim again later, when the crocodile gets back.'

She pulls a face. 'Promise?'

'Cross my heart.'

'Can I have an ice-cream?'

'Yay, baby.' I sweep her into a fireman's lift and head out of the water. She thumps my back with her fists, 'I want to swim, I want to swim,' but she's laughing, not whining. She's fine.

We arrive, and Oz smiles up at me with Matilda's rare smile. Who could hate him, a loser in possession of one of the most winning smiles ever handed out? He has detached the lining of the beach bag, and Yvonne's spoiled things are spread around him.

I set Matilda on her feet and grin back at him. I'm glad the others have pissed off. Maybe I'll tell him how Cremorne Point went on Tuesday.

'Great swimming,' I say. 'I'm going to fetch us some ice-creams. Look after each other. How about finishing the castle, Matty?'

She seizes the bucket and begins to ram sand into it. 'I'll make it extra, extra good,' she says, 'and when Tom and Ella get back, I'll knock it flat so they can't play with it.'

'Tom and Ella are nice kids,' I tell her. 'They're only little. Don't be mean to them.'

Oz is on his feet flourishing a ping-pong ball that fell from Yvonne's bag. 'We'll add a twisty ramp for this to roll down,' he says.

He looks chuffed to have something to do. I'm chuffed too and smiling. I fish my wallet from my discarded trousers and set off towards the café I saw in the Pavilion.

The woman ahead of me is ordering for six kids who

take forever changing their minds about flavours, and it's a while before I'm heading back down the beach towards the striped umbrella, shielding three vanilla cones from a snatch-and-grab gull. The first thing I see is, bloody hell, the crocodile's back, with Sue, Tom and Ella in tow, and she's making a god-almighty fuss about her bag.

The second thing I see is that I can't see Matilda. I break into a run towards Oz and the others, spinning as I go, hunting in all directions for the sight of her pink swimsuit. 'Where is she? Where's Matty?'

Yvonne looks up, startled, then around at the beach. 'I thought she was with you.'

My heart's in my throat. It's hard to speak. 'Oz, where is she?'

He has shrunk beneath the umbrella to escape Yvonne's strop. He shrinks further. I yell at him, 'For fuck's sake, where is she?'

'I couldn't leave the stuff,' he says.

I'm scanning the sand as though she might have dug herself into it.

No bucket.

'The bucket's not here,' I say.

'She went to fetch water,' he says. 'I was watching, but then Yvonne—'

I've dumped the ice creams in the sand, and I'm hurtling towards the ocean, leaping over kids on towels, shouldering people out of my way, my eyes hunting everywhere, finding her nowhere, checking each child in the shallows, each bobbing head in the waves. 'Matty,' I yell till my throat hurts, but nobody answers. 'Matty!' Oh Jesus. I scrape my lungs from my chest and hurl them impotently in every direction. 'Matty!' I don't know where to run, where to look. 'Matty!'

And, yes, Jesus, God, thank you, here she is, clutched to the chest of a bronzed lifeguard who is wading towards me, and she's alive because her arms are tight

274

round his neck, and her face turns to mine, scarily white but alive and unharmed.

'Daddy!' She reaches for me.

'The drag was too strong for her, mate,' says the hunk, handing her into my arms.

She clings to me like an orphan monkey, shaking and savage, gripping my flesh till it hurts. My knees give way, and I sink to the sand with her, managing to find a hoarse, 'Thank you.'

'No harm done,' he says, 'but don't take your eye off her, right? You need to get her enrolled in the Little Nippers.'

He's off along the sand, scanning the bathers.

The rain is back suddenly, thrashing down on Matilda and me, fused to one another like limpets.

'The sea wouldn't let go,' she says.

'Not without me, I said.'

'The crocodile came back—'

'No excuse. Never do that again.'

She nods into my chest.

'I love you, Matty.'

Eventually I stagger upright and carry her through the downpour towards Oz. He's under the umbrella with Yvonne, Sue and the children, watching us approach.

There is nothing I need from these people.

'It was up to you to watch her,' Yvonne says.

I ignore her. Bring my face close to Oz's under the drumming canvas. 'You couldn't leave the stuff?' I hiss.

He has no answer. He gnaws on a thumbnail.

'My child might have drowned, and you couldn't leave the stuff?'

I fish Matty's T-shirt from my rucksack, set her down and yank it over her head. She's immediately drenched with rain. I drag my own clothes on, strap on my watch, check I have everything.

And then I see it. Oz's hand drops from his mouth

and reaches for Yvonne. Her fingers close around his, and she squeezes. A child and his mother. 'What a fuss,' she says. 'Where's the bucket?'

There's a commotion of gulls, one driving off others before snatching at the dropped ice-cream that's fast vanishing in the rain. The ping-pong ball comes skidding across to my feet. I scoop it up and straighten to my full six-foot-three.

I flick the ball hard at Oz. It bounces off his cheek and lands in the sand. His hand shoots back to his face.

'Keep your stuff,' I say.

I pick Matty up and head through the rain towards the bus stop.

'I'm sorry I messed up your birthday, Little,' I tell her. 'Do you still want to go to Luna Park? As many rides as you like?'

Early one morning, a couple of days before Oz was due back, Nancy travelled out to the suburb where he lived. The bus, nearly empty, motored past shops not yet open on deserted community high-streets that all looked the same, before meandering through a succession of drab residential estates towards the end of its route.

With luck, seeing the reality of his home and neighbourhood would loosen the knot that had begun tying itself in her innards. She wanted to be calm and relaxed when she rang him on Monday to say, 'Hello there. Yes, it's me. Here in Sydney. Flying back tomorrow. Kicking myself that I missed you. Would you have time to meet up for a drink?'

She must get some proper sleep by then. She'd been awake since four thirty this morning, escaping a dream about losing her shoes and not being able to find them. Complete nonsense, as dreams were when you remembered them afterwards. She glanced at the red flip-flops on her tanned feet, planted on the juddering floor of the bus. She banged her heels together and smiled.

She got off a short distance from Oz's road and stood watching the bus turn the next corner. It was foolish to be nervous. The house was empty, she was only having a look, yet it felt odd to be doing this, not at all comfortable.

She consulted the map, then set off, dawdling past close-packed bungalows with gravel drives and scruffy front gardens. Strange to think Oz must have come along here many times. Yvonne and Ben too. They would walk here again and never know that she'd been.

This early the air smelled as fresh as a summer's day in England, but everything else shouted Australia. The crackle of dead eucalyptus leaves under her feet, the cockatoos' squawks, the endless nag of the cicadas, the big, harmless spiders dangling from bushes. She tried to breathe evenly, to relax her shoulders, moving ever more slowly, slowing almost to a stop.

Beyond this corner, past this white flowering bush, she would see it. Across the road would be the bungalow that had been Oz's home for more than two decades. She would see the loft extension he'd built with the help of a friend, the front garden he'd never mentioned that she'd never thought to ask him about. She inhaled, held the breath and stepped forward.

Then ducked back. Because there he was on the driveway, unloading luggage from a blue hatchback. Just a glimpse, but something about the shape and stance of him was imprinted: her recognition was instant and entire.

Her vision swam; she felt dizzy. She put a hand to the fence and bent double to bring the blood to her head. She took several deep breaths and a swallow of bottled water before peering again between the white flowering branches.

A small woman in salmon-pink shorts and a yellow shirt had come out of the bungalow's open door and was stooping to pick up a box of beach things. Her voice was audible but not the words. She disappeared back into the house.

Nancy stared at Oz. The same, absolutely, but also quite different, a grown man. He straightened, a hand in the small of his back, and for a moment did nothing, looked up at the racketing cockatoos in the spindly gum trees that grew in his patch. Then he picked up two suitcases and went inside.

The house and car doors remained open. There was stuff still on the drive.

They came out together. Yvonne took the last case. Oz locked the car, gathered up the last box and a clutch of carrier bags and followed her in. The door closed behind them. A cockatoo flew down and strutted around on the driveway, flaunting its bright yellow crest.

Nancy lingered awhile, but there was nothing more to see. A man and his wife were in a bungalow. Possibly their son was there too. They were unpacking their luggage, opening the mail, maybe boiling a kettle for coffee.

She began to walk back to the bus stop. She could try ringing Oz later today; he might be answering his phone before Monday. But she wasn't sure any more that she wanted to. To go home without making contact seemed possible, no longer such a waste.

She was torn. She was curious. If they met, if they spoke, they would have so much to tell each other. Yes, but also nothing at all. The past was the past, and the rest was nostalgia.

There would be a valentine when she got back to London. She smiled to think of it. His messages made her happy; she didn't want them to stop. The rare sound of his halting, shy voice on the phone would always make her heart quicken. But in between, how much did she think of him, or he of her? Here he was with Yvonne, opening his mail, drinking his coffee.

She walked faster. She didn't want to miss a bus. What she suddenly wanted more than anything, she realised, was to get started on moving from Muswell Hill to somewhere new, somewhere fresh, maybe south of the river. The tension was draining from her body, through her flip-flops, into the crackling leaves underfoot. She was hungry now for a proper breakfast, a fry up, and when she had eaten she would go back to the hotel and sleep for a while.

2009

When I come in from the balcony, Matilda has fallen asleep. I pull up the armchair, lower myself into it and watch her. Luna Park was heaven for her, hell for me. The hurdy-gurdy music and clash of machinery, the stink of burgers and candyfloss, the garish colours and hair-raising rides, the screams and shouts of the kids, all had her in ecstasies, while it was tough even getting my feet to carry me in under the giant, grinning, swallowing mouth of the gate. A fairground is no place to weather despair.

I still haven't told her. I can't bear to tell her. But I have to, and this is my last opportunity to do it without strangers listening in. She's sleeping; don't wake her. She's happy; don't make her anxious. Look at her little chest rising and falling. I remember watching her sleep those two single-dad weekends in Battersea, the way it felt right to have her with me, the peacefulness of it.

It was the same peace I felt four years ago in Kilburn when she slept through the night for the first time in her life. The bliss of that reprieve never fades from my memory. My body wasn't primed to expect it. I kept jerking awake, thinking I would see her little three-year-old self in the doorway, chattering and demanding, but instead there was absence and silence. Was she all right? I raced to her and found her slumbering, just as now, on her back, hands flung above her head, eyes closed, staying closed. I went back to bed. Allowed myself to believe. Slept until morning.

By the second night my body had begun to put trust in the miracle. Every muscle relaxed, my brain emptied, I slid into unconsciousness and stayed there, taking on new reserves of sanity and wellbeing before a leisurely surfacing into daylight and the barely credible sense of having slept well. There was no sound from Matilda, and I knew she was fine. The only sounds on that January morning in Kilburn four years ago were the rain on the window and Gina's breath on the pillow beside me.

For Gina too was asleep, her eyelids barely flickering, her face serene among her tangled dark curls. She was completely beautiful, and I should have desired her, but I found that I didn't. Instead an empty sensation opened up in the pit of my stomach where desire should have been. I slid from the bed, left her sleeping, channelled my bliss into making breakfast for her and Matty whenever they should wake.

I rise from the armchair now and close the balcony door. The afternoon's tropical downpours have passed. The rain is soft, pattering against the glass like the English rain four years ago.

I had stopped liking Gina; that's what had happened. Back then I scarcely acknowledged the fact or examined it. I was high on good sleep; nothing was going to dent my bliss. We were out of the habit of liking each other, I told myself. Everything would go better. I would surely warm to my wife again.

During three years of sleep deprivation we had witnessed each other *in extremis*, and the sight wasn't pretty. She'd seen my laziness, my mendacity, my bad temper, negativity and a whole lot of other ugly sides to my psyche. I'd seen her rigidity, her imperious blaming, her self-pity, her manipulation and a few other things too. Exhausted and trapped, we'd turned on each other, yelling insults above the head of our child.

But none of that should have mattered. I'd have forgiven Gina every character flaw, and I hope she'd have forgiven mine too. We'd been souls in hell, cats in a sack, having to scratch and bite to survive. With the purgatory over, we'd sleep again, night after night, regaining our humanity, and all would be well.

But it wasn't. I never warmed to Gina again: that's what I'm realising. For four years I've been battling the dislike I refused to face up to that morning, denying it to myself, occasionally berating myself for it.

Why? What has kept me from liking my wife?

I lean close to the window. The raindrops tap on the glass, trying to tell me something.

Then I get it. And groan, it's so awful and obvious. Plain as day. She can't help it, but that doesn't excuse it. I understand it, forgive it even, but I can never accept it. I've held the knowledge at bay, not wanting to face it.

Gina dislikes Matilda.

Not just in desperation, in the grip of wild, cornered moments of anger, but coolly and quietly from the day our baby was born. She's never said so. She has stiffened her Connecticut backbone, bitten her lip, soldiered on.

I stand for a long, wordless moment staring out at the rain. I'm seeing a different solution. I haven't signed the consent form. How hard would she fight? Would she win?

I turn back to the bed, lean over Matilda and kiss her damp forehead. She is best off with me. There's no question about it. Somehow I have to persuade Gina to agree, or battle to convince whoever needs convincing.

I leave Matilda sleeping and head for the lobby. I go by the stairs not the lift, because new thoughts keep coming, and I must take time to get this one right. All the way down I'm thinking about Gina. It isn't so simple. I'm not being fair. I don't dislike Gina. I loved her. I still do. At least I still can when I see glimpses, but they've only been glimpses. She stopped laughing, I realise. Before Matilda was born Gina laughed and saw fun in everything. She even seemed to like Mum.

I'd forgotten that. My mother and my beautiful wife laughing together. It's so long since Gina laughed, I'd forgotten she could. Although, wait, she was laughing on

New Year's Eve, telling her friends she was going home to the States. I hated her because she was kicking me in the teeth, but she wasn't kicking me in the teeth. She was happy, that's all.

The lobby's empty and quiet. From behind the desk, the clerk from Monday night nods, 'Good evening,' and goes back to her book. Here I am again at the phone. Okay. Take a breath. Try to relax. Put the card in the slot. Dial.

Gina picks up and says, 'Hi.' She sounds happy.

'Hi there. It's me.' My voice is light too. I concentrate on keeping it so. 'Look, Gina, I want you to listen—'

Her happiness crashes. 'What's up, Mark?'

'Everything's fine,' I assure her. 'The flight's fine, and we'll be on it, never fear. But, Gina,' I say, 'listen, because I've been thinking.'

I pause, and she waits.

'You need to be free,' I say.

'Yeah,' she says eagerly. 'That's it exactly. I need to start over—'

'So hear me out. Let me say the whole of this, okay?'

'Okay,' she says.

'So... here it is. Here's what I think.' I take a breath. 'I could look after Matty. Give you a proper, long break to get back in touch with America and with yourself. You're a good person, Gina, so am I, just no good for each other, and Matty gives you no chance to be yourself, so...' I rush on, giving her no space to speak, 'so, at least until you get settled into this job, I won't mind at all, I can cope with her in Battersea, and you can catch your flight. You don't need the hassle of a child on the plane. You don't need the stress of her throwing tantrums in Connecticut. You don't need your mother on at you about your parenting skills. Your parenting skills are just fine, so are mine, and we can take our time sorting this out. I'll bring her to see you at Easter.'

I keep talking, repeating myself, telling her again she's a good person, remembering what a good person she is. I don't dare to stop speaking, because the moment I stop, I'll have lost. She'll ask, am I kidding her? She'll tell me no way. Insist I stop stalling and hand Matty over. I'll have to drag the whole thing through the courts.

I stop.

My life contracts to a point.

I wait for Gina to speak.

HOME

November 2009, Tuesday

'Y,' they shout, 'Y,' and suddenly everyone's laughing, and the sound fills the room and gusts out through the door, which we've propped open to let in some air. A passing student peers in from the corridor, wondering what can be so hilarious.

We're jam-packed, the extra tables allowing for seven left, seven right and seven facing me: twenty students and a volunteer classroom assistant, nearly all of them new this term. To my shame, last year's English 1 lot mostly stopped coming, but big Keith, tippler Wayne and Comfort are still here.

I've been explaining how 'y' at start or end of a word makes the 'ee' sound. Ee-esterday. Ee-ellow. Ee-ou. Happ-ee. Joll-ee. I've got them taking turns thinking of words that end with the 'ee' sound. Prett-ee. Smell-ee. Craz-ee. Love-lee. 'So what letter makes the 'ee' sound?' I've been asking each time, pausing before writing it on the whiteboard, and 'Y!' they've been shouting until it feels like a pantomime, and suddenly for no reason they're laughing.

'Sudden-lee,' I offer, writing it up. 'That's 'sud', 'den', and what letter makes the 'ee' sound?'

'Y!' they chorus.

Unless there's an inspector present or a test looming next week, I spend almost no time on the syllabus these days. I plug away instead at phonemes and key words, as often as each student needs. I spend hours at home producing dozens of word-games, picture-games, rhymes and puzzles to suit their individual quirks and abilities. And it's working, it's working.

'Okay. Just one more. Your turn, Comfort. Tell me another.'

'Fancy,' she says.

'Fanc-*ee*!' they yell as I write it up. My phone vibrates against my leg, and Nanc-ee, I'm thinking. Oh heck, Mum.

I've been thinking about her all day. A year ago this morning, I was here at the whiteboard, interrupting a lesson to take that devastating call from the hospital. My stomach does a nauseous little drop now at the memory.

The phone remains in my pocket. I grab the stack of dictionaries and race around the tables, handing them out. 'Remember alphabetical order—A, B, C, D—and how the words in the dictionary are listed in alphabetical order? See if you can find the words *beginning* with 'Y'. Spend five minutes copying some down. Then we'll put a few up on the board.'

The room hushes as they turn pages, but then the classroom assistant chuckles, sharing a joke with muscle-man Keith. Valerie is grey-haired, tweed-skirted, and at least ten years older than Mum, but her laugh has me double-taking that Mum's in the room. I ride the illusion, half-imagining it's true.

With Valerie to coach him, Keith is fast getting the hang of how to link sounds to letters. He smells sweeter too these days—is he in love with her? She's the best volunteer yet.

When I nagged Alison about classroom assistants, she admitted to a heap of 'letters from do-gooders' gathering dust at the bottom of a filing cabinet. She handed them over reluctantly. 'Oh Mark, do you have to? Volunteers are nothing but trouble. They haven't a clue, or else they have loony ideas they won't stop banging on about.'

'Such as?'

'Oh, you know. The way they learned to read themselves sixty years ago. Phonetics by rote. Jane and John—all that old crap.'

'Janet and John,' I said.

'Exactly. And they need special security passes. It's a headache.'

'I'll interview them, I'll train them, I'll sort out the passes,' I said.

Valerie sits between Keith and Wayne. Phonetics are lost on Wayne, but she's discovered that repetition eventually works. Show him a word over and over, and he guesses wildly, nonsensically, as if there's a part of his brain that refuses to buy into the con-trick of reading. But then the ninety-ninth time, or the one-hundred-and-seventh, the word sneaks past his defences and into his memory. He and Valerie jump up shouting 'house!' or 'tomorrow!' and rush to my table to prove he can read it and write it, each as proud as the other.

He's acquired about fifty words so far. He never pops out for a drink any more. Valerie has spent her own money on primers for him, and he happily turns pages, recognising his words in new contexts, guessing at others from the pictures and syntax, unabashed by the infantile content. The story kids are Peter and Jane, not Janet and John, but same difference and all power to the pair of them.

Comfort doesn't need a volunteer beside her; she can go it alone now, make her way slowly through the longest of words, following the print with a false fingernail, sounding it out. Her hair's elaborately braided and beaded; her broad, beautiful smile is untroubled. Toddler Matthew is happy in the crèche, her other two kids are at school, and Kwaku lives with his mother and has a new woman, heaven help her.

Valerie chuckles again, and I give my head a quick little shake, remembering the missed call. I sneak a peek and see it was Lizzie. And now there's a text from her. *Sharing ur sadness today Mark. Look fwd to raising a glass to Nancy with you next weekend. Can't wait :-) xx*

I'm warmed by her kindness. She must have asked

me when Mum died and made a note of the date. She and Mum met only twice, briefly, thirty-one years ago, but her sympathy's genuine. Lizzie needs kindness too. Why haven't I thought of this before? I'll invite her up from Bristol for New Year if that cold-fish husband of hers is off again with his mistress. And while I'm at it I'll ring Dad tonight too and get him here for Christmas. Roast chicken and plenty of Guinness.

Two good ideas. Yes. The next trek to Connecticut isn't until Easter.

'Okay. Time's up,' I say. 'So who's found a good word beginning with 'y'?'

'I have,' shouts Keith, egged on by Valerie. 'Ee. Og. Hurt!'

The class falls about laughing.

Riding home on the bus, I give in to nostalgia. Catching the 77 is routine now, but I kid myself this is the first time. Standing room only as over the traffic lights we go without killing anyone's mother, and on through the winter dark towards the absence of mine. And before long I'm on her doorstep again, in the flicker of light from a passing train on the embankment. She left here only this morning, I pretend, hung-over from the party last night. Music and dancing. Less alert than she should have been. *Girls Just Wanna Have Fun.*

I turn the key. Ease the door open and take a breath of the air inside, trying to conjure a faint smell of curry. But it's gone. There's no trace of her. No old cat rubbing my ankles.

I close the door, climb the stairs in a dream, turn and sit on the top step. For a long while I look down at the coloured tiles, thinking idly how that mosaic floor has been here for what, a hundred years, witnessing arrivals, departures, laughter, loss. Secrets.

Through the wall come sounds of the kids home

from school: a shriek, a laugh, Jane's raised voice. I get to my feet and go down slowly. Stand a while in the hall, feeling Mum's presence recede.

Outside I pull myself back to the present. Stick on a grin before ringing Jane's bell.

Her new man opens up. Malcolm. West Indian. Deep-voiced and smiling. 'Hi there, Mark.'

And then Matilda comes running, and I sweep her up for a hug, warm and alive. Her tangled red hair smells of... yuck... what?

'Kittens, Daddy! The kittens have come! Three of them, come and see. Can we have one? Please, please, can we? The ginger one. I'll look after it properly, I promise.'

Oh bloody hell. And I open my mouth to start arguing.

Acknowledgements

Big thanks to Amanda Cooper for telling me about Bondi Beach in the rain, Lucy Crook for winkling the date of the gate out of New South Wales Maritime, Sara Francis for advice on the law on removing a child, Rebecca Killian for help with Connecticut dialogue, Federay Holmes for the inside story of long-haul flight with a 7-year-old, Ian Jewesbury for patient ruminations in the pub, Jim Palfreyman for help with Aussie dialogue, Andy Quin for putting me in touch with Frances Ratford, Frances for telling me where to park and buy ice-cream at Bondi Beach, Dinah Wiener for insisting on one final chapter, Elizabeth Barton for indefatigable help and support, and Jan Fortune at Cinnamon Press for saying yes.

For their invaluable insights, my thanks go also to Kathryn Blundell, Chris Boyd, Bob Boyton, Joe Britto, Peter Higgins, Adam Lechmere, Paul Lyons, Ellen Macdonald-Kramer, Magda North, Julie Nuernberg, Julia Rampen and Angela Trevithick at Writers Together; to Anthony, Belinda, Catherine, Joanna, Natalie, Nick, Peter, Richard and Stephanie at Original Writers; to Christine Armstrong, Alan Bevan, Jennifer Everett, Jodie Hill, Wannie Jones, Anna Roads and Rosemary Watts at Clapham Library Book Group; and to Edmund Bealby-Wright, Margaret Clare, Jon Harper, Nick le Mesurier, Jonathan Masters, Janet Mitchell, Sarah Rayner, David Roberts and Pip Wheldon.

Lightning Source UK Ltd.
Milton Keynes UK
UKHW011812301221
396406UK00001B/104